LOST GIRLS

CELINA GRACE

ALSO BY CELINA GRACE

NOVELS

The House on Fever Street

SHORT STORIES

A Blessing from the Obeah Man and Other Stories

LOST GIRLS

For Jethro, Isaiah and Mabel, with my love

PROLOGUE

In the dream, it is always the same. Up ahead, I can see the holed stone outlined against the sky; drawn in shadow, a monochromatic sketch in my mind's eye. The moon is so bright, it's almost like daylight. I can see the glint of Jessica's eyes as she comes and crouches down beside me, as I wait by the hedgerow. Behind us, the stream runs over the rocks and flows through the weed that grows like thick green hair in the water.

"Come on, stupid," Jessica whispers and then she's gone, creeping forward towards the rocks that are just a few steps away from the hedgerow. They are huge. Monolithic, they rise up and up and up, outlined against the harvest moon; a craggy jumble of stone, all sharp edges and depthless shadows in the moonlight. The Men-an-Tol is enormous, far bigger than in real life – a great stretching circle of stone, the hole in the middle of the rock gigantic, filled with a darkness that ripples like moonlit water. Jessica's blonde hair shines in this weird, bleaching light, the same colour as the cornfields that grow all about the farm. She creeps away from me, her long, thin legs in their red shorts flashing pale in this strange landscape that is at once a memory and a fantasy. I watch as she draws near the rocks. I can't move from this spot, I can't throw off the weight that presses me to the ground. It's as if unseen hands are holding me to the grass and earth beneath my feet.

I manage to move my head. I look down and I am dressed in the clothes that I wore that summer, my favourite outfit of nineteen eighty-two; blue-spotted shorts and a yellow t-shirt, but it's all wrong because my body is the body I have now, the body of an adult. Jessica has reached the rocks, her blonde hair a puff of corn silk blown by the midnight breeze. She stands in front of the Men-an-Tol and puts her ten-year-old hands on the rock and somehow I can feel the chill of the stone under my own palms. And at last I can move, can get up and run forward, released from whatever bondage held me to the ground. But it's too late, I look up, and Jessica looks up, and I see her mouth fall open as, emerging from the blackness of the hole in the centre of the stone, is a creeping arm, a bulbous leg, as if the blackness itself is coalescing into a hideous form.

Jessica turns to run. I see her mouth wide open, the gleam of moonlight off her teeth as behind her the black figure shakes itself free and rears up against the moon, monstrously big, moonlight glinting off fangs and claws and its dead black eyes. It swoops on Jessica and smothers her blonde hair in blackness; she disappears as if an inky curtain has been drawn across her.

I stand there in the moonlight and scream, and scream, and scream.

Always, in my real life, I wake up then, my heart thrumming. Kicking and flailing, I run from the dream into wakefulness and I lie there in the dark. I remember that I am an adult, no longer ten years old, and the realisation hits me once again; I am grown but Jessica is not. A quarter of a century later, she is eternally ten years old; lost back there with the rocks and the cornfields and the dead white moonlight.

PART ONE

CHAPTER ONE

The day of the funeral dawned cold and bright, sunlight filtering weakly through the curtains. The fine weather didn't last. As I dressed shivering, after my bath, I could see dark grey clouds massing over the distant mountains and a thin white mist beginning to rise from the valley. By the time we went down to breakfast, the sunlight was gone; the sky sagging with imminent rain.

By the time I finished dressing, Matt had already left the room. He'd rested his hand on my shoulder before he left, had given me a reassuring squeeze, but he hadn't said anything. What was there to say? I sat at the dressing table and drew a thick, black line over each eyelid. My hand was almost steady and it only took two attempts. My skin looked too white, dull and lifeless. I pinched each cheek.

Caernaven was as cold as it always had been. Despite the clanking radiators in every room, I could almost see my breath as I walked down the corridor, my heels muffled by the carpet runner. I hesitated outside Angus's room. They'd found him here, just by the door which was now firmly shut, thank God. I looked at the floor, as if there would be some mark, some stain. Nothing, of course. I felt a sudden rush of nausea and swallowed it down. It must be hunger - I hadn't eaten much lately.

The dining room was as dark as ever. In the blackened fireplace were the ashes of last night's fire. Mrs Green, or someone, had switched on a little electric heater which stood in front of the hearth, both bars glowing red but sending out a pathetic heat that barely warmed the patch of floor in front of it. I stood for a moment in front of the fire, feeling my shins scorch in their covering of fine black nylon, putting off the moment I'd have to start making conversation.

The others were already sat down to breakfast; Matt, with my empty chair next to him, Aunt Effie opposite, and next to her, Mr Fenwick, my father's solicitor. I poured myself coffee and gave one to Matt, just the way he liked it, black and strong. He smiled at me and I managed to smile back. I directed the remnants of the smile towards Aunt Effie and Mr Fenwick. So far, so good – I was holding it together. As I sat down, I could feel my eyes being drawn towards the empty chair at the head of the table. For a moment, I could almost *see* Angus there; dark-suited, his pewter-haired head bent towards the copy of *The Daily Telegraph* folded next to his plate. He would turn his eyes to me, like twin points of metal. But of course, I didn't really see him, because he was dead. Angus was dead. The knowledge kept thumping me in the stomach. I kept wanting to laugh, it was so ludicrous. It kept coming in waves; I was afraid at some point I wouldn't be able to control it. I poured myself another cup of coffee, trying to distract myself. The coffee pot chimed once, twice, on the edge of my cup.

Aunt Effie and Mr Fenwick were carrying on a stilted conversation about the order of procedure at the funeral, and various travel arrangements. Matt sat beside me, saying nothing. He ate almost silently, staring across the table, and I wondered what he was thinking. From here I could see the glints of silver in the hair above his temples; they matched the frame of his glasses. I squeezed his thigh under the table and he glanced at me and smiled, briefly. I smiled back, or tried to – I'd been pushing down the scream that had wanted to emerge for so long my face wouldn't react properly – the smile came out all wonky.

"You'll be doing a reading today, Maudie?" said Aunt Effie.

"What?"

"You'll be reading today, dear?"

I took a moment to reply.

"Yes," I said.

"What will you be reading?"

I struggled for a moment. I felt Matt give my own leg a comforting squeeze and managed to get the words out.

"A poem. One of the writers from Katherine."

Aunt Effie looked pleased.

"Ah, of course. Very suitable, I'm sure."

We were all silent for a moment. I crumbled the toast left on my plate. Matt raised his coffee cup to his lips and took a sip.

"Yes," said Aunt Effie, "he would have liked that."

She looked down at her plate, eyes glistening behind her glasses. Something about her tears made me suddenly feel faint. I wasn't hungry anymore. I took a scalding mouthful of coffee, the cup chattering against my teeth.

Mr Fenwick excused himself from the table and we soon heard his brisk steps echoing back from the polished wood of the hallway. Matt put his coffee cup back in its saucer and the tiny sound rang out into the silent room.

"I'll be upstairs, okay? Just got to get a few things before we go to church," he said. He put a hand on my shoulder as he walked passed, and nodded to Aunt Effie as he left. "Put something warmer on, darling, you're shivering."

His comment warmed me more than a thicker jumper would and I managed a real smile. It was strange, seeing him dressed in a black suit and not one of his ratty old jumpers and his tweed jacket with the corduroy patches on the elbows. He'd had that jacket so long the corduroy had worn smooth, like velvet. He looked different in black;

older, more serious. I suddenly had a glimpse of him as his students must see him. He left the door wide open, as he always does when I'm in the room, and I felt a rush of affection for him, for always thinking about me.

I pushed my chair away from the table and stood up. Aunt Effie did too, rather more slowly.

"Maudie."

Shit. I stopped just before the doorway and turned around slowly, trying not to let my feelings show. Oh, I know I should have been more patient but I couldn't be around anyone else's grief.

She made her way towards me, walking stick tapping out a staccato message on the floorboards. I forced myself to wait for her. As we walked slowly towards the hallway, I concentrated on my breathing.

"Matthew is looking well," she said.

"Yes," I said, looking at her sideways. I had never quite ascertained her feelings towards my hasty marriage to a man thirteen years older than myself. Not hasty, let's not say that – let's say *impulsive* instead. She's not one to talk of her feelings – we aren't, in our family - but I thought – wondered – whether she really approved.

She startled me then. She put a hand out to my arm and pressed it.

"I know you don't show your feelings much, dear," she said, almost whispering. I stared at her, shocked that her choice of words could mirror my own private thoughts. "But you're so like Angus; I know you must miss him dreadfully, dear. As we all do."

I opened my mouth but she interrupted me.

"I know things haven't always been easy – " I made some sort of sound and she increased the pressure on my arm. I had to stop myself shrinking away from her touch. I felt peeled, as if I were missing a layer of skin. "I know things haven't been easy but – well, Maudie – "

"What are you trying to say?" I said. I resisted the urge to move my arm away. It wasn't her fault, after all.

"I'm just saying that sometimes things have to be done for the best. We all have responsibilities. It might not always be what we want to do but it has to be done, anyway."

I made a non-committal noise. I had no idea what she meant.

She looked down. I was close enough to see the fine dusting of powder on the withered peach-bloom of her cheek.

"Don't let me down," she said quietly.

"What – "

"At the funeral. Please – just do what you've been asked to do."

She was looking at me directly. Her eyes were the same colour as Angus's; pale grey. For a moment, it was like looking at him and I couldn't stand it. I wanted to say *why wouldn't I* but I couldn't get the words out.

"Okay," I gasped, finally. I pulled my arm away, too roughly, but I couldn't help it. I managed to nod goodbye. I could feel her looking at me as I made my way up the stairs and had to force myself not to run.

I found Matt up in the bedroom, looking out of the window at the distant mountains, his hands in his pockets. I hesitated for a moment and then wrapped my arms around him from behind, laying my head against his shoulder blades. I could feel the steady thud of his heart reverberating through his body, beating gently against my face. The suit had that dry, new-clothes smell. I sighed.

On hearing me, he turned around and took me into his arms properly, rocking me back and forth.

"You're shaking," he said.

"I'm just cold."

He let the lie pass. I burrowed my face into his shoulder.

"What a horrible day for you," he said.

"I'm alright," I said.

He drew back a little and held me at arm's length.

"Are you?" he said. His eyes met mine and I blinked and

looked away.

"I'm alright," I said again. I kissed him briefly, just a quick peck on the lips. He pulled me closer to him again.

"Don't worry," he said, the slow metronome rock of his arms bringing me a little comfort. "I'm here for you. Don't worry about anything."

He gave me a final squeeze and released me.

"I'd better go down and see if I can help out with the cars," he said. "Wrap up warm."

I nodded.

"This is really shit, Maudie," he said. "I know it is. But you'll get through it. I'll help you get through it. You know that, don't you?" He looked at me with such concern, I had to look away. "You do, don't you?"

I felt my face twist and fought it. I managed to nod again. Matt put his arms around me again.

After he left the room, I waited in the same spot, wrapping my arms around myself, trying to recreate the same sense of comfort that Matt's embrace had given me. It didn't work. Out of the window, I could see Matt walking across the driveway, stopping to speak to Mr Fenwick, their faces serious. The black limousine stood on the gravel forecourt, chugging clouds of white vapour into the air. I felt a momentary qualm because Angus wasn't a limousine type person; he thought they were too brash, too vulgar, but the funeral director had suggested it and I'd agreed, too bleary with shock to think of saying no. Would he have disapproved?

My head swam. I couldn't get through this day, I couldn't... One thing would help, if I could find it. I went to the wardrobe and knelt down, throwing old shoes aside, pushing past the litter of paper and plastic bags that cluttered the bottom of it. It was a faint hope but...my questing fingers felt the sharp edges of a shoe box and something leapt up inside me. I took a quick look over my shoulder at the firmly closed bedroom door. Then I lifted the lid of the box. Still here, after all these years. There was at least a quarter of a bottle left. Thank God. I felt the heat of it slide down my throat, the wonderful burn of it hitting my stomach. I finished the vodka in six quick gulps and pushed the bottle back into the box, hiding it under a welter of old clothes. My head swam as I got up from the floor but this time I welcomed it. I began to feel that wonderful sense of distance, a glass bubble surrounding me. In the bathroom, I rinsed my mouth with mouthwash. Then I buttoned my coat tightly about me, ran my finger tip under each eye and went to join the others.

"Angus, as you know, lived most of his youth in Scotland and always retained a great deal of fondness for his native land – "

As the vicar spoke, I glanced around the packed church. Angus had had few close friends but very many acquaintances, nearly all of whom were here. My eye picked out various members of the board of governors from Katherine, all of whom I would need to speak to later; several young faces, who looked like students, or recent graduates; a few ancient family members down from Scotland; what looked like all of the directors from the company, down to the lowliest executive: a smattering of what had to be press, packed into the last few pews; faces, young and old, that I didn't recognise at all. I slid my gaze back to the front of the church. Coffins always look too small to hold the person they enclose. I looked at the wooden sides, French-polished to a deep lustrous shine, and thought: how *can* Angus be in there? How can he be dead? A rush of unreality hit me, and I jerked a little in my seat. All of a sudden, I felt swamped with heat. *I'm going to faint*, I thought, and for a moment could not decide what would be worse – to faint in full view of everyone in the church, or to disturb everyone by rushing pell-mell towards the exit...

"Darling?"

Matt's whisper jerked me back to reality. I reached out

for him, my other hand pulling at the hair that lay hotly against my neck.

"Angus inherited the family business on the death of his father in the late sixties and under his leadership, Sampson and Sons became one of the most successful manufacturers in the United Kingdom, if not Europe. By the age of forty, Angus had increased turnover of the business by two hundred percent, and as we all know, became one of the most successful – "

"Are you okay? Maudie?"

"I'm okay." I breathed deeply in and out. I was okay – the panic was receding. I put my shaking fingers to my forehead and wiped away a thin film of sweat. My fingertip ran over the familiar ridges of my scar, a jagged L-shape that linked my eyebrow and my temple.

"However, unlike some entrepreneurs, Angus wanted to use his fortune for good. As well as generous donations to a host of charitable foundations, Angus founded the Katherine College of Art and Creative Writing in nineteen ninety-two, enabling many young people to follow their dreams and ambitions in the creative arts, and I know he would be so pleased to see so many alumni here today. Named after his wife Katherine, who died so tragically young, the College quickly became a – "

Matt was still looking at me anxiously. I dredged up a smile from somewhere. I was still damnably hot – I began to surreptitiously unbutton my coat.

"He was, in short, a most generous benefactor to the Arts, a benevolent entrepreneur and a man devoted to his friends and family. Here to read a poem from one of the first graduates of the College, is Angus's only daughter, Maudie."

I could feel eyes swivelling toward me as I sat struggling to release myself from my coat. Blushing, I wrenched at the last remaining sleeve and felt the lining give in a purr of ripped stitches. I managed to stand up, clutching my notes in a sweating hand. Matt gave me a strained smile as

I manoeuvred my way past him and made my way to the front of the church. I felt the pressure of two hundred pairs of eyes boring into my back. I was sure my scar was glowing red, as if a branding iron had been laid against my face. I just about managed to restrain myself from putting my hand up to cover it. Then I was level with the coffin.

I could only do this if I didn't think about it, about any of it. I could feel that weird sense of disconnect again but this time I welcomed it; I felt as if I were watching myself from afar. *See, there's Maudie climbing the steps to the pulpit.* I could feel the cool slip of the little banister beneath my palm but it was as if it were happening to someone else. I stood facing the packed rows of the church, all those eyes on me. Out of the corner of my eye, I could see the hard edges of the coffin. *Angus*, I thought, *where are you now?* Was he in this church, waiting for me to mess up, once again? I wouldn't give him the satisfaction. I began to read, as professionally as my quavering voice would allow.

It was later. I manoeuvred my way slowly through the drawing room, clutching an empty wine glass. People were drinking a lot, although discreetly, and conversation was at a subdued hum. I kept my face fixed in a restrained smile and moved through the little groups as though I had somewhere specific to go. As I made my way across the room, squeezing past elbows and shoulders, I looked at all the different pairs of feet shifting back and forth; polished brogues, black court shoes, a pair of grubby trainers, which marked their owner out as either a disrespectful teenager or an arts graduate from the College.

I found Aunt Effie sitting on one of the drawing room sofas. She looked exhausted, as if she'd shrunk a little during the afternoon. For a second, pity softened me. She'd had her eyes closed and I began to move away but she opened them and spotted me.

"Would you like a drink, Auntie?" I said, pretending I hadn't been trying to leave.

"A cup of tea, thank you dear." The bulbs of her knuckles shone bluishly through her skin as she clasped her walking stick. "Mrs Green has some Earl Grey in the kitchen, I believe."

I just nodded. It would give me something to do.

The kitchen was relatively empty. Mrs Green was busy in the pantry, stacking more canapés on white plates. She pointed me in the direction of the tea and I made it, hastily and badly. I could see a nearly full bottle of brandy on the shelf behind Mrs Green's head and wondered if it would sound too strange if I asked to have it. I decided it probably would, and picked up a bottle of wine as a substitute.

As I handed Aunt Effie her tea, Matt came up to me.

"What can I do?" he said after a moment.

I seized the opportunity and asked him to get me a glass of brandy – "just a small one". He nodded and hurried off to the distant kitchen. I sat back down, feeling slightly better. Aunt Effie and I sat in silence, the subdued hubbub of the wake swirling around us. I tried to think of something to say, something bland and inoffensive, but I couldn't think of anything. I looked around the room, at the ornaments, the pictures and glassware and sculpture. Angus likes to collect beautiful things. *Liked.* I looked around the crowd to see if I could see any of his women, but I didn't recognise anyone. Perhaps that tall redhead in the corner, in black velvet? I thought I'd spotted the young one earlier; I couldn't remember her name - the one who'd been here when Becca and I had visited - but that had been a few years ago and I couldn't be sure. I put my hands up to my head, massaging my temples.

Matt came back with the brandy. He poured me a glass and stood over me until I'd had a sip.

"That's better," he said. "You looked like you were about to keel over. Just sit there for a moment and keep Aunt Effie company. I'll be back soon."

We both watched Matt move slowly about the room,

topping up people's drinks, helping with coats, having his hand shaken. Occasionally, he'd look back at me, and smile. I sipped at my brandy, my mouth puckering.

"Matthew's been very helpful," said Aunt Effie. I nodded. He was good at this stuff, putting people at their ease, making sure everything ran smoothly. He was so much more interested in people than I was. Sometimes I admired this trait in him. At other times, I regarded it with a half-contemptuous amusement.

Aunt Effie was still speaking.

"I haven't had much of a chance to get to know him since your wedding," she said. I smiled, guiltily. "Being so far away from you. You must come up to visit more often, Maudie. Particularly now..."

She was waiting for a reply. What else could I say?

"Of course, Auntie."

I looked up and caught Matt's eye as he made his way to the kitchen with an empty wine bottle. He gave me a ghost of a wink, just a bare flutter of an eyelid behind his specs. Despite the awfulness of the day, I felt my heart lift, just a little.

I watched him move about the room, his face serious. He stood for a while talking to the Dean of Katherine and I tried to catch his eye, but the light slanted across his glasses in a way that made them opaque; I couldn't tell which way he was looking.

After I'd finished my drink, I roused myself. I made myself do the rounds of the rooms, thanking people for coming and receiving their condolences in turn. The same phrases kept coming up: *always seemed so strong, such a shock, painless, sudden, no-one quite like him.* The afternoon seemed to stretch on forever; I felt as if I'd lived my whole life talking to black-clad mourners with their careful words, and their pats on the hand, and the tremulous, strained smiles that were turned my way. Eventually, I reached the hallway, thick with more people. I could see Matt's dark head over by the foot of the stairs, talking to Mr Fenwick and another younger man. For a moment, I stood still. In the dark hallway, everyone's funereal attire blended into one shadowy mass. Then I noticed, right over in the far corner, a flash of blonde hair. I looked again. The woman had her back to me; she was tall and very thin, wearing a white shirt that glimmered dully in the little light that penetrated the hallway. Her hair was a bright, true blonde, hanging to her shoulder blades, which I could see clearly through the thin material of her shirt. Who was she? I hadn't noticed her before. I moved forward and my eyes dropped away for a second. When I'd managed to get closer to her, she'd gone. I stood for a second, blinking.

"Maudie?"

Matt was calling me. I shook my head and made my way over to his little group by the stairs.

"Are you okay?" he said.

"Fine, I'm fine," I said. It was the mantra of the day. I held up the bottle of wine. "Just doing the rounds. Anyone want a refill?"

Mr Fenwick held his glass out and I dribbled the last of the wine into it.

"Who's the blonde girl?" I said.

"Which blonde girl would that be, my dear?" said Mr Fenwick. He had a bone-dry sense of humour and a way of talking which made him sound perpetually faintly amused. I once thought he'd cultivated the tone deliberately, judging it to be exactly that of an old-fashioned, family solicitor. I liked him though. I'd known him since I was five; he had a blunt kindness that shone through his professional manner.

"Oh, it doesn't matter," I said. "I just saw this blonde girl over in the corner and didn't recognise her. I just wondered who she was. She was quite thin. I couldn't see her face."

"I didn't notice her," said Matt. "But we were busy talking. Mr Fenwick – " he hesitated for a second. "Mr Fenwick will stay behind afterwards to – to read the will."

The will. It sounds stupid but it hadn't even crossed my mind.

"Now, my dear," said Mr Fenwick, who must have noticed my contorted face. "Please don't distress yourself. It's a very straightforward will, nothing to be alarmed about. I'll go through it with you step by step later but you really mustn't worry, it's all perfectly straightforward. No hidden surprises."

I wasn't quite sure what he meant.

"Thank you but it wasn't – I mean, I hadn't thought about the will. It was just – "

My voice wobbled despite myself and I clutched at the slippery glass of my empty wine bottle, needing to feel something tangible beneath my fingers. I felt Matt's arm go around my waist and leaned into him.

I didn't think about the blonde girl again, until right at the tail end of the wake, when we were once more gathered in the hallway. Matt was helping an elderly guest on with his coat when over his shoulder I caught sight of her again, just her thin back in her shimmering shirt and her fall of bright blonde hair. She was standing in the same place she'd stood before.

The elderly guest tottered off and I nudged Matt in the ribs.

"There's that blonde girl again," I said. "Do you know her?"

Matt turned to look. He stared for a moment, turned back to look at me and gave a half-stifled laugh. A few disapproving tuts were heard from the remaining guests, but Matt took no notice.

"You idiot," he said. "That's *you*."

"What?"

He was still trying not to laugh. "It's you. It's you reflected in a mirror. Or two mirrors, actually, a reflection of a reflection. Look, shake your head. There – see? It's you."

I began to blush. "Oh yes. What an idiot."

I looked more closely. I craned my neck and turned my head and in the mirror, the blonde girl did the same. I turned more fully and saw my own scorching face reflected in the mirror, the scar standing out livid against my temple where my hair had fallen back. What a fool. I looked at Matt and he took my hand, pulling me against him.

"You've had a day of it," he said. "Don't worry."

Later, I took a good look at my naked self in the bathroom mirror. Seeing my reflection had shocked me, not just in the silly way I'd mistaken myself for someone else. I hadn't realised I'd got so thin. There was a hollow underneath each side of my ribcage; there was a smudge of shadow beneath my collarbone, where the flesh fell away. I dabbed some more concealer onto my temple and pulled my hair forward. On the bathroom window sill, my mobile phone jittered as an incoming text came through. I picked it up; it was from Becca. *Didn't want to call cos time difference. Wish cld be there, thinking of u, sending love n hugs. Becs xxx.* It made me smile and I held the phone against my cheek briefly, as if those kisses on the end of the message could be transferred to my face.

There was a knock on the door and Matt's voice outside.

"I'm okay," I called back. "I won't be long."

I turned the hot tap on again and, under cover of its gushing water, upended the brandy bottle into my mouth. I'd managed to sneak the bottle upstairs after Mrs Green had left. I drank down six gulps, screwed on the cap and hid the bottle in the toilet cistern. Head swimming, I climbed into the hot bath that I'd run and settled myself against the curved porcelain. The water folded itself around me, soothing as a caress. I tried to breathe deeply, tried to empty my mind of thought and visualise nothing but the white sheets of steam hanging in the air.

Matt was in bed when I came back into the bedroom, not reading, just staring up at the ceiling. He seemed to fill the bed – his hairy-chested bulk looked incongruous against the white frills of the pillowcases. Normally the sight of him lying half-naked against the sheets would have struck a spark of desire in me. Today I felt nothing. I hesitated a moment and then crawled into the bed next to him and reached out a tentative hand. I wondered whether he'd be able to smell the brandy on me. I had a good excuse, if he did.

"Just a moment, darling," he said. "Are you finished in the bathroom?"

"Yes."

He pressed a quick kiss on my cheek, then rolled out of bed and left the room.

I curled my legs up beneath me and turned my face into the pillow. It smelt of the particular brand of washing powder that had always been used here – the smell of my childhood, up until the age of ten. After that, it was boarding school sheets that my nose was pressed against, boarding school sheets that, more often than not, were soaked with my tears, a faint silvery crust of salt visible upon them in the morning light.

The bedroom door opened and made me jump. Matt turned the light out as he got into bed and we lay there in darkness and silence.

"Come here, you."

I was suddenly near tears. His arm reached out to roll me against him and I put my face against his chest, breathing in the smell of him.

"Oh Matt – "

"What, darling?"

I was silent for a moment, struggling not to cry.

"It's been such a horrible day."

"Yes. You're tired now and no wonder."

"Yes."

I could feel the thud of his heartbeat in my ear, as it echoed through the bones of his chest. Its quick, steady pounding soothed me. I pressed myself closer to him, feeling – at last, thank God – some measure of peace. My eyes closed and when he spoke again, I had to ask him to repeat himself.

"I *said*, who did you think you were? I mean – did you really not realise that was you?"

"What?"

"Your reflection. You know – this afternoon – "

"Oh that." I gave a tired giggle. "I don't know."

I was so tired. I could feel unconsciousness gathering itself in a slow crashing surge. My mouth seemed to move independently of my brain.

"Blonde. She was blonde."

"Who was?"

"Jessica… Jessica was blonde."

"Oh Maudie, darling. You're not thinking of that again, are you?"

I wrenched my eyelids open one last time. How could I explain that I thought about her all the time, that she dogged my footsteps, that she hung about me, always that one step out of reach?

"She haunts me," I said, my voice barely a whisper. Matt may have said something in return, but by then, I was fast asleep.

CHAPTER TWO

We left Caernaven early the next day. We could have stayed on, I believe Mrs Green was expecting us to, but Matt had a seminar and a lecture the following day and he wanted to prepare. As we drove away from the house, I kept my neck rigid, unwilling to look back. Angus had always come to see us off. I could see him now in my mind's eye, his tall spare figure on the top of the stone steps by the front door, the raising of his palm and the glint of sunlight on his wedding ring. *He just wants to make sure we're really going*, Matt had once joked.

We drove without speaking. The radio played softly in the background, the sort of middle-aged, easy listening type station that Matt loved and I liked to tease him about. He had a habit of singing a line of a song very loudly, just a random line, not the chorus or anything, and not from a song that was playing on the radio or stereo, but from one that was obviously running itself in his head. It always made me jump, and then laugh, and he would look over at me in surprise. He didn't realise he was doing it but something today was obviously stopping him as he was silent, and so was I.

I looked out of the window, watching the countryside scroll by. I thought of all the times I'd left Caernaven before, by foot, by car, by train. By ambulance.

I drew in a deep shaky breath.

"Do you remember our first meeting?" I asked, suddenly.

Matt gave me a quick, quizzical look.

"Remember it? Why wouldn't I remember it? Of course I do."

We drove on for a moment without speaking.

"Why?" he said.

"Why what?"

"Maudie, come on. Why are you asking me that question?"

"I don't know." I turned my face to the window, at the banks of the motorway rolling past. "I was thinking about the past."

"Always a dangerous thing."

He said it in a joking voice but there was an awkward undercurrent. He was right, I thought. The past can be dangerous. Or did he just mean that thinking about it was the dangerous thing? I had a sudden, ferocious urge for a drink.

"Could we stop for lunch? For a break?"

Matt shrugged. "Don't see why not. Probably a good idea."

"Somewhere nice. Not some dismal little service station."

As Matt found the motorway exit and began the search for the somewhere nice I'd stipulated, I thought about Angus once more. It was usual for me, when visiting Caernaven, to take the train up. Partly it was to avoid the fag of a drive but partly it was so I could bolster myself up on the journey with a few drinks. The trick was to pace oneself; I had to arrive fully armoured but comprehensible.

Angus normally met me at the station. Before I walked out of the entrance hall to the tiny car park beyond, I would always pause for a minute to check that the appropriate feelings were in place; mild irritation, the fretful contemplation of two days of idleness and boredom. Did other people get the same heart-sink sensation when they went back home or was it just me? The wine I'd have drunk on the journey had numbed me. There was no fear, only the vaguest tremor of anxiety that was dispelled with a shake of my head.

"How about this?" said Matt.

I came back to the present with a jerk, blinking. He was indicating a pub up ahead. It served alcohol, it was open. I tried to sound suitably grateful.

"Looks fine to me."

When we were inside and Matt was at the bar, giving our order, I thought again of our first meeting. It had been at Caernaven, at a dinner party given by Angus. I'd come up from London, a long overdue visit; I'd stayed away deliberately, not wanting to return unless I was sure of myself. As I'd unpacked my suitcase in the bedroom, I'd looked out of the window at the familiar view – the fields and hedges spreading in a patchwork of gold and green and, far beyond, the smoky blue bulk of the mountains, the sky heaped with masses of white cloud above their peaks. Angus had sprung the dinner party on me, I remembered, and I hadn't packed anything suitable to wear. I'd told him so at the first opportunity.

"Angus, I've got to go into Hellesford and get something to wear for tonight, I haven't got anything suitable."

He looked irritated.

"Christ, Maudie, haven't you brought anything? Why not?"

I stammered a little.

"Because I – I didn't realise – "

"You haven't got time to go now, I need you here for six. Have you checked the spare rooms?"

"No – "

"There's a few dresses of your mother's still hanging about. Wear one of those."

I felt a slight shock, as I always did when he mentioned

her. She was always there but not there; not exactly censored, but rarely openly spoken of. I thought of arguing the point and gave up.

"Alright," I said. "I'll have a look."

Once, I'd looked at these dresses all the time. As a small child I used to climb into the wardrobe and pull the door shut and sit there, wound about with my mother's old clothes. I'd like to have said that they smelt of her but of course they didn't; they smelt of washing powder and fabric softener, not of human skin. As the years went by they smelt less pleasant, stale air beginning to permeate their fibres, until one day I closed the door of the wardrobe for the last time and left childish things behind.

There were three spare rooms on the first floor. In the second room, a bank of wardrobes stood against one wall. I flicked through the hangers, each garment wrapped in its own shroud of plastic. I found a plain black dress that looked as if it would fit. It would have to be washed and dried before I could wear it – perhaps Mrs Green would see to it. I held it for a moment against myself, imagining my mother wearing it, sometime in the late sixties. I'd seen photos, although never of her in this actual dress. She had blonde hair like mine… I put a hand up to my head, running a strand through my fingers. I was eleven months old when she died in a car crash. I was in the car with her, but I'd escaped almost unhurt. Flying glass had cut open my face, the blood sheeting down the side of my neck like a red scarf. Otherwise, there hadn't been another scratch on me. *Like a miracle*, Angus had once said to me, in an unusually unguarded moment. But I sometimes wondered whether some part of me had been hurt, as well as my face; some hidden, inner part of me. I thought that every time I saw the scar in the mirror. I shook my head. *I'm better now*, I told myself firmly, and marched to the door of the room.

"Penny for them?"

"What?" I said, startled. Matt was holding a glass of wine

in front of my face. I tried not to grab for it.

"You were miles away."

"I know," I sighed. "I'm sorry."

"Christ, darling, you don't have to apologise. I can imagine what you're thinking about."

"Actually, I'm not," I said. "I was thinking about meeting you for the first time."

He raised his eyebrows.

"Well, that's a happy memory for a change." He paused, then grinned. "Isn't it?"

"Of course."

"I even remember what you were wearing."

"Oh yes?"

"Some lovely old dress of your mother's. Very sexy you looked in it, too."

I snorted.

"You were wearing that bloody awful old jacket. As usual. You did not look sexy in it at all."

"That must have been why I asked you on a date, and not the other way round."

"I said yes, though."

"Eventually."

We regarded each other over the table, and smiled.

I hadn't actually spoken to Matt that first night until after dinner, when everyone was out on the terrace. It was a beautiful evening, the air soft and scented with the heavy, drowsy smells of summer. Insects flickered about the outside lamps and midges came to bite us, until I went to light the citronella candles that were dotted about on the walls of the terrace. Matt saw me casting about for matches and offered me his lighter, a beautiful thing of old, polished brass, a faint design of vine leaves on its surface worn almost smooth by years of wear. He'd already lit a cigarette; I watched him smoke it slowly and thoughtfully, his eyes closing slightly on every intake of breath. I handed him back the lighter and he took it from me, his fingers brushing mine.

"I'm so pleased to meet you, Maudie," he said, once more. "Angus talks about you a lot."

"He does?" Momentarily, I was wrong footed. What had he been saying about me? Had he mentioned my – my illness? *You've got to think of it as an illness, Maudie*, I heard Margaret say in the confines of my head. *You have to get over an illness. You have to convalesce.*

I quickly put on a smile.

"I hear you're from America," I said. "You don't sound very American."

He laughed. "I'm not. Just spent two years teaching over there – the University of Vermont. Do you know Vermont?"

I shook my head.

"But I'm really from here, from England," he went on. I watched the smoke he'd inhaled seep out from between his lips and drift off in a wavering blue scarf that dissolved into the twilight. "From London. You live in London, is that right?"

"Yes, sort of Crouch End area. I have a flat there."

"In Crouch End?" He pronounced it with the ironic French accent that every Londoner affects when they talk about the area – *croooche en*.

"Now I know you're a real Londoner. They all say it like that."

"Well, there you go. The Yanks haven't crushed old Blighty out of me yet."

I laughed.

"You definitely don't have an American accent, either."

"God forbid," he said and our eyes met. I felt an odd tremor that, for a second, made me catch my breath. I blinked and looked away.

"Anyway," said Matt, as if I'd just spoken. "Crouch End is very nice, I hear."

"Well, actually, it's really more Highgate," I said.

He looked amused.

"Well, you're doing alright for yourself, aren't you? What

do you do?"

I smiled, rather brightly. How much did he know about me? And was he just making small talk, or was he really interested? Was he patronising me?

"Oh, this and that. I work at a charity. Only part-time at the moment."

"Interesting," said Matt.

"It's really not," I said, grinning. "But thanks for being polite. Want another drink?"

"Not just now," he said, which slightly annoyed me as it meant I couldn't go and get one for myself. "Stay and talk to me."

"About what?"

"About – about vampires," he said. I gave a little huff of laughter and his smile widened. "Highgate Cemetery," he said "That's where the vampires are, aren't they?"

"So they say."

He looked at me with one corner of his mouth turned up.

"Not been bitten yet, have you?"

My hand went up to my throat automatically and made us both laugh.

"Not yet," I said, and we laughed again.

*

After we'd left the pub, I fell asleep almost as soon as we rejoined the motorway. It must have been very boring for Matt, having to drive the rest of the way home with no one to talk to, but he let me sleep; I think he could see I needed it. He shook me awake gently when we were parked outside the flat.

"Wakey, wakey," he said. "You were dead to the world. We're home now."

I stumbled blearily out of the car. In the lift on the way up to the flat, I looked at myself in the mirrored wall; mussed hair, pouched eyes. My scar looked very red. I shifted my gaze to Matt, who was rubbing his face, dragging a hand over the bristles of his chin.

"God, I'm bushed," he said. "That drive never gets any easier."

I dropped my gaze to the floor. I wondered whether he was thinking the same thing; that perhaps we wouldn't have to do that drive anymore. Despite that, as we walked into the living room I went automatically to the phone and picked up the receiver, ready to call Angus to tell him we'd got home safely. Then I remembered and dropped the phone with a little cry and burst into tears. Matt was by my side immediately.

"Maudie – "

"I'm fine," I said, choking. "Just – just let me be for a bit."

"But – "

"Please."

He stepped back warily. I lay down on the sofa and pushed my face into a cushion.

"I'll get you a drink," he said.

I nodded into the pillow. I couldn't see what he was doing but I heard his footsteps move away from the sofa and into the kitchen. There was the creak of the refrigerator door and the chink of a glass bottle, the glug and trickle of liquid into a glass. Soon I heard his footsteps walking back.

"Here you go," he said tenderly, like it was medicine. I sat up. He was holding out the brandy glass to me. I took it, rubbing the tears from my face.

"Thanks."

He watched me drink it. Then he sat down beside me and pulled my head down onto his shoulder. I could feel his stubble catch on my hair as he rubbed his cheek against my head.

"One thing about grief," he said. "You'll never again feel as bad as you do right this moment. And tomorrow night, you'll never feel quite as bad as you do tomorrow morning.

And so on, and so on. That's what they mean by time being a great healer."

I nodded but I could have told him it wasn't true. *Time heals all wounds.* It was a kind-hearted lie, a benevolent myth. Unless it took more than twenty-five years to come true.

CHAPTER THREE

"Darling…"

I could hear Becca's voice from across the room. I turned in my chair, watching her plough through the restaurant like a galleon in full sail.

"Darling!"

Her voice went upwards as she spotted me. I grinned and waved and, two seconds later, was enveloped in her chest, the fronds of her lacy scarf muffling my face as she pressed me to her. For a moment I smelt Chanel Number Five and the sweet powdery scent of her make-up before she released me and I staggered back.

"How *are* you, darling? I was so worried about you, at that ghastly funeral. It's so hard to lose a parent, it doesn't matter how old you are. No, sit down, sit down. Have you ordered? Christ, we can't even smoke here anymore – darling, let's just pop out for a sec – I can have a quick smoke and you can tell me all about it – what do you say?"

As always, I felt slightly breathless. Becca has that effect on people. I always feel like throwing my hands up and saying 'whoa, whoa'. Bless her.

"Go on, then. I can see I'm not going to get any peace until I let you have your nicotine fix."

We took up our stations outside the entrance, huddled alongside with the other smokers who were talking and shivering and breathing out great long streams of smoke into the icy night air.

"Go on then, hon," said Becca, inhaling with a gasp. "Are you okay? I'm so sorry I couldn't come up to be with you, but those bastards at work would just not hear of me missing that Boston trip…"

I rolled my eyes.

"Don't worry about it, Becs. It's fine. It's not as though you and Angus really got on or anything, did you?"

Becca protested.

"Darling, that's a bit harsh. I only met him a couple of times. I thought we got on perfectly well, what little time we spent together. Why, did he say differently?"

I cursed myself mentally.

"No, not really. You know what he was like though. Or rather, what I told you he was like. Oh, you know what I mean – "

Why had I said that? I could hear Angus's summation of Becca clear as day in my head, after I'd taken her with me to Caernaven that one time. *Too tall, too loud, too unfeminine.* It was my own fault, I'd wanted to know what he thought of her. I'd wanted him to approve of her and our friendship. I should have known better. Had there been anyone in my life that Angus approved of, ever? I had a sudden unwelcome thought: if Jessica had – had lived, had been known to us as an adult, would he have approved of her?

"Becca, I'm fine. Really. I know you would have come if I'd asked you to."

She smiled and took another lung-busting drag on her cigarette. I regarded her with affection. Darling Rebecca; henna-haired Amazon, cloaked in cigarette smoke; fond of emphatic statements; fiercely intelligent, bossy, extrovert. I'd known her five years; she was my best friend.

"Let's go inside and order, if you're done," I said. Becca gave me a strong, one-armed hug.

"We need to feed you up," she said. "Look at you,

skinny-malinky. Matt's not been taking care of you. Where is he, anyway?"

"At home. He sends his love but he had a paper to do for next week's conference."

"He's going away?"

"Just down to Brighton. Some dullsville academic thing. It's only for a few days."

"So you'll be all on your own? Want to come and stay with me?"

"Really, Becca," I said, slightly annoyed. "I can cope on my own for a few days."

"So how are you coping?"

"What do you mean?"

"Oh, you know. Just – coping. With everything."

We'd reached the table by now and seated ourselves.

"Becca, I'm fine, honestly. I don't know why –"

I stopped.

"I don't know why what?" she said.

"Oh, nothing." I pushed my hair back from my face. I felt suddenly hot and cross. "I just don't know why everyone's treating me like some kind of fragile doll, all of a sudden."

Becca reached for my hand.

"You idiot," she said, with a soft edge to her voice. "You've just lost your *dad*, that's why. We just want to know if you're okay."

It was the way she said 'your dad' that got me. Angus had never been a dad. A father, maybe, but never a dad. *I'm an orphan*, I thought suddenly. The word seemed so archaic. My throat felt tight. I turned my face away for a second, getting my voice back under control.

"Thanks Becs," I said, after a moment. "I'm fine but thanks."

We applied ourselves to the menus.

"Christ, I'm starving," said Becca. "I'm going to have a starter as well."

"Aperitif first?" I said. "Or straight onto the vino?"

"Ooh, G&T for me. And let's get a bottle as well, to start with. The service here is always a bit hit and miss."

I signalled to the waiter. I felt that wonderful sense of relief I always had in her presence. Becca didn't care much what anyone thought. She just went for it, whatever it was, and it was as if I suddenly had permission to join.

The waiter brought our drinks and we raised them to each other.

"Cheers."

"Cheers, my lovely."

When I got home that night, Matt was still working at his computer. The room of the study was dark, his face lit only by the bluish glow of the laptop screen.

"Still at it?" I said, surprised. "You must have been flat out all night."

He raised his hands above his head in a 'don't shoot' gesture. Then he flipped the screen of the laptop down and swung round in his chair to face me.

"I have been, truth be told. But it's time I called it a night and this is the perfect excuse. How's the fair Rebecca?"

"She's fine." I slurred a bit on the sibilant but that didn't matter; Matt was used to me coming home tipsy from a night out with Becca.

"Did you finish your paper?"

"Just. A few footnotes to sort out and I'm done."

"That's good," I said automatically. I wandered about the study, picking things up and putting them back down. It drives Matt mad when I fiddle with things, but it's a nervous habit, I can't seem to stop it.

"Maudie – "

"Sorry," I said. I touched a finger to his big glass paperweight. It was like touching a bubble of solid ice. I picked it up, liking the feel of it in my palm.

"Listen," he said, watching me. "Why don't you come with me? To Brighton?"

"Oh, no – "

"It'll be good for you. Change of scene and all that. You can amuse yourself during the day and come to the functions at night."

I groaned inwardly at the thought of all those academics and their endless, impenetrable conversation, the way they all seemed middle-aged, even if they weren't; the glasses of cheap white wine in plastic cups; the dehydrated sandwiches and sad little bowls of crisps laid out on scratched formica-topped tables. I imagined myself standing next to Matt on the periphery of each group, trying to yawn with my mouth closed.

I tried to sound regretful.

"Darling, I would but...I don't really feel up to socialising."

"You've just been to dinner with Becca. Put that thing down darling, please, and don't fiddle."

"That's different," I said, putting the paperweight back on the desk. "She's my best friend. I don't have to – "

"Don't have to what?"

"Nothing," I muttered. I picked up the paperweight again.

"No, what?"

I put the paperweight back down with a loud clack.

"I don't need to pretend with her," I said.

"*Mind* that, you'll break it. What do you mean, pretend? You don't have to pretend with my friends. Do you?"

I felt very tired suddenly.

"Oh nothing, I didn't mean it. Let's just forget it."

He opened his mouth and then reconsidered.

Despite my mood, I felt a spasm of drunken desire. We hadn't made love since before the funeral. In fact, not since the day of Angus's death, an hour after the phone call from Mrs Green. Sex with Matt could be such an escape and that day, that was all I needed; to be as far away from reality as I could possibly be. I'd made him fuck me over and over again, until he collapsed, gasping and said 'no more'; until I was raw with it, a welcome physical pain to take my mind off the other, deeper kind.

But Matt didn't make love to me that night. I lay awake beside him in the darkness of our bedroom for a long while, listening to him breathe, locked away from me in a thicket of dreams. I turned on my side and tried to empty my mind. Eventually, I did sleep, and dreamed again of Jessica, although not of the rocks and the monster. In the dream, we were riding our bikes along the harbour road in Penzance. Jessica pedalled faster and faster – she flew further away from me, as if her bike had wings. I watched her blonde hair flutter behind her as she dwindled in my vision.

I woke up suddenly. I'd been pedalling in my sleep – the covers were bunched and twisted about my legs. I had to pee and I was thirsty.

After my visit to the bathroom, I drifted to the kitchen to pour a glass of water. I didn't turn on the light. The kitchen was lit with an orange glow from the streetlamp outside and the plane tree outside the window tossed its branches in a night breeze, the flickering shadows of its leaves moving across the kitchen counter. I shuffled into the living room and went to the window, idly twitching aside the curtain.

There was a woman standing in the street below, a tall, thin, blonde woman, dressed in a long black coat. She was staring up at the living room window. My eyes caught hers and I gasped in fright. The expression on her face was unreadable but even at this distance, I could sense a concentration of emotion; some kind of fixed energy pulsing through her, concentrating her gaze. It occurred to me that I was still dreaming. I closed my eyes for a long moment, afraid to move. When I opened them again, she was gone. The street was empty. I felt light-headed again and clutched at my cool water glass. For a mad second, I contemplated running downstairs and out into the street, to see if I could catch a glimpse of her; that blonde hair, that burning gaze, the enveloping black coat. No. I put my glass down on the windowsill and made my way back to bed. I lay under the covers, against Matt's warm, sleeping side, my eyes wide, unwillingly awake.

CHAPTER FOUR

I took Becca to Caernaven with me once. Just once. It was the only time I'd invited a friend back there. I don't know why but the person I was in London was not the person I was in Cumbria and I could never seem to reconcile the two. But Becca was different - we'd known each other for long enough for that not to matter. At least, not to matter much.

Some of it was Angus as well. It wasn't that he was rude, exactly, it was just that he didn't treat people the way I wanted him to. Some small childish part of me wanted him to be a dad, a proper Dad, capital D; tweedy and avuncular, paunchy, eyes twinkling benignly from behind his glasses. A pipe-smoker, a cheek-pincher, a winker. No matter that he didn't actually wear glasses and wouldn't have dreamt of wearing tweed. In reality, he was tall, broad-shouldered; he kept his steel-grey hair cut savagely short; he smoked cigarettes and no lightweight versions either; Marlboro Reds. He veered between being curt and abrupt, or completely charming, depending on who he was talking to. Once I moved away from home, I seemed to lose the ability to read his moods – on my visits back, I got it wrong all the time; being skittish and cheeky when I should have been grave, solemn when I should have been light-hearted. I found myself embarrassing then, so how must he have felt? No, it was better to be by myself when I went back, less painful all round.

But Becca was a bit different. For a start, she was one of the least judgmental people I'd ever met – it was a big part of the reason I liked her so much. Supremely self-confident, she assumed everyone else had the same breezy attitude to life and all its challenges as she did. I knew she'd cope effortlessly with whatever mood Angus was in, and this helped me feel more relaxed myself. It was so simple when I looked at it in these dispassionate terms; I don't know why it was so hard to carry it out in practice.

In keeping with this theory, I'd bought a couple of bottles of wine with me on the train, which Becca was keen to help me demolish. I'd never enjoyed the journey so much before; the two of us swigging wine and eating peanuts, swapping stories and giggling. I arranged for us to get a taxi from the station, so I knew there would be no awkward journey home with Angus. We'd arrive at dinner time, which would mean we'd all have something to do other than talk. It was all going to be fine, I told myself as I sloshed the last of the first bottle into our glasses.

"Bloody hell," said Becca several hours later, as the taxi pulled up in front of the house. "It's huge. You never told me it was going to be so big."

I was pierced by the memory of Jessica's reaction on first seeing Caernaven. It made me struggle for words but, after a second, I managed to make some flippant comment. I paid the taxi driver and we clambered out, retrieving our cases from the boot.

Becca stood for a moment, taking in the monolith that was the front of the house, then turning to survey the view.

"Lovely spot," she said. "And you grew up here, you lucky thing. I grew up in Croydon, for God's sake. There's no comparison."

"Oh well," I said, rather awkwardly. I never knew what

to say when people said things like that. "Let's go inside and get a drink."

Angus opened the front door as I put my hand out towards the handle.

"Angus, this is Becca, my friend. Rebecca, I mean."

"Pleased to meet you," said Becca. He gave her a look I couldn't decipher but shook her hand and smiled.

"Welcome, Rebecca. How was your journey?"

He put a hand on the small of her back, steering her through the front door. I gathered up as many bags as I could and struggled after them. Becca had stopped in the middle of the hallway and was exclaiming over the staircase.

"I'll just dump these here," I panted and let most of the bags fall with a thump. "I'll take you up to your room later." I turned to Angus. "I thought Becca could go in the Blue Room?"

He was already walking away and waved a hand at me.

"I'm sure that's fine. Come and join us for a drink when you're ready."

Us? I stopped lugging Becca's suitcase across the floor.

"You alright?" said Becca.

I immediately put a smile back on my face.

"No problem. Sorry about Ang - my father - he's sometimes a bit preoccupied. Don't take it personally."

"I hadn't," said Becca. "Taken what?"

I shrugged and rolled my eyes. "Oh nothing," I said. "Forget it. Let's go and get a drink, shall we?"

We made our way to the drawing room, Becca exclaiming all the while about the house, the antiques, the art and the sculpture. "So *beautiful*," she kept saying and lingering at one thing or the other until I virtually had to push her through the door of the room. I was sniggering under my breath at our childishness and it took me a few moments to notice that Angus was indeed not alone. Sitting very close to him on one of the couches was a young woman, almost as young as I was, with a cloud of soft brown hair and a very red mouth.

"Oh," I said, nonplussed. Then I collected myself. "Hello."

"This is Theresa," said Angus. He got up from beside the girl and moved towards the drinks cabinet. "Teresa, this is my daughter Maudie and her friend Rebecca."

We all shook hands and there was a moment's awkward silence, then Becca stepped into the breach.

"How do you know Angus?" she asked.

Carnally, was my guess. I'd been wondering recently whether he had some new woman on the go – when something like this was starting up he became even more distant, and I'd noticed his usual phone calls to me had become even more sporadic. Theresa looked a little uncomfortable. I wondered whether she'd been told we were coming.

"I'm a teacher at Katherine College," she said. Becca and I made encouraging noises but she didn't seem to have much more to say. Angus brought us over some drinks.

"How long have you been teaching?" asked Becca.

"Not long," said Theresa. "This is my first job."

"What a surprise," I murmured. I must have said it a little too loudly as she glared at me.

"Theresa will be joining us for dinner," said Angus. He put a hand on her waist, just a little too close to her backside. I had to look away. "We'll sit down at seven."

"Will we be dressing for dinner?" said Becca, grinning. I began to smile and then saw Angus's face. He didn't get it. He gave me a look.

"That would be lovely, Rebecca," he said. "But I'm sure what you're wearing would be quite adequate."

I snorted and got another look. Teresa was looking out of the window, or at least towards the window. I didn't think she was thinking of anything much.

The silence stretched out uncomfortably.

"Well, I'd better show Becca to her room," I said eventually. Angus nodded and we were dismissed. I'm not sure Teresa noticed we were going.

Becca and I both hefted a case and headed for the stairs.

"God," said Becca when we were halfway up a flight. "Your dad likes them young."

I shivered. "Don't."

"Sorry," she said. There was a moment's pause. "This house is truly amazing. I can't believe you grew up here."

"Well, I was at boarding school for some of it," I said. We had reached the Blue Room. "Here you go. The loo's just across the corridor."

Becca walked in and looked around.

"It's amazing. Thanks." She gave me a quick look I couldn't quite decipher. "I was only joking about dressing for dinner."

"God, I know that," I said. I rolled my eyes. "Don't worry about my father, anyway. He'll be too taken up with what's her name to pay us much attention, you'll see."

In that, I was wrong. When we came down for dinner, I could see Angus had switched into charming mode. Perhaps he was bored with Teresa – and I could quite see why – or perhaps he'd become aware of his previous shortcomings. He talked a lot to Becca and sometimes to me. Teresa pushed her food around the plate in a sulky manner. I tried to talk to her but gave up after a while.

I'd thought she'd leave after dinner but again I was wrong. We went back into the drawing room for coffee.

I may have over done it a bit on the booze that night, I'm prepared to admit. I was wound up and anxious; hoping Becca was enjoying herself, trying to please Angus, trying to alternately include Teresa or ignore her as politely as possible.

It meant I had to get up in the middle of the night, my bladder almost bursting. I was staggering down the corridor when I heard the sounds, sounds so immediately strange that at first I thought I was dreaming. I'd been dreaming when I woke up, thick tangled dreams of wolves and forests and these were sounds straight out of the dream; feral, rough animal sounds. In my befuddled state, it took me a moment to realise what they were, and that they were coming from Angus's bedroom.

I managed to get to the bathroom before vomiting. At least I managed to do that. My croaks and gasps drowned out the noises Angus and Teresa were making and when I'd finished vomiting, my tears and sobs were able to drown them out too. I went back to my room and lay rigid, my fingers in my ears, trying not to hear, listening to the thunder of my heartbeat and the gallop of blood in my veins.

CHAPTER FIVE

It was a while before Becca and I could meet again. We chose a bar we both liked for our rendezvous, a little subterranean cavern with lots of tucked away nooks and crannies. Since the smoking ban had come in, visibility had improved a little but I still had to screw up my eyes against the dimness as I threaded my way through the tables and chairs, looking for Becca.

I couldn't find her anywhere in the bar; I was obviously the first to arrive. I found a little table right at the back with two spare seats and sat myself and my glass of wine down. I'd bought a bottle for us; I knew I'd be needing it. A candle in a votive glass holder cast a flickering golden light over the rough surface of the table. I pushed it further back against the wall and took out my book but I couldn't concentrate. When I realised I'd read the same line five times, I shut it and put it away and concentrated on drinking my wine.

Becca came around the corner in her usual rush, trailing scarves and her battered old handbag.

"God!" she said, flinging herself into the chair opposite. "What a night! Total overload at the office and then I get here and make a beeline for someone who I was sure was you and obviously it wasn't. Oh, excellent, you've got us a bottle - slosh some in there would you, darling? How are you doing?"

We talked about inconsequential things through the first half of the bottle. Becca asked after Matt, although I didn't have much to tell her.

"He says hello," I said. "He was pleased I was going out again. I think he's worried I'm just going to closet myself away at home."

"Well, it's understandable," said Becca. "You do have a tendency to get a bit hermit-like."

"I do not!"

"Okay, well, only sometimes." Becca wasn't interested in arguing the point. "*Anyway…*"

"Anyway, what?" I was stalling and both she and I knew it.

"What's upsetting you? I know it's not just your Dad. What's wrong?"

I emptied the rest of the wine into our glasses. I could feel the two glasses I'd already swallowed warming my stomach and I basked in the feeling. It was such a comfort.

"How long have we known each other?" I said.

Becca looked surprised.

"Five years? No, more. Six years? Ever since we both worked at Whitfords."

"Whitfords, that's right." Or 'Shitfords' as I'd overheard Becca calling it, one day in the canteen there. It had been a good time in my life, relatively; it was before I'd started to fall ill. Becca had left Whitfords not long after that but by then we were drinking partners, buddies, friends. That we still were, despite my illness, despite Angus's disapproval, seemed something of a minor miracle.

I was aware I'd fallen silent. Becca looked at me through the candlelight, frowning slightly.

"Want another drink?"

I gave her a wry look.

"What do you think?"

She grinned and pushed her chair back. While she was

waiting at the bar, I was thinking about my options. To tell, or not to tell? If I told, how much to tell? Should I just lie and make something up, for the sake of another few months of peace before she got curious again? It would be easier, but... in a strange way, I wanted to tell her. I hadn't spoken of this to anyone except Matt for years. Matt and my therapist.

Becca came back with another bottle, bless her. She poured us both a generous glass and I watched the condensation bead on the glass and run in a shining droplet to splash onto the table.

We didn't clink glasses this time.

"Look," she said, gently for her. "I know something's bothering you. You've got that look again." I opened my mouth to ask her to elaborate but she waved me down. "It's just – well, I want to help you. I'm your friend, after all. You don't have to tell me anything but, you never know, I might be able to help."

I nodded. I took a sip of wine, pondering. Becca sat back and smiled at me, gently still, but in her eyes I could see a glimpse of something that was almost greedy. For a second, I felt a tiny flash of dislike for her, and stamped down upon it. Of course she was curious, I'd been so mysterious about my past. I couldn't blame her. I felt the old impulse to pretend it didn't matter, to turn the subject. But what had Margaret said to me at our last session? *It's nothing to be ashamed of, Maudie. I think it's time you started letting people in.*

Guilt gripped me around the throat and I coughed. I took a sip of my drink. I talked to myself, like I so often did. *Becca's my friend, she won't judge me. Much.*

"Well," I began. I didn't know how to start. "It's not – I mean, it's not as if I've got something really terrible to tell you. Well, terrible in that it's something I've done. It's not. It's just – hard – for me to talk about."

Becca didn't say anything but she reached across the table and took my hand. Touched, I tightened my fingers around hers for a moment, before speaking again. I was finding it easier now, the words were coming more fluidly.

"When I was ten, I was on holiday in Cornwall with Angus. He'd bought two cottages out in the middle of nowhere, about a half an hour's drive from Penzance, which doesn't sound like much but really, they were incredibly remote, or so they seemed to me. It was the first time we went there - we had the one cottage and the other cottage – " my voice clogged and I coughed and started again, "the McGaskills took the other cottage."

"Who were they?" said Becca.

I looked down at the table, watching the flickering light of the candle.

"We'd all been – friends – for ages, but we'd never had a holiday at the same time. Do you see?"

"Yes."

I took a sip of wine.

"The McGaskills had a daughter. She was the same age as me. Jessica –" my voice cracked again and this time I took a gulp of wine. "Jessica. Her name was Jessica. We were best friends."

"Ah," said Becca, smiling. I felt a pang, knowing that what I was going to say would wipe that smile from her face. I knew she would be upset and distressed. But how could I spare her, when she wanted to know, and why should I spare her, anyway? I had to live with this every day. Let someone else share the misery, for once.

"We were best friends," I repeated. "We were both only children and we lived in the same village back at home, up in Cumbria. We went to the same school. We even looked alike, you know, skinny and blonde and little. We liked to pretend we were sisters, it was almost as good as having a real sister. People often took us for sisters. Mrs McGaskill – Jane – she was like a mum to me. I know people always say that, but she really was."

I'd drained my glass of wine. Becca saw me swallow.

"More?"

"Yes, please. Could I – sorry to ask you, but would you mind if I got myself a brandy before I go on?"

Her eyebrows went up.

"Of course. But don't worry – I'll get it."

She went to fetch the drink. I sat back in my chair, trying to breathe deeply. I felt panicky, trapped underground with the rest of my tale to be told. Over by the toilets, I caught sight of a flash of bright blonde hair and felt my stomach clench in fear. God – not now. I shut my eyes for a brief moment. I was not going to crack up now. Becca was coming back to the table, glass in her hand. I took a cringing look over her shoulder. No blonde woman in sight. *Get a grip*, I told myself.

The brandy helped. I tossed it back in one and felt the burn of it light a fiery trail all the way down to my stomach.

"Easy," said Becca.

"I'm okay," I gasped. I took a deep breath. "Where was I?"

"You were telling me about the Mc-something. The McGaskills."

"Yes. Jessica and I – we had such a good time – we'd go to the beach and go walking, bike riding. There was a farm next to the cottages where we used to go to look at the animals and help feed the calves if we could." Remembering this, I smiled. "I'm sure the sun didn't shine all the time, but it seemed like it did."

"A golden summer," said Becca, in a non-committal tone.

I looked at her. "Yes. Yes it was. It didn't matter so much to me, growing up without a mother, you know, because I had Jessica and her family. That was why – " my voice failed for a second. I coughed. "That was why it was so terrible, what happened. It ripped us all apart."

"What happened?"

"I'm coming to that." I took a deep breath. "There was an – an ancient place near the cottages. An ancient place of worship for the druids, or the Celts – there's similar places all over Cornwall. Not exactly a stone circle, but there's this one stone with a hole in it, and another you can see through... Jessica and I – I don't know – we just got obsessed by it. There was lots of folklore about it, you know. There still is. In the old days, the villagers used to take their sick children down to the Men-an-Tol at midnight and pass them through the hole, to heal them."

"The what?"

"The Men-an-Tol. It means 'stone with a hole'. Jessica and I made our own folklore up, except we kind of forgot we'd made it up and I think we almost believed it. She *did* believe it. Jessica said that when it was full moon, at midnight you could climb through the Men-an-Tol and you would go back in time." I saw Becca smile and smiled myself, unwillingly. "Oh, I know it sounds ridiculous now but you know what kids are like. We were so romantic, we just yearned for it to be true. I think we did honestly believe it."

I stopped talking for a second. The bar had become very crowded, people pressing in on our tiny table from both sides. People shouted and called across the room to one another and laughed loudly. I was glad of the tumult; it made me feel safer. I was too close to the story; I felt as if I could be pulled back into the past at any time.

"What *happened?*" said Becca. She leant across the table towards me, frowning.

I took another sip of wine. My tongue felt as if it were coated in glue. There was a part to this story that I was going to leave out, I just decided. It didn't have any bearing on what happened anyway and it was – private.

"That summer we were there, when we were ten... Jessica found out there would be a full moon during our holiday. Well, you can imagine how excited we were. We were going to go to the Men-an-Tol at midnight and climb through the hole. Jessica had planned it all. She was always more of the ringleader. She came up with most of our schemes but, you know, I was happy to go along with her. Anyway, we plotted and planned the whole thing. We were going to meet by the farm, by the hedgerow, and walk up to the circle, just before midnight."

I stopped talking.

"And? You did?"

I didn't answer for a moment.

"I didn't. She did."

"What?"

I felt tears prick at my eyelids.

"I meant to," I said. I pinched my nose to stop myself crying. "I woke up and got dressed and went downstairs. I got to the front door and I – I-"

Becca held my hand again.

"It's alright."

"I meant to," I said. My voice wobbled. "I got scared. I didn't go. I – I told myself that Jessica wouldn't go either."

A teardrop escaped and hit the polished surface of the tabletop. We both looked at it. I smudged it with my finger. I had the image of the front door in my head, slightly open; outside the night frosted with moonlight, the sky filled with ragged clouds and star-specks and behind it all, an abyss ready to pull me in.

"I just got scared," I said. "I'd never been out at night on my own before. The world just looked too big."

Becca squeezed my hand.

"Well, I don't think that's so terrible," she said. "You were only ten."

I snatched my hand back. How dare she misunderstand?

"Jessica did go."

Becca raised her eyebrows. "She did?"

"Well, we think she did," I said. I looked down at the table. "She went somewhere. She disappeared."

"What?"

"Just that. She disappeared. She was never seen again."

Becca's mouth fell open.

"What, *never*?"

"Never." I clenched my hands together under the table. "I don't think her mother ever forgave me."

Becca didn't appear to hear my last sentence.

"But – but – wasn't there a search? Didn't they find her?"

"Of course there was a search," I said. The brandy and wine were mixing uneasily in my stomach. "It even made the news, there were reporters down there and everything. But they never found her or her body. She'd just vanished."

Becca's eyes were wide.

"My God. That's – that's terrible."

"Yes."

"My God. They never found her. *Never*?" I shook my head. "Jesus," she said, "What do you think happened?"

I pressed a hand to my stomach. I was feeling steadily sicker. I could see the outline of the door in my head, the shadow behind it.

"I don't know."

"Are you alright?"

"Not really." I pushed myself up from my chair. "Sorry, Becca. I've got to go."

"What, now?"

"Yes. Sorry."

I grabbed my bag and coat and pushed my way through the crowded room. I could feel my stomach start to cramp. Bent double, one hand over my mouth, I just made it to the toilet in time.

CHAPTER SIX

"So, how have you been?"

My therapist always opened our sessions with that question. I pondered the answer, looking across at her seated in her sagging leather armchair, her legs neatly crossed. Margaret Greggs had clear, grey eyes and she always wore brightly coloured blouses.

I told her about being alone for the past couple of days while Matt was in Brighton. I told her something of what happened at the funeral. She nodded occasionally but mostly she just say there, calm as a Buddha statue, letting the words spill out of me. I normally found this room relaxing but today I could feel myself hunching in my chair and biting at a shred of dry skin on my lip.

"You seem anxious, Maudie. Is there something in particular that's bothering you?"

I was silent. I had been thinking about mentioning the thin, blonde woman, the woman I'd seen outside the flat.

"You know this room is a safe space, Maudie. There will be no judgement, no pronouncement on you. You can trust me."

I struggled for a moment and gave in.

"I've been seeing this – woman," I began. "I'm not sure – I mean, it's hard to say – "

"Go on. Take all the time you need."

"There's this woman. I keep – seeing her." I suddenly realised how that sounded. "I don't mean *seeing* her. I mean – " I stopped for a moment, flustered. "I don't mean seeing her as in sleeping with her, or anything. I'm not sexually seeing her. I mean – "

I stopped and took a deep breath.

"I mean, I've been really seeing her. I look, and she's there. You know."

Margaret raised her eyebrows encouragingly.

"How do you mean, Maudie?"

I swallowed.

"I actually see her. In real life. Oh God, I'm not explaining this very well. I mean, I suppose, that I keep *noticing* this woman. She keeps – turning up. Outside my flat."

"Mm-hmm?"

"Well, she has once," I said. "I mean, I've seen her once." I was floundering a little. It all sounded so insignificant. Would I be able to convey to Margaret just how frightened it made me feel?

"It's just – it's that - I'm not sure if she exists or not."

There was a moment's silence. I replayed the conversation in my head and clenched my teeth. "Sorry, it's just that I've seen her standing in the street. And – oh, I don't know – it's as if she… hates me – or something. Some really strong emotion. She has this intense stare."

Margaret said nothing. She sat there, inscrutable in her shabby chair, fixing me with her gaze, nodding slightly every time I paused.

"I thought I saw her at the funeral, but I didn't – I thought it was someone else but actually, it was me – "

Margaret held up a hand.

"Sorry, Maudie, could you repeat that? I don't quite understand."

I told her about the mirror mix-up, smiling as though it was a mildly funny anecdote. She didn't smile, just gave me a crisp nod.

"Then I had a bad dream a few nights later, at home and got up to get myself a drink of water. I saw her in the street, I mean, I saw her really for the first time. She was looking up at the flat, staring right at me."

Margaret frowned. "And do you think she wasn't really there?"

I chewed my bottom lip. "I don't know."

"And you haven't seen this woman since?"

"No. Although I keep thinking I see a flash of blonde hair and tense up, thinking it's her."

"You don't know who this woman is? Until recently, you've never seen her before?"

"No."

"So you have no idea who she is?"

I looked down at my hands. Somewhere deep inside me, I wanted to answer in the affirmative. I couldn't bring myself to do so. That would mean acknowledging what I knew to be impossible.

"No," I said, again.

There was a short silence. I looked down at my hands, noting I'd chewed most of the polish from my nails.

"Do you have any thoughts?" I said, quietly, not sure whether I wanted an answer.

Margaret put a hand up to her face, rubbing a finger along her jaw bone.

"To be honest, I'm not sure. I have to say this is a bit odd, Maudie. Now – " she held up a hand as I looked up in panic, "Now, I'm not saying there's anything to be worried about. But, I have to be honest, I would be easier in my mind if you could confirm that someone else had also seen her. Although I'm sure there is a perfectly rational explanation."

I nodded, miserably.

"But," said Margaret, "I also think we need to ask ourselves the question that doesn't seem to have occurred to you, just yet."

"What's that?" I whispered.

She smiled at me, kindly.

"Well, what is it that she wants? Why does she keep appearing?"

I could feel my eyes widening. Margaret went on.

"Had you thought of that?"

I shook my head.

"Well, then," she said. "It's probably something perfectly explainable. I think you need to ask her what she wants."

"But – " I struggled to find the words. "What if – what if I never see her again?"

"Do you think that's likely?"

I thought for a moment and shook my head.

"No," I said.

Margaret brushed a lock of hair from her face and tucked it behind her ear.

"Maudie, what do you think of the woman? What are your real feelings? How does she make you feel?"

I gnawed at my thumbnail, realised I was doing it and put my hand back down in my lap.

"Scared. She makes me feel scared." I thought some more. "And guilty. And I don't know why I feel guilty, except that's my sort of default setting."

"Why do you think that is?"

I looked at her quickly.

"You know why."

"Jessica?"

I nodded.

I took a taxi home from Margaret's house. I couldn't face the streets full of people, or any form of public transport, although she only lived a mile or so from my flat. I always emerged from a session feeling as though I were missing a layer of skin; I felt peeled, my nerve endings exposed to the outside air. And I was always cold, huddling myself into the taxi seat, my arms and legs crossed and hugged together for warmth.

I asked the taxi driver to drop me off at the end of the street. I needed to pick up a few things from the corner shop.

As I walked back along the street, I looked towards the flats, to the car park at the side of the building, hoping to see Matt's car parked there but not really expecting it – I knew he probably wouldn't be home until much later. His car wasn't there. I sighed inwardly and looked towards the entrance to the flats and as I did so, a tall figure in a long black coat came out of the doorway. Their back was towards me but flowing over the collar of the black coat was a fall of bright blonde hair.

I felt my heart begin a fast and painful thudding. Laden as I was with carrier bags, I began to walk faster, then faster still. The blonde figure was walking quite slowly towards the pedestrian crossing at the other end of the street. I put on a final burst of speed and caught up.

I heard my voice say 'excuse me' in a high, breathless gasp but before the figure could react I saw my hand go out, the heavy bag swinging from my wrist. I grabbed at an arm, quickly and roughly.

The person I'd accosted gasped and spun round. Facing me, thinly plucked eyebrows raised high, was the face of a stranger, a middle-aged woman. I released my grip, stuttering out an apology. Close to, I could see the greying roots of her bleached hair.

"What is it? What do you want?" she demanded

"I'm sorry," I said again. The carrier bags dragged painfully on my wrists. "I'm sorry – I thought you were someone else."

I stepped back and one of the bags broke. A bottle of wine fell to the ground and smashed; a small tidal wave of merlot flowed like blood over the concrete. I let out a cry. The woman looked at me and looked at the wine that had just splashed her shoes and her face twisted in something that was almost disgust. She shook her head and walked away quickly.

I hurried back to the flat, holding the remaining carrier bag close to my chest. I was shaking. I pictured the wine puddled on the pavement, little rivulets running into the gutter. I had picked up the pieces of the bottle as best I could and cut my finger in the process. I was a mess.

Where was Matt? I missed him as much as I had ever missed him. I turned the heating on high, put on some classical music, lit some candles. I opened one of the remaining bottles of red wine and drank the first glass down quickly, wanting the anaesthesia. I needed to feel safe.

Matt returned home an hour later and I felt a rush of relief at the sound of his key in the lock.

"I've missed you," I said with my arms around him a minute later.

"I've missed you too." He gave me a squeeze and his hands slipped down my arms to take mine. I winced and pulled away as my sore finger was touched.

He kissed my finger gently.

"There. All better now?"

I laughed. "Yes, thanks."

He went to the drinks cabinet and rooted about inside. He was wearing his tweed jacket and, for once, a tie with his shirt.

"Could I have one of those?"

"Aren't you already on the vino?"

"Yes," I said and fiddled with the controls of the stereo, turning away slightly. I didn't want to tell him I'd almost finished the bottle. "I just fancied a whisky, that's all."

He handed me my drink and sat down on the sofa with a long sigh of exhaustion, dropping his head back. I hesitated and then sat next to him. I told him about Becca coming for dinner, about seeing my therapist, about the new film I'd watched the other night on my own. I didn't tell him about the blonde woman. Perhaps I should have, but I so wanted him to think of me as stable, and capable; not someone to be pitied.

"How was your session with Margaret?" he asked. "Do you think that new thing she's got you on is doing any good?"

I picked up the TV remote and tapped it against my palm. It always made me awkward when Matt and I talked about my medication. I wanted to forget that I took pills.

"I think so," I said, not really caring whether it was true or not. "I feel fine, anyway."

"Don't do that," Matt said, taking the remote away from me.

"Sorry."

For a moment there was just the sound of a violin concerto coming softly from the stereo in the corner.

"So how was the conference?" I asked.

"Oh fine," said Matt, "Some quite exciting lectures, actually. I'll tell you all about it later."

"Great," I said, trying to sound enthusiastic. He had closed his eyes while he was speaking and I took the chance of studying him. He really did look tired, his skin dull and papery. He had dark circles beneath his eyes, visible even behind his foggy glasses.

"Oh, by the way," said Matt, opening his eyes. I leaned forward, smiling, eager. "Did you call the solicitor?"

"The solicitor?"

"Mr Fenwick, darling... Did you call him like I asked you to? We were supposed to contact him to discuss the estate and so forth, this week."

"We were?" I said, blankly.

"Yes, I asked you to do it before I left. When we were having dinner. Don't you remember?"

"No," I said, feeling guilty. Not only had I forgotten to do what I was asked, I'd forgotten Matt even asking me. I must have been more pissed than I realised.

Matt frowned. "But I asked you specially. I distinctly remember asking you. You really can't remember?"

"No," I said. "Sorry. I've –"

"You've what?"

I reached for the whisky bottle again and topped up my drink.

"I've had a lot of my mind lately," I said. "I'm sorry. Please don't be angry with me."

"I'm not *angry*," said Matt, "It just worries me how much you forget things, that's all. It really does. I can't believe anyone can be so absent-minded."

"I'm sorry," I said. "I'll phone him first thing tomorrow, I promise I will."

Matt sighed.

"Oh, I shouldn't be so hard on you," he said, reaching out his arms. I settled gratefully into them. "You've had a tough time of it lately, God knows."

That was when I should have told him. I should have confessed my worries, my anxiety that I was slipping. I didn't. He began to kiss me and, with relief, I kissed him back.

CHAPTER SEVEN

I asked Matt to marry me on Boxing Day, six months after we met. It came as something of a surprise to me, as well as to him, but it wasn't the first time I'd done something life-changing on impulse.

We were walking in the garden at Caernaven, trying to work off some of the Christmas dinner of the day before. Our breath steamed away before us; the ground was brittle with frost. The sky was grey and low and as we walked, I watched a solitary crow flap across the clouds, a little moving inkblot against the dirty white sky.

"Oh, the fish pond's frozen," I said, as we turned the corner of the walk and came back onto the terrace. "We'll have to pour some boiling water on the ice so the fish can breathe."

"Wouldn't it be quicker to smash it?" said Matt, who was stamping his feet and blowing into his cupped, gloved hands.

"No, the shock waves can kill them," I said, happy to tell him something he didn't know. We both looked at the frozen water, grey ripples of ice powdered with a dusting of snow. A blackened water lily leaf protruded from the surface.

"Come on," I said, somehow saddened by the sight.

"Your whole childhood is here, isn't it?" said Matt as we walked away.

"I suppose so."

Cornwall came into my mind. Eight weeks out of a lifetime spent there, just two short months and yet it had affected the rest of my life... I wasn't going to tell him that yet though. Suddenly it came to me that I would be able to tell him one day; that I *would* be able to tell him everything about me, and be comfortable doing it. I stared at him as we trudged through the frosty grass, dazzled by the realisation. As I had this revelation, my path forward became clear. I wanted that one day to be this day. I wanted our future together to start right now.

"Matt, will you marry me?"

The moment the words were out of my mouth I wanted to laugh, they sounded so silly. Matt stopped walking.

"What?" he said.

I cleared my throat and asked again.

"Are you being serious?" he said. He'd turned to face me fully, and his eyes were darting from one part of my face to the other. He was trying to spot the hidden smirk, the inward smile that would signal to him I was joking.

"I'm not joking," I said. "I'd like to marry you. Would you like to marry me?"

I think it started sinking in then. He put a gloved hand up to his mouth and I saw his breath huff out in a surprised cloud.

"You *are* serious." A smile started to break through on his face. "My God."

"So what's your answer?"

I felt irresistibly light hearted, all of a sudden, nothing like the solemnity the occasion was supposed to provoke.

Matt started to laugh.

"Of course I'll marry you."

I began to laugh too. We didn't touch each other, not then; we just stood opposite, laughing at each other's expression, our high spirits visible on the frosty air as smoky white clouds. Despite the cold, I had warmth blooming within me, as if a giant sunflower had spread its yellow petals in my chest. *I was going to marry Matt.* I felt light-headed, oddly dreamlike.

We carried on walking, holding hands. Every so often a giggle would bubble out of me. Matt kept glancing sideways at me, half incredulous.

"I keep thinking you're going to say 'got you!'" he said. "And it'll all have been a hilarious joke."

I turned to him and put my gloved hands up to his face. The pale winter light bleached out his skin, removing the crows feet from the corner of his eyes. His stubble looked very dark; I could feel it catch on the wool of my gloves.

"I wouldn't joke about that," I said.

He kissed me and then drew back.

"Aren't I supposed to ask your father for your hand in marriage, or something?"

I'd been smiling and at his words, I could feel the smile die on my face. I hadn't thought of Angus once since I'd asked my question; a small miracle. Was I scared of Angus's reaction? I wasn't *scared* of him, I decided, I just couldn't stand his relentless negativity. I just knew he wouldn't approve of what I'd done. Maybe – and this was another thought I pushed away as soon as I'd had it – maybe that was why I'd done it.

"Oh, don't worry about that nonsense," I said as carelessly as possible. "I'm a modern girl, I'll go and ask him. Tell him, I mean."

Matt looked uncertain.

"If you're sure – "

I nodded and took his hand.

"Don't worry about it," I said. "It'll all be fine. Leave it to me."

Angus was in the sitting room, in his usual chair by the fire. The door was fully open. I paused in the hallway, out of his sightline. Matt stood beside me and I turned and whispered to him to leave me.

"Are you sure?" he asked. I nodded. He walked away and I watched his long, flat back disappear around the turn of the staircase. Then I took a deep breath, and knocked on the open door.

Angus looked up from his paper. I had a smile on my face that at once felt forced and over-bright.

"Maudie," he said, nothing more than an acknowledgement.

I remembered him sitting by the side of my bed, during the bad time. The bedclothes were tight about me; I couldn't move my arms properly. He said something to me; what was it, now? *You're all I have.* That sounded like something born out of love, but was it? Perhaps what he meant was that I wasn't enough.

"Angus," I said, hesitantly.

"What is it?"

I stepped forward and warmed my hands at the fire so I didn't have to look at him directly. All of a sudden I was quaking.

I took a deep breath. Angus had put down his paper and was looking directly at me.

"Maudie?"

I forced a smile on my face as I turned to face him.

"I've got some wonderful news. Matt and I – " my throat closed up suddenly and I couldn't finish. I coughed and tried again. "Matt and I are going to be married."

It still sounded ridiculous. Angus was very still.

"Is that so?"

I nodded, again unable to speak. There was a long moment of silence, but I kept the smile on my face. After a moment, my cheeks began to ache.

Angus still said nothing. His hard grey eyes were fixed on my face, his gaze pinned to mine.

"Aren't you pleased?" I asked, immediately cringing. Why had I said that? Why did I say things like that, why did I ask, when I knew the answer was never, ever what I wanted to hear? Why did I lay myself open, scraping and bowing for his approval, when it never, ever came?

There was another moment's silence.

"I assume by your demeanour," he said, "that you've replied in the affirmative?"

He didn't need to know that I'd actually asked Matt, rather than the other way round. I could just imagine his incredulity at the idea. I made a mental note to warn Matt not to say anything.

"Yes," I said. Courage came to me from somewhere. "And I'm very happy about it."

"I'm pleased to hear it," he said, in a neutral tone. At long last he moved his eyes from my face to look at the fire and I felt as if two long sharp pins had been removed from my face.

I floundered for something else to say, to fill up the silence.

"We haven't set a date yet. Or where it's going to be, or anything really. I don't know exactly what you're supposed to do first – do you have to register something? Or fill in a form? It's all new to me, I haven't a clue what you're supposed to do."

Angus picked up the fire tongs and added another log to the fire. Sparks flowered out of the glowing coals in the grate.

"I assume," he said. "That you've already spoken about a pre-nup?"

I'd been watching the fire, half-hypnotised by the flames and didn't hear him properly. Or, if I did, I didn't understand him.

"Sorry?"

"A pre-nuptial agreement," said Angus. "I assume you and Matthew have already spoken about one?"

"No," I said blankly.

"If you haven't mentioned it to him already, that's the very next conversation you should have."

I hesitated. I began to feel that familiar flutter of

confusion, of not knowing the right thing to say. I knew I must have that look on my face, the look that drove Angus's voice to sharper, louder depths.

"Maudie, you must have thought about it. How could you not have?"

"I don't – I mean, I hadn't – " I started to stammer and shut my mouth.

"Maudie," he sighed, exasperated. "I know you're old enough to make your own decisions, wrong-headed as they might sometimes be. But I'll tell you this now, I cannot sanction this marriage, or give it my blessing, unless you promise me to enter into a full and appropriate pre-nuptial agreement with Matthew."

I stared into the fire. I could feel something, some emotion, begin to swell inside me and I couldn't work out what it was. I took a deep breath, trying to choke it down.

"You're not serious," I said.

He continued to look at me.

"I am completely serious."

I laughed a laugh that had no mirth in it.

"That's ridiculous."

Angus stood up. I took a step back. I knew what I was feeling now; it was anger. My entire neck felt stiff with it.

"Maudie," said Angus, quietly. "You are my only child. At some point in the future, you will be an extremely wealthy woman. It would be remiss of me not to give you every opportunity of protecting yourself for the future. You're so naive about the world sometimes – you think you know everything about it, but you don't."

The anger had reached my throat, my voice. I couldn't stop the words coming out.

"And what I want doesn't come into it?" I asked him through a stiff jaw. "Do you actually think I would be stupid enough to marry someone who's just in it for my money? Do you actually think that little of me?"

"Maudie, listen to me – "

"No, you listen to *me*! How dare you say that about

Matt? Do you think that he thinks like that? Do you think I am some stupid little girl who can't even be trusted to pick out her own husband? Would you have preferred to get one for me yourself? Or would you prefer that I never had one at all? Yes, that's it, isn't it? Why can't you just admit it?"

"Oh, stop being so melodramatic, for Christ's sake," said Angus. The contempt in his voice penetrated the fog surrounding me. I dropped my eyes to the dancing flames of the fire. I had more words inside me, a torrent of them, all the words I'd never said to him before. I put my hands up to my mouth, clamping it shut to stop them flowing out.

Angus sighed and sat back down. His hands fell loosely against the arms of the chair and I noticed for the first time how the bones of his fingers were beginning to protrude through skin growing papery. *He's getting old*, I thought. I couldn't work out if that made me feel better, or worse.

"You're overwrought," he said. "There's no point having this conversation now, you're not in any sort of mood to listen to me."

I was shortly going to cry, hard. I had to leave before that happened.

"Just think about what I've said," said Angus. His gaze was fixed on the flames, his body twisted away from mine. "That's all I ask. Just think about it."

*

I slept fitfully that night and woke at nine, feeling unrested. I wondered whether Matt had also passed a restless night. Just think, when we were married, we'd be able to share a room here. I missed his solid warmth in the bed. The house had never seemed colder.

After breakfast, I asked Matt to come for a walk with me. I could see by his smile that he thought I was taking him somewhere to celebrate properly, although God knows it was far too cold for any kind of *alfresco* antics. We pulled on our coats and scarves and walked out into the garden, stepping back over the same ground we'd walked yesterday.

"Maudie?"

I realised I'd been standing still, looking at nothing for nearly a minute. Matt was observing me with a half-smile. His nose and cheeks had pinked in the cold; he looked younger than usual, more carefree, more boyish. Was that because of my proposal? It was a lovely thought although there was something a little worrying about the fact that his happiness rested so firmly on a decision of mine taken on something of a whim.

"Sorry," I said. "I was miles away."

"Not having second thoughts, are you?"

"No!" I said, a little too quickly. "Not at all. It's just that – "

"What is it, sweetheart?"

I stood with my fists clenched for a moment. Then it burst out of me.

"My *fucking* father – " I said.

"Maudie!" said Matt, shocked. "What on earth – "

"He wants me to have a pre-nup," I said, talking over him. I clenched my teeth for a second. "It's such a stupid idea, it's so insulting, I won't blame you if you're furious, I can't believe he's making me ask you – "

"Whoah, whoah, whoah," said Matt, putting both his hands on my shoulders. He put a finger under my chin and tipped my face up to his. He was frowning, but more in puzzlement than in anger. "Slow down, and tell me from the beginning."

Falteringly, I summarised the conversation of the day before. Again, at moments, a choking anger overwhelmed me. *Thanks Angus*, I thought. *Thanks for managing to ruin what should be one of the happiest days of my life*. If Matt broke the engagement, would I be able to bear the humiliation? If he does, he's not the man I thought he was, I told myself, but it didn't really help.

After I finished speaking, I held my breath and waited for the explosion from Matt.

"Well," he said, after a moment. "I can't see that that would be a problem."

I let out my breath in a gasp.

"Oh Matt, really? You don't mind? You're not terribly insulted?"

That made him laugh a little.

"No, Maudie, I'm not. I can't believe you've got yourself into such a state over this."

"Really?"

He nodded. Then he pulled me closer and kissed me on my scar.

"You idiot," he said, "You're so daft, sometimes. You just don't think about all these practical things, do you?"

"It's not that –" I began. His words reminded me of what Angus had said. *You're so naive about the world.*

"It's alright," said Matt. "God darling, let's not even think about such awful things as divorce, not today."

"God, no," I said, limp with spent emotion. "I don't care about the stupid thing, it's just that Angus – " I stopped myself. "It doesn't mean anything anyway." I was babbling a little but mostly out of relief. "Money's not important, is it, anyway?"

"Of course not," said Matt.

"It's all ours to share anyway. And - " and I laughed lightly, "I'd never divorce you."

He pulled me close to him again and kissed me, properly this time. His mouth was warm against my frozen face.

"And *I'll* never divorce you either, sweetheart," he said, rolling his eyes.

"Let's never mention that word again."

Later that afternoon, I went into the room which

contained my mother's clothes. I found myself at the wardrobe, staring inwards at the racks of garments, her dresses and jackets and coats. I ran my hand along the row of hangers, rattling them against one another on the rail. My hand stopped at the last hanger; my mother's wedding dress, shrouded in rustling plastic. Slowly, I pulled it towards me and tugged at the zip. The long, silky white folds spilled out over my hands, glossy and cool against my skin.

I lifted the dress out and held it against me. I could never wear it – whilst beautiful, it was so obviously a dress of its time. I would look as if I were on my way to a fancy dress party. I hugged the dress tighter, moving so the slippery folds rippled against me. And I felt again the old, old longing, for a mother I couldn't remember, for a person I'd never known. She should be here with me right now, laughing over her old wedding dress, talking to me about my own wedding plans. I let the dress slither through my fingers and drop to the ground in a cold puddle of silk. There were tears pressing at the back of my eyes.

Chin up, Maudie. Be happy. Matt will be your husband. Be thankful for that. I told myself all these things, as I put the dress back into its bag on the hanger and replaced it in the wardrobe, before I left the room to join my family, the two of them, the old and the new.

CHAPTER EIGHT

Matt reminded me about the call to the solicitor's office as he kissed me goodbye. The sun had barely risen and I moved about the kitchen in a fog. I didn't think I'd drunk that much last night but I felt badly hungover, my head aching and my mouth parched and dirty. Outside, a drizzling rain made the air look grey and dirty. I pulled my dressing gown more tightly about me as I made coffee, wincing as I raised my head to look for the cafetiere.

"Got a headache?" asked Matt.

"No," I said. "I just slept badly."

"Right." He was pulling on his tweed jacket. "So you won't forget?"

"Forget what?" I said. I pushed my hair away from my face, yawning.

"The *solicitor*, darling, you remember? You said you'd ring Mr Fenwick to see what he wanted? God, Maudie – "

"Alright," I said, grumpily. "I don't see what the hurry is."

Matt gave me a cold look.

"It's not a question of hurry, Maudie, it's just that it's something that has to be sorted out. There's the estate, and the property and all sorts of things." He pulled on his black leather gloves. "I've asked you three times to do it.

You don't know how bloody tired I get of nagging you about it."

"So don't then," I said. "I said I'd do it."

"I shouldn't have to ask you three times," said Matt. "You're a grown woman. Christ, if my students were as slow to get things done as you are – "

"*Alright*," I said. "I'll do it today. Satisfied?"

"Yes," he said stiffly. He picked his briefcase and turned away.

I heard the front door slam and then watched for him as he walked out of the front door and came into my line of vision, stationed as I was at the kitchen window. I hoped he would look up so I could wave, perhaps pull a silly face, but he didn't. The rain was coming down harder now – I could see it darkening the shoulders of his jacket.

I felt a twinge of guilt. How easy it was for me to take things easy, whereas poor Matt had to trudge off to work at that second-rate college, every day. But he loved his job. He always said that teaching was one of the most rewarding things one could do. I remembered he was still waiting to find out whether he'd have a permanent place on the faculty. I hadn't asked him about it; I hadn't been encouraging or sympathetic. I finished my coffee and marched to the bathroom, determined to call Mr Fenwick as soon as I was dressed.

As I washed my hair, I thought again about our future. Perhaps, if I'd had to earn my own living, I would have been an entirely different person. I'd be quicker, tougher, smarter. As it was, I often felt as if I were drifting through life, acknowledging this but not really wanting to change it. I mean, no one really likes work, do they? Unless it's their vocation – as I'd always seen Matt's teaching. I blushed to think of that now; it seemed so patronising. Perhaps he would rather live my lifestyle, my easy, comfortable lifestyle; getting up when I wanted, reading books and watching TV, walking, swimming, visiting museums and art galleries, shopping, eating out, going to bars, seeing friends. What sort of person wouldn't like that? I wrapped a towel around myself and stepped from the shower, resolute. Today I would do *something*, something concrete, something I could report back to Matt.

I telephoned Mr Fenwick's office and spoke to him directly. I was still slightly hazy about what Matt wanted me to ask but, after the preliminaries, I made a tentative enquiry about the transferral of funds.

"We're still waiting for a few bits and pieces to be tied up," he said. "But it won't be a long before we're able to transfer the money. A matter of weeks, if that. Are you short of funds, Maudie? Because I'm sure the Trust can advance you something if it's needed."

"No, no, it's fine," I said, pinching a fold of my jeans between my fingers as I spoke. I'd never really given much thought to how the money in my account ended up there. It was just there, always, endlessly replicating. I pictured a cash point machine, and behind the screen, a treasure-filled cavern, glinting with jewels and glittering golden coins. "I just – it was just I wanted to make sure everything was – was going smoothly." Now I sounded like I didn't think Mr Fenwick knew his job. "I'm sure it is but – it's just a big responsibility and I just wasn't sure what I'm supposed to be doing – "

Mr Fenwick soothed me.

"Maudie, my dear, please don't distress yourself. Dealing with the outcome of a will can be a very upsetting time, despite the obvious financial – advantages, shall we say, that it brings your way. I'm sure Angus knew that you would be sensible in dealing with things. I'm sure he knew you would be reliable and not, well, get carried away."

I almost laughed. How little he knew me. And it made me realise that Angus must have lied about me or perhaps just evaded the truth. It was grimly funny, in a way. I muttered something appropriate in a response.

"That reminds me," said Mr Fenwick. "I know Angus was keen for you to get involved with the Board. Had you thought about that at all? I know it's early days but – "

"The Board?" I said, interrupting him.

"Yes, my dear," he said. "The Board of Directors at Katherine College. Surely Angus mentioned it to you?"

"The Board of *Directors*?" I said, knowing how stupid I sounded but unable to stop myself.

"He was very keen to have you involved."

I was silent for a moment, struggling for words.

"Mr – Mr Fenwick – sorry, but I'm a bit thrown – Angus wanted me to be on the Board at Katherine?"

"Yes, my dear," he said, unfazed. "I know he meant to talk to you about it and I just assumed he'd done so. From your tone, it seems not. I'm sure I didn't mean to upset you – "

"Oh - oh, you haven't," I stuttered, not wanting to upset him. "I was just – it just threw me a little, I had no idea. Angus didn't mention it to me. Perhaps he was going to before he – before he – " I couldn't bring myself to say *died.*

"Well, perhaps it's something to think about?" said Mr Fenwick. "Now that you know it's what your father wanted?"

"Yes."

"I would talk it over with Matthew, if I were you Maudie," he suggested. "I know that some of the directors are keen to meet with you when you're ready."

"Right," I said, helplessly. "Yes, I – I will."

"Jolly good, my dear." After saying goodbye courteously, he rang off.

I sat for a moment on the sofa, staring across the room. I felt winded. Why had Angus wanted me to take over his role on the Board? I put my hand up to my face, biting my nails. It just seemed such an unlikely thing for him to have done – to endow me with all that responsibility. For a moment, I couldn't remember what we ever *had* talked about, when we were together. The weather? My health?

And now this. Was this Angus's way of saying he – he

forgave me? That he thought I was someone whose judgement could be relied on? Was he saying that he believed in me, finally, after everything? Or was it just his way of keeping me within his grasp?

*

"To us," said Matt, clinking his champagne glass against mine.

"To us," I said and sipped my drink. The bubbles tickled my nostrils. I felt just fine; happily tipsy but still coherent, buoyed by my successful day.

"What a good idea this was," Matt was saying, "I'm amazed you got a table though."

"Angus had an account here," I said.

Matt rolled his eyes.

"Of course he did. Not that I'm complaining."

The waiter came to refill our glasses with the last of the champagne. I waited for him to leave, took a deep breath and relayed to Matt the conversation I'd had with Mr Fenwick earlier.

"The Board of *Directors*?" said Matt.

I had to laugh.

"That's exactly what I said."

"Well – " said Matt, doubtfully. "Well, I'm not sure what to say."

"That was pretty much my response at the time."

He put his glass back on the table.

"I'm sure – I'm mean, Angus wouldn't have wanted you to do it if he thought you weren't up to it," he said.

"Up to it?" I said.

"Well, yes," said Matt. "Come on, you know what I mean."

"I know I'm not very clever – " I began.

"That's not what I meant. You're not an *intellectual* or anything but that's not what I meant at all. "

I looked down at my plate. "You mean, I might not be

up to it – well, mentally."

"Yes," said Matt. He looked awkward. "Come on, darling, you know it doesn't matter to me. You can't help your past. But, well, that's not to say you should be put under any more pressure. I'm not sure you could handle the responsibility of a role like that. I mean, it's an executive position. You'd have all sorts of things to worry about."

Inside my head I agreed with him but the words still stung. Perversely, I wanted to disagree. I opened my mouth and shut it again.

"You don't have to decide now, do you?" said Matt. "I mean, that's the sort of decision you have to sleep on, surely? You don't want to rush into anything."

I nodded in agreement. He gave me a grin and squeezed my knee under the table.

"Let's have some more champagne," he said.

The waiter brought another bottle and poured us both full glasses. I watched the thin golden stream of champagne flow and froth in the glass. The waiter set the bottle back in the ice bucket and melted away.

"Cheers," I said.

"Cheers," said Matt. "We could drink to Angus. We haven't done that yet, have we?"

"No," I said. Suddenly I felt near tears. I swallowed hard. Matt reached for my hand.

"I know you're finding things a bit hard, lately," he said. "You're putting a brave face on it, for me, which I really appreciate, but you don't fool me. I can see that it's really affecting you."

His fingers were cold at the tips from grasping his champagne glass. I looked down at my plate, feeling something akin to panic. *You don't fool me.* What else could he see through? Was I fooling anyone? Even myself?

"Thanks," I said in a watery voice. The waiter, thank God, brought our main courses and broke the tension between us. We ate in silence for a little while. I was trying to think of a new topic of conversation.

Perhaps it was time I told him of my problems of the past few weeks. Perhaps I should tell him how I'd been feeling and about the strange sightings I'd had of the thin blonde woman. I took a decisive sip of champagne and made up my mind.

"Matt."

"Hmm?" he said, intent on his plate.

I took a deep breath.

"Some strange things have been happening to me." I never normally said things like this to anyone; I wanted to be thought of as sane, calm, normal. I attempted a light laugh. "I've been seeing – well, some odd things – "

I looked up, away from Matt's face, my eyes drawn across the room by something, some movement or flicker of light. I felt as if I were plummeting floorwards, out of control in a runaway lift. The sounds of the restaurant faded away, the chime of cutlery on crockery and the hum of the other diners' voices were sucked away from me as if into a vacuum. The blonde woman was standing not ten feet from me. Our eyes met. She had the same frozen expression that she wore the last time I'd seen her, concentrated emotion pouring from her eyes. I gasped. My champagne flute went flying, struck by my hand that flew out in an instinctive warding-off gesture. At the musical smash of glass, the woman wheeled around, her long black coat flaring out like a funereal flag. She walked quickly away and I heard the bang of the restaurant door as it slammed shut behind her.

I acted without thinking. I stood up and my chair fell backwards. I saw Matt's face change, and then I was past him, running through the restaurant, slipping through the tables, my only goal to find the woman, to hunt her down until she told me what she wanted. I ran past the astonished maitre d' and neatly sidestepped a couple that were just coming through the door. Then I was out in the street, the icy night air a shock of cold against my hot face.

I paused for a second, looking left and right for my quarry. Way off down the street I caught sight of a gleam of blonde hair as she walked beneath a streetlight. She was moving at a fast pace, her high heels ringing against the concrete of the pavement. I took a deep breath and ran after her.

I was almost hit by a car as I crossed West Street but I took no notice of the screech of brakes or the volley of obscenities. My whole being was concentrated on that distant halo of hair. I pounded down the street. Soon I was out of breath and holding my side. I passed hordes of people. Some of them shouted after me in derision or encouragement.

As I got within twenty yards of her, she looked round. Perhaps the thudding of my heart was audible. She looked at me – our eyes met – and, incredibly, I saw fear. She was scared of me. Her face contracted and she began to run herself, her coat flaring out behind her as she ran away from me.

"What do you want?" I shouted, voice raw in the icy night. The woman didn't flinch; she never looked back. As I ran, I saw her turn the corner of a street, out of my view. Ten seconds later, I was there myself, bent double, gasping. I looked along the street, expecting to see a fleeing figure. Nothing. She was gone. I slowed and stopped, one hand pressed to my side, pulling in air in great, noisy gasps. Nothing. I felt a great surge of anger and frustration, strong enough to blur my vision with tears. I dug my fingernails into my thighs. Nothing. I balled my hand into a fist and hit my leg, hard on the thigh, once, twice. *Fuck*.

"What the hell were you doing? What's wrong with you?"

I slipped back into my chair, my face throbbing. I tried smiling but it didn't come out properly.

"It's a long story."

"Well, it had better be bloody worth it." Matt's eyebrows were low, his mouth turned down at the corners. I reached for my drink, remembered I'd smashed the glass on the floor and withdrew my hand. My fingers were trembling.

Matt's voice was icy.

"*Maudie* – "

I sighed. The waiter came up with another champagne flute. I wondered whether he'd mention my sudden flight from the restaurant and my sheepish return. Of course he didn't; he'd been too well trained.

"Matt – "

"Would you mind telling me what the hell is going on?"

I picked up my new glass and took a sip. Now my breathing was returning to normal, I was beginning to feel foolish. The shot of adrenaline that had propelled me down the street was ebbing away and in its place was only embarrassment. I had ruined our night out. I made up my mind not to make things worse.

"I'm sorry, darling," I said, managing a real smile at last. I even laughed a little. "I just thought I saw someone I knew go past the restaurant. Someone from where I used to work."

Matt looked unconvinced.

"Who?"

"Katy," I said, improvising wildly. "Actually, I still have a book of hers and I suddenly remembered that and thought I might just catch her and explain..." My voice trailed off into silence.

Matt made a sound of disbelief.

"Sometimes I think you do it on purpose," he said. I could see a muscle twitching in his jaw, almost hidden by his dark stubble.

I shook my head.

"No, that's not – "

Matt withdrew his hand and picked up his fork.

"Okay," he said. "Let's leave it."

"I'll get dinner," I said on impulse, hoping that would

help.

"Thanks," said Matt, grimly. He kept his eyes on his plate.

I nodded again and we sat in silence, until the waiter came with the bill for me to pay.

CHAPTER NINE

"You look fine," said Matt. "Stop fidgeting."
Immediately I put my hand back on my lap, having just reached for the windscreen visor mirror.
"I'm not."
Matt glanced over at me and smiled.
"I don't know why you're so nervous. It's only a little gathering. A get-together to celebrate Bob's book. That's all."
"I'm not nervous."
"So why do you keep fidgeting?"
We were driving through an area of South London I didn't recognise, somewhere beyond the borders of Brixton.
We drove in silence.
"What's Bob's book about?" I finally asked.
Matt breathed out sharply through his nose.
"Semiotics."
"Oh," I said. I opened my mouth to say something of what I knew about semiotics, realised it was nothing, and shut it again.
"I'm surprised you don't write a book," I said, after a moment. "Why don't you?"
Matt gave me a pained glance.

"Because, Maudie –" he began and then sighed and didn't say any more.

"What?" I said.

"Nothing."

"No, what?"

"Oh, just leave it, for God's sake. We're here now, anyway."

I'd been feeling anger, rather than anxiety, but at this announcement my heart rate leapt up a notch. I wasn't very good with crowds of strangers. I'd managed to sink a couple of glasses of wine before we left the flat but it wasn't enough; I could still feel everything. I needed more to drink. I needed numbness.

"Maudie, there's nothing to worry about," said Matt, taking pity on me. "They're all perfectly nice, normal people. They won't eat you."

"I know," I said. Anxiety made my voice shriller than normal. I sounded ridiculous.

"You'll be fine."

The author, Bob, was throwing the party, along with his wife Carla. This much I'd managed to ascertain from Matt but as to the dress code, the number of people there and other such vital pieces of information, I'd drawn a complete blank. I'd ended up wearing my red silk dress and my new heels but was it too much? Too formal? Would everyone be laughing at me behind my back? I found myself clenching my fists.

The woman who opened the door was short and dumpy. She wore the sort of glasses you saw on actresses playing secretaries in films from the 1950s, jeans and a black shirt. No jewellery. I began to feel a slow sinking feeling. I was completely overdressed.

"Matt!" she said. She smiled at me. "I'm Carla and you must be Maudie. It's so nice to meet you finally. Do come in."

We followed her into the narrow hallway. I could smell cigarette smoke and dog. The place was a mess;

comfortable and homely, but a mess all the same. I thought about keeping my coat on but knew I'd never get away with it.

"What a gorgeous dress!" said Carla. "Come through and meet everyone." She must have realised how nervous I was. "It's alright, we don't bite!"

I should have been grateful for her understanding but I felt like punching her. I put on a weak smile and followed Matt. I was soon swallowed up in what seemed to be a crowd of about fifty people; all in their forties and fifties, all dressed in jeans and shirts and casual shoes. I stood out like a beacon. I quickly lost track of people's names and inter-relationships. I was too busy fixing the smile on my face and trying to hold onto Matt's hand.

They were all what Matt had said they were – kind, nice people. It wasn't their fault that I found their topics of conversation by turns incomprehensible or boring. There was a lot of talk about teaching, about living a middle-class life in London, a little about various current topics of news. I didn't say much, really; I didn't feel there was much I could contribute.

I was introduced to Bob, who looked like Merlin and wore a tweed jacket even more decrepit than Matt's. I managed to say "Well done on the book," which drew from him extravagant thanks.

The one thing I could do was drink. In my defence, the wine was flowing freely and my glass was constantly being refilled, so it wasn't as if I actually set out to get drunk, but I did. My trips to the downstairs loo became every more wobbly. I started to join in conversations with comments that I thought were witty and hilarious. At first people responded, but as my voice became louder and more slurred, their smiles began to be a little more fixed and their glances at Matt became ever more frequent. I'd stopped waiting for my glass to be filled by our hosts and simply helped myself from the big fridge in the messy kitchen. Carla kept bringing round little plates of food;

rough, handmade canapés, and bowls of crisps and bits of cheese, and I had a few handfuls but after a while I didn't feel so hungry any more.

I have a vague recollection of being in the hallway and watching Carla's glasses winking in the light from the ceiling. She seemed to have three pairs of glasses, on three heads and I tried to focus on one by shutting one eye and squinting. Matt was saying something and I knew I had to say something too but nothing was coming out properly; all I could manage was a garbled mess of words. There was the shock of cold air outside the door and the dreadful, inexorable feeling of vomit travelling upwards towards my mouth. I didn't make it to the street; I was sick on the pathway. I was too drunk to feel any shame - my overriding sensation was one of relief. I vomited again by the car and again by the side of the road after Matt pulled over. I could feel his hands gripping me about the waist as I heaved and choked. Then there was nothing but a few scraps of tattered memory left in my head and a merciful, inky blackness that saw me through to the next morning.

Death would have been a merciful release compared to the effort and horror of having to wake up, get up, of dealing with the torment of having to face Matt again. What I could remember of the evening made me want to curl into a ball and scream into the pillow, except I couldn't have made that sort of level of noise without my head exploding, so I merely lay in a foetal position with my face in my hands. I moaned quietly to myself until that hurt too much and then I just lay there.

The door to the bedroom opened and I froze. How could I deal with this? Would it be best to be sobbingly remorseful or should I try to joke it off? I hadn't lost control like that in front of Matt for a long time.

"I thought you might need a coffee," said Matt.

I tried to gauge his tone but my head hurt too much. I took a deep breath and hauled myself into a sitting position. My head thumped painfully.

"Thanks," I said. I took the mug from him, not daring to look up.

"How are you feeling?"

Was he being sarcastic? I risked a glance. He looked fairly neutral.

"Not too bad," I muttered. "Bit of a headache."

"I'm not surprised."

I thought I'd be able to make a joke of it but I felt so bad, in all ways, that the tears suddenly welled up. I started to cry.

"Oh Matt," I wailed. "I'm sorry. I made such an idiot of myself. I'm so sorry."

He didn't say anything. He didn't make a move towards me. But he didn't turn on his heel and leave. I started stammering out excuses, promises, anything to make him react in the way that I wanted.

"I'm sorry, I'm sorry - I don't know how I could have made such a fool of myself." I flung myself back down on the pillows and pushed my wet face against the cool cotton surface of the pillowcase. "I'm sorry."

Still he said nothing.

"I'm sorry, sometimes I just can't cope with things and I know it's not a solution but I find things really hard sometimes. You know I've been ill and sometimes it just comes back and I can't do anything about it."

Silence still from Matt. I cried a little bit louder.

"I'm sorry. It's just - sometimes things are so hard." I wiped my hand under my running nose. "I'm still grieving. I've just lost my father."

I heard him sigh and then the creak of the bed and the dip to the mattress as he sat down beside me.

"Maudie - "

I wriggled round to look at him. A small part of me was aghast at presenting my tear and snot-soaked face to him but if it would get me off the hook, it needed to be done.

"I'm sorry," I said, sniffing.

"I just don't get why you needed to get that drunk," he said. "Did you mean to? Honestly, Maudie, it was a stupid thing to do. Completely childish. You're not a teenager anymore."

"I know," I said, eyes downcast. "It's just -"

"Just what?"

"Oh, nothing," I said. My voice caught again. "I just - sometimes, it's just too much."

"What is?"

I lay back down again, staring into the white cotton of the pillowcase.

"Everything. Angus and Jessica and – everything."

Matt was quiet for a moment. I heard him draw in a breath.

"You can't blame every bit of bad behaviour on what's gone wrong in your life, Maudie," he said. "Sooner or later you have to take responsibility for yourself."

I said nothing. I could feel anger and self pity sweeping over me in a giant, poisonous rage.

There was a short silence. Then Matt got up off the bed.

"I think I'll let you sleep it off," he said. "Then later you can ring Bob and Carla and apologise. *Yes*, Maudie - " as I made a sound of protest."That's only fair."

I pushed my face into the pillow, hating him, myself, the world. I heard the door close gently behind him.

Later that evening, when I was lying on the couch and feeling marginally more human, although no less terminally wretched, Matt came back from wherever he'd been. I sat up and tried to smile. He didn't say anything and he didn't kiss me. I felt my heart sink. He went to the kitchen and I could hear the clink of bottles.

When I heard him walking towards me, I turned my head. He was holding out a glass of what looked like murky tomato juice.

"Here you go," he said. "Have a hair of the dog. I think you've suffered enough."

Immediately, I felt ten times better. I reached for the

glass and took a sip. He'd made it strong; for a second I felt myself gag as the burn of the vodka hit my poor, abused stomach.

"Thanks," I said. "I phoned Bob and grovelled."

"Good," said Matt. "Well done. I'm sure it's nothing he's not seen before; he teaches freshers, for God's sake."

I laughed a little, weakly.

"Thanks for the drink."

"You're welcome," he said. "Idiot."

I laughed again and relaxed back against him as he sat down next to me. I smiled up at him and kissed him. The vodka was making me feel almost normal again. He tightened his arm around my shoulders.

"I shouldn't have been so hard on you," he said. "You've been through a lot lately, it's understandable you're going to react in some way. "

"Thanks," I said. I snuggled myself more firmly into his arms.

"Just don't do it again," he said.

"Of course not," I said, and laughed lightly. "Don't worry about me. I'll be fine."

CHAPTER TEN

Forgiveness or not, Matt was stiff with me the following morning. Our breakfast was normally punctuated by the singing of random song lyrics (Matt had a particular fondness for Bob Dylan in the mornings) but today, quietness reigned over the cornflakes. I kissed him goodbye at the front door and he kissed me back but with lips that did not yield.

Alone in the flat, I mooched around, picking up a magazine and dropping it again, collapsing on the sofa and then getting back onto my feet. I looked at the clock; eleven am, surely not too early for a gin and tonic? A pre-lunch aperitif? I gathered together a few bills and shuffled them about on the desk, swigging at my drink. God, I hated paperwork. I was bored again, bored and restless. Stupidly I thought that perhaps I should think about getting a job. Then I remembered the money that would soon be ours and told myself not to be so ridiculous.

The G&T went down so nicely I poured myself another. The telephone rang as I was flicking through the television channels, in the faint hope I might find something worth watching. Mr Fenwick's dry, correct voice greeted me as I picked up the handset.

"It's the estate, my dear," he said after the preliminary

pleasantries. "I'm so sorry to bother you but we really do have to have a think about what we're going to do with it.

"Yes," I said. "I didn't think – I mean, I know I have to decide what to do about the house and so forth."

"Indeed. You'll have to decide whether you want to keep it, perhaps rent it out, or sell it. Mrs Green will want to know if her services are required, plus there's the casual staff and so forth."

"Yes," I said again, hesitating. I didn't want to think about it, about any of it. "Perhaps – perhaps I might take a trip up there and see if I can help – I mean, I can decide what to do."

"I think that's a fine idea, Maudie. Oh, I am sorry to have to pressure you but really, I think it should be your decision, yours and Matthew's, of course. If I thought Matthew would be happy to take charge – do you think he would?"

I answered without pause.

"Oh no, Mr Fenwick, he's far too busy at the moment. I'll be fine, I can do it."

"Well, that's marvellous then Maudie, as long as you think it won't be too much for you. Perhaps you could give me a call when you get back to London?"

After I put the receiver down, I sat for a moment, staring out of the window at a grey-skied winter day. I had no idea what to do about the house, or the staff. I wanted to ask Matt his advice but I thought it might be better to present myself as capable and able to take care of myself; to reassure him after my behaviour at the restaurant and at the party. I decided to present him with a fait accompli.

"I'm heading up to Caernaven tomorrow," I said to him over dinner.

He raised his eyebrows. "Oh, really? Why's that?"

I told him of Mr Fenwick's telephone call.

"And he thinks we should sell it? Well, I suppose we should at least think about it. We've got to do something about it, sooner or later."

I pushed at the food on my plate before answering.

"I don't - "

"What is it?"

I put down my fork and reached for my wine.

"I don't know if I want to sell it."

Matt looked at me steadily.

"Why not, Maudie? It's not like we spend a lot of time there. You're not saying you want to live there, are you? Darling, it's so far away! We'd spend half our time driving back and forth."

"I don't *know* what I want to do. I'm just – I'm just going up to have a look, that's all. To have a think."

Matt had paused in cutting his steak. Now he picked up his knife again.

"I'm not sure you should drive all the way up," he said, after a pause. "It's a very long drive for you to do alone."

"Oh, I'll be fine," I said. "I've done it hundreds of times."

"Well, I'll worry about you."

"Oh really," I said, uncomfortably. "I'll be fine."

"I'm not sure it's a good idea."

"Matt," I said, without a thought of what I was going to say next.

"What happens if you have another – another episode like the one the other night?" he said, not looking at me.

I was struck dumb for a moment. I thought, with a quake of shame, that I didn't know which episode he was referring to.

"What do you mean?"

"You know – at the restaurant."

"I've *explained* that," I said, hating the querulous sound of my voice. "And I've said I'm sorry."

Matt sighed. He put his knife down again.

"Alright," he said. "I don't want to argue. Just – just be aware that I worry about you, that's all."

He got up and took his half-eaten steak over to the counter.

"We all worry about you," he said, so quietly I barely heard him.

I didn't eat much after that. I put the plates in the dishwasher and watched television desultorily for an hour. I opened another bottle of wine. I was thinking hard. Perhaps I *should* sell Caernaven. It was no doubt worth a huge sum of money and I knew it cost almost as much to run. But it wasn't as if we were going to be strapped for cash anytime soon. Perhaps it would be the best thing; let some other family fill it up and make their own memories there, happy ones this time.

I decided to drive up and left early the next morning, so early I was out the door before Matt had got fully dressed. I kissed him goodbye and he told me to drive safely.

I hesitated before I left, wanting to say something else, but I couldn't think what. As I drove out of London and joined the motorway heading north, I began to feel angry. Why was Matt acting so continuously hard-done-by? I seemed to annoy him constantly at the moment. Alright, so I'd forgotten a few things and drunk a bit much a couple of times, but so what? *My fucking father's just died*, I said to him, arguing with the version of Matt that I carried around in my head. That was my excuse and I was sticking to it but I felt a momentary qualm. I'd tried for so long to seem normal. It hurt to think that he might soon look at me and think I was about to slip. Perhaps he was already thinking that, after my behaviour at the Ivy. *But I'm not*, I told myself fiercely. *I'm perfectly fine.*

It was raining when I finally pulled into the driveway of Caernaven and made my way slowly down it, the gravel under the tyres making a sound like rushing waves. For the first time, there was no Angus to greet me at the door, no exchange of awkward kisses. I paused for a moment after shutting the door, breathing deeply. Mrs Green had long since gone home to her tied cottage that lay about half a mile down the estate lane. She'd left a note for me, telling me she'd see me in the morning, and a casserole kept warm by the Aga. I ate it at the kitchen table, unwilling to bear the dining room with its frigid temperature and the empty chair at the head of the table. Then I went down to the cellar.

The kitchen was always warm from the Aga but walking down the cellar steps was like plunging into a cold pool. The air down there smelled dank and the dusty bottles in their serried rows glinted dully in the wan light that fell from the doorway at the top of the stairs.

The only light switch was at the bottom of the stairs so there was always the terrifying descent into darkness when walking down the steps, and the equally frightening, panicky run back up, with the dying of the light behind you and the darkness that came snapping at your heels. I took an armful of bottles, not checking the labels, and bolted the cellar door behind me when I got to the kitchen.

I poured myself the first glass and wandered through to the hallway. I had taken off my shoes at the door and my socked feet moved almost soundlessly over the chessboard tiles on the floor. *This is all mine*, I thought. I felt oppressed by the knowledge. Despite the high ceilings and the wide hallways, the house felt as if it were shrinking, pressing itself closer and closer about me. I walked up the stairs, trailing my free hand up the polished banister. At the first landing, the stairs split in two and I followed the left-hand stairway, walking up to the first floor where the majority of the bedrooms were. I paused outside Angus's room, my hand on the door handle. Then I pushed the door open and went inside, walking over the spot where he'd fallen and died. I only realised this once I'd done it and a shudder went through me.

I stood in the centre of his bedroom. It was tidy, the bed stripped bare, the fireplace empty save for a few flecks on soot on the grate. For all that, it smelt musty, unaired. I realised I had one hand up to my mouth and I kept swallowing. There was an old photograph of my mother on his dressing table, but no image of me. I felt a jab of anger. Why didn't he have a photograph of me? Was I that much of an embarrassment, that he couldn't bear to be reminded? The anger cooled as quickly as it had appeared and I felt my eyes burn yet again. Abruptly, I turned and left, banging the door behind me.

I had some thought of going into the rest of the bedrooms on this floor but I had finished my wine. I went back to the kitchen to top up my glass, slopping it over the side.

I decided to go to bed early, to turn my back on the day and make a real start tomorrow. There were papers to go through and documents to find. All of a sudden, I felt weary. It was this twitchy, fraught state that frightened me in London; it was then I had strange thoughts and fancies. I thought for an instant of the blonde woman, but somehow knew I would never see her here. She belonged to London and all its tensions.

I had a missed call from Matt on my mobile, asking if I'd got there safely and to please call him as soon as I could. I rang him and waited, a little nervously, for the phone to be answered but my call went through to the answer machine and his mobile was switched off. He hadn't mentioned he was going out. Perhaps he'd fallen asleep. I left him a loving and light-hearted message, trying to sound as carefree as I possibly could, hoping that would reassure him. Then I trailed up to bed and sat down, stretching my legs and wincing at the ache in my back. I put the half empty wine bottle and another, full one on the bedside table. I felt jumpy and nervous. The house felt too big; I could feel the space of it behind my bedroom door, its creaks and echoes and empty rooms. I returned to my bed and the wine bottle and began drinking determinedly, seeking a measure of bravado, or alternatively, sledgehammering myself into oblivion for the night.

CHAPTER ELEVEN

True to her word, Mrs Green was in the kitchen cooking breakfast for me when I stumbled downstairs at half past eight, my head throbbing. Her greying hair had recently been crisply permed and her broad, capable hands were following their familiar routine; breaking eggs into their poaching pans, measuring coffee grains into the percolator, wiping crumbs from the surface of the breadboard.

"How have you been, Maudie?"

"Well," I said, tentatively. The smell of coffee caught in my throat. Nausea hit me and I turned away, breathing deeply.

"Oh, I'm sorry dear. Of course you haven't been here since the funeral, have you? It must be hard." She sighed. "It's not been the same since he's gone, you know. Well, of course you know. It's not the same at all."

The nausea receded. I managed to mutter something in response.

"Breakfast won't be long," she said. "Are you alright? You look a bit peaky."

"I'm okay," I said. "Just a bit under the weather." I kept my distance, in case she caught the reek of wine fumes from me. "I'm sure a bit of breakfast will do me good."

After I'd forced a plate of food down my reluctant throat and sat for a moment, struggling not to vomit, I levered myself back up and went outside for a bit of air. My head was killing me.

The sun was struggling feebly through a bank of grey cloud. I could barely see the mountains; they were cloaked in mist. I took a few deep breaths, trying to quell the nausea. This house was bad for me, in all ways. Perhaps I should sell it.

After a while, I went back inside and straight up to the study. Angus had been an organised man, a skill I didn't think I'd inherited. I waded through neat reams of paper and countless files, all correctly labelled. What exactly was I looking for? Why was I even *here*? I was just fumbling around, as usual, getting in the way, not knowing my purpose. Halfway through the morning I called Matt's mobile, just to say hello, but it was turned off. He probably had a class. No matter, I'd try him later.

There was really nothing for me to do in the study. I drifted back to my room and began to poke around in the cupboards. Within minutes, I'd found a whole heap of absorbing stuff; stuff I'd forgotten about for years – school certificates and books and faded photographs. There were several from boarding school, including a group photograph of all the girls in my final year. I'd framed it, for some reason; God knows why I'd thought it worthy of that. I picked it up, wiping the dust from the surface of the glass. There was my fifteen year old self, third row, fifth from the left; my hair in an unfortunate fringe and the knot of my school tie slightly askew. I wasn't smiling.

I dropped the photograph and wiped my hand on my jeans. I sifted through a few old textbooks and dog-eared notebooks. There was a battered old teddy bear wedged underneath another heap of exercise books. I picked them up to see if I could free him and then recognised the writing on the front page of the top book. My God, my old diaries. I picked up the topmost one and weighed it in my hands. I felt a sudden reluctance to open it. If only I could be sure of the year, without opening it, to see if it was safe for me to read... I took a deep breath and turned over the front cover.

I'd been holding my breath and when I read the first entry, I sighed out with relief. This was from nineteen eighty; I had written about starting the new school year and how I didn't much like my new teacher, the unfortunately named Mrs Spot. How Jessica and I had giggled over that name. Seeing Jessica's name on the page in my eight year old handwriting gave me a jolt. I read on a bit further, slowing turning the faded pages. Some entries were written in pencil and almost illegible.

After a while, I sat down with my back to the radiator, the warmth of it pushing against the whole length of my spine. Gradually, as I read on, the central heating went off and the metal cooled against me until I looked up from the diary and levered myself from the floor, cramped and stiff. I creaked across the carpet, leaving the diaries in a heap on the floor.

My hangover was finally abating and a cup of coffee should see it off for good. Down in the kitchen, waiting for the kettle to boil, I tried Matt's mobile again and this time he answered.

"Hi, it's me."

"Maudie, where the hell have you been? I've been worried sick. Why didn't you call me when you got there?"

"But I did," I said, blankly. "I called you when I got here, didn't you get my voicemail?"

"No I did *not*. I saw you'd called me this morning but there wasn't a voicemail. It was that that stopped me calling the police."

I quailed – he was talking in the clipped, precise way that meant he was completely furious.

"I'm sorry," I said, not knowing what sort of tone to use. I *had* left him a message. Hadn't I? "I did leave you a voicemail when I got here yesterday, I'm sure I did."

"Well, I didn't get one. I got some garbled nonsense that

cut off halfway through but that could have been anyone; it didn't even sound like you. Were you drinking last night?"

"No," I said, my automatic response. I tried to think of something plausible. "I was really tired. Maybe I sounded a bit weird."

"It wasn't just that, it just didn't even sound like a human voice, it was just a load of static. Why the hell didn't you call me again?"

"I'm sorry." I felt like crying. "Maybe it was the reception here. It's never been that good."

"God," he said. "You'll be the fucking death of me."

"I'm sorry," I said for the third time. I hit myself on the leg a couple of times and clenched my face in pain. I kept my voice at a normal level.

I heard Matt take a deep breath in and sigh it out.

"Alright. Alright. Just as long as you're okay. Have you made any decision about the house?"

"Er – not yet. I'm still looking through things here. We can talk about it when I get back."

"I don't particularly *want* to sell it," he said. "It would just be one less thing to worry about."

"I know," I said. I thought of him in the flat, sitting in his study, the ashtray on the desk piled high with cigarette stubs as he waited for me to call him. I was a shitty wife. I would do better in the future. I made him a silent promise in my head.

"Look, I've got to go, my break is almost up. Please, please call me before you set off tomorrow so I know what time I can expect you."

"I will, I promise," I said. "I love you."

He sighed again. "I love you too. Bye."

I took the phone from my ear and looked at it as the buzz of a broken connection sounded in my ear.

"Bye," I said, to empty air.

Mrs Green had lit the fire in the bigger drawing room

and I curled myself on the sofa in there after lunch, my pile of diaries beside me. Although the sight of Jessica's name still gave me a jab of pain whenever I saw it, I was becoming more and more absorbed in my half-remembered childhood. In some ways, it felt as if no time at all had passed since I'd actually been the age I was describing in the diaries.

I read through my eighth year and my ninth. Then I reached the last book, the last diary I ever wrote. I read the sentence that began *Angus says we're off first thing tomorrow. I can't wait. I've never been to Cornwall before and this year will be brilliant...* before I closed the cover and put the book down. I didn't want to read any more. I would take the diaries home with me, even if I never read them again. At least they would be there, safe with me, ready and waiting in case I was ever able to read the last book. I looked out of the drawing room window at the darkening garden and thought, unwillingly, about the past.

CHAPTER TWELVE

"I don't know why I let you drag me into this," I said to Becca.

"What?"

I repeated my question in a shout. Becca winced.

"Come on," she said. "I knew it would do you good. Stops you sitting at home and festering. Besides, I haven't seen you for ages."

I felt a little pang of guilt.

"Yes, I'm sorry. Things have been a bit hectic, what with having to go to the Lakes and Matt working so hard and so forth…"

"What?"

"I said – "

"Oh God, this is ridiculous, I can't hear a word. Let's go outside for a bit."

We squeezed ourselves through the crowd in the corridor and headed for the street outside. Becca's firm had hired L'Amour for their Christmas party and she'd invited me along. Music was throbbing from the largest room, bouncing off the glittering white walls, shaking the enormous chandelier that hung from the ceiling in a frozen waterfall of crystal shards. We eased ourselves through the scrum of people hanging around the back door of the club, into the dingy back alley and stood teetering on our heels.

"Christ, that's better," said Becca. "Some fresh air at last."

She lit a cigarette immediately and I grinned.

I felt better, despite the cold. The heat and the crowd and the noise inside had made me jittery; it seemed a long time since I'd been around so many people.

"How was your trip up North?"

I grimaced.

"Weird. Sad. A bit stressful."

"Well, it would be, wouldn't it?" Becca patted my shoulder. "Bound to be a bit strange going back to the house without your Dad in it for the first time. Have you decided what you're going to do with it yet?"

I shook my head.

"How's Matt?" she asked.

I blinked and smiled.

"Oh, okay."

"You don't sound very sure."

"No, it's not that – " I shrugged, suddenly flustered. "Well, he's still not sure whether he's got this thing at work. Whether he's passed his probation. I think it's weighing on his mind a bit."

"Yes?"

"I think so. He's not said anything, but I think it's bothering him."

"Oh well, " said Becca. "I'm sure he'll be fine."

"Yes," I said. I thought back to last night, how I'd woken up in the middle of the night to find the bed empty. I'd gone to the study, knowing what I'd see; Matt, hunched over his laptop, smoking and frowning. He'd looked up when I'd appeared in the doorway and for a moment, his face had been the face of a young boy, vulnerable and innocent. This time it had been him who'd come to me for comfort; in bed, he'd clutched at me as if he were falling and I was the only thing holding him up. Even afterwards, in his sleep, he'd kicked and groaned and thrashed around, as if he were fighting his own version of the monster in the

Men-an-Tol. At breakfast this morning I'd hoped to hear him sing, and he did once, just one line, something about a shadow he was seeing...

"You're right," I said to Becca, as firmly as I could manage. "He'll be fine."

We danced, swaying and sweating beneath the kaleidoscope lights.

"God, I'm hot," said Becca. "I'm going to get another drink. Want one?"

I knew I shouldn't. I already felt light-headed, a little blurred around the edges. But I needed something to soften me up, help me feel a bit more removed from the ragbag of emotions that made up my life.

"Go on then."

Becca left me and I moved back to lean against the wall, feeling suddenly exposed. The drumbeat of the song currently playing thudded through my body like a giant heart beat. I felt breathless. All around me people were shrieking and laughing and dancing. I looked up, searching for Becca's familiar face at the bar.

Then I saw her. Not Becca. *Her*. It was almost funny, the way the crowds parted for just that instant, long enough to allow our eyes to meet, just like a clichéd love song. The blonde woman stood there, her hands in the pockets of her long black coat. She was looking at me directly and for a long moment, we both stared at each other. Her face was almost expressionless, perhaps the faintest touch of sadness apparent in her eyes. She wasn't smiling or glaring. She just stood, and looked.

I shut my eyes. When I opened them again after a moment, she was still there, still looking at me. I felt a jab of fear hit me in the pit of the stomach. She continued to look steadily at me. I blinked again and she was still there, still looking me full in the face.

The pounding of the music, the noise of the crowd faded away. For a frozen moment, her face was my entire world. Suddenly I wasn't afraid any more. As I watched, the woman raised her hand, a long, thin white hand, and began to beckon. Dazedly, I felt my legs begin to move of their own volition. She was a siren, drawing me in, trapping me with an unseen noose trailed from her long, sharp-nailed finger. I moved across the heaving dance floor, stumbling against people, pushing my way past them. Her gaze was a tractor beam, I had no power to resist.

I didn't take my eyes off her. The music pounded at my ears. We couldn't speak. She beckoned again and turned, moving through the crowd like smoke, one hip forward, another, the edge of her black coat flowing like water. I followed her, my mouth dry, mesmerised. I was lost.

We were out in the corridor, I think, I couldn't see properly. She turned to face me and I looked at her, her face, her eyes, her fall of bright blond hair. I was dumb. I could scarcely breathe. It was like being opposite a lover.

"Who are you?" I said. I could feel my heart, punching away at my ribs like a small muscular fist. "Who are you?"

She was silent for a long while. The music pushed and throbbed in the background. Her eyes were so blue. I could feel recognition dawning, deep within me, something I'd known since I'd first seen her, something I'd not allowed myself to confront, something I'd pushed down and pushed down, unable to believe it. The impossible made real.

"Why, Maudie, don't you know me?" she said.

I could feel my legs begin to shake beneath me.

"Don't you know me?" she asked, again.

"No," I said. I croaked it. It was a lie and I knew it. I knew her. I knew who she was.

"It's me," she said. "It's me. I'm Jessica, Maudie. It's me. Jessica."

PART TWO

CHAPTER THIRTEEN

When I met Jessica for the first time, we were seven years old and she wore the most beautiful pair of red leather shoes. On the toe a flower was appliquéd in blue and yellow petals and in the centre was a shining brass button.

"I like your shoes," I said shyly.

"Oh - thanks."

Jessica was taller than me, her hair was longer and she seemed altogether more grown up. She'd been assigned to show me around the school and by the set of her resentful shoulders, I guessed she would rather be out in the playground with all the other kids.

We walked a little further up the corridor.

"Why do you talk funny?" she asked.

I hung my head, stung.

"I'm Scottish. Well, I was born there. My Dad's really Scottish but he doesn't talk funny because he went to school in England."

"Oh," said Jessica and we walked on in silence.

We sat next to one another in the classroom. By then, she'd thawed a little. She showed me where she'd written her name in tiny red letters on the underside of the desk. I gaped in amazement at her daring.

"You can write your name there too," she finally said, conspiratorial.

Sweating with fear, I scribbled my name on the grain of the wood.

"Cool," Jessica said, and from then, on we were friends.

We sat together in the classroom, we played together at lunchtime. Jessica had two other friends, Sophie and Beth, who were giggly and friendly but didn't have the same force of personality Jessica exhibited, even at seven. She was the leader of our little group, the one who told us what we were going to play, the one who directed us, scolded us, encouraged us. When Robert Fallway made fun of my scar, calling me Frankenstein and making me cry, Jessica was the one who chased him off and punched him, just for added emphasis. She got a talking to by the headmistress for that and I loved her even more.

I think that was the same week she invited me to her house for the first time. Normally, I was collected from school by whichever *au pair* Angus was employing at the time, or sometimes Mrs Green. That day though, Jessica and I walked home from school to her house, right in the middle of the village, next to the post office. For me, shepherded about, overseen and driven everywhere, it felt rather thrilling to be walking along the pavement with my best friend, swinging our bags and chatting. It was a beautiful day; we kept turning our faces to the sun and shutting our eyes, half blinded by light.

I knew most people didn't live in a house as big as Caernaven but even so, the first sight of Jessica's house momentarily surprised me. It was a tiny cottage, one of the many stone-built terraces that made up the majority of our village housing. The front door was painted a cheerful shade of blue and the door knocker was of the same shiny brass as the button on Jessica's shoe. She had her own key to the door which impressed me.

Jessica's house was empty, humming with silence.

"Mummy's at work," said Jessica, showing me into the tiny kitchen. "She leaves me my tea - look, there it is. She's done yours too."

There were two plates on the kitchen counter, both covered in clingfilm, heaped with salad and a slice of quiche and some grapes. We each took one and I followed Jessica through to the back garden. It felt rather delightfully like a picnic and I felt envious. I wanted to come home to this tiny cottage and have my dinner in the garden too. After we'd eaten our tea (and that was another thing that I found strange, as tea in our house was always drunk in a cup), Jessica showed me the playhouse that her Dad had built, the old robin's nest in the hedge, the fourteen goldfish in a tiny, weed-choked pond.

Finally, we climbed the stairs to her bedroom.

The front door opened as we were halfway up and a tall, grey-haired man walked in. He was thin and slightly crumpled and, for an odd second, I thought he looked as though he were made out of paper.

"Hi Dad," said Jessica. She bounded down the stairs and kissed him. He seemed to fold in half as he bent down to her.

"Hello darling. Who's your friend?"

I stood where I was on the stairs, one hand on the banister. I was shy with adults I didn't know.

"This is Maudie, she's from Scotland."

He smiled at me from his withered face.

"Hello dear."

It was fully dark by the time the front door opened again and Mrs McGaskill appeared.

It's hard for me to remember how I felt about her then, untainted by subsequent events. I know that from very early on, I liked her. Very quickly, I loved her. By the time of our holiday in Cornwall, I almost worshipped her. It was that intensity of feeling that made what happened later so exquisitely painful. Of course, I was looking for a mother-figure and any woman would have done.

She was thirty-two when I met her. In looks she resembled Jessica. She was tall and slim and her messy blonde hair fell to her shoulders. Both she and Jessica, and myself, were the same 'type'; Scandinavian in colouring, fair-skinned, blonde and blue-eyed; lanky and fine-boned with delicate joints. I was a little frecklier than the both of them and didn't tan so well in the sun, but for all that, my secret pleasure was to imagine they were my mother and sister. I felt a fierce, private joy when strangers mistook us for just that.

Jessica and her mother had a tempestuous relationship. Both were quick to anger and they constantly pitted their wills against one another. There were often raised voices, slammed doors, short storms of tears. "You're driving me mad!" I heard Mrs McGaskill shout one day and Jessica retorted, "I'm not - I'm not even *trying*." But lying underneath all these histrionics, like a solid slab of bedrock, was a deep love obvious to all. Perhaps it was because Jessica was an only child.

I wasn't aware of any rift between her mother and father, not really. I was too young. But even then, I could see how dismissive Mrs McGaskill was of her husband, how easily he seemed to fade into the background when Jessica and her mother were there. When he wasn't directly before me, I had trouble remembering what he looked like. I had my own father, hard and forbidding as he was; I wasn't looking for another.

It was Angus who suggested Jessica come to our house for a change. For once, he was waiting for me at the school gates when classes finished and a *tsunami* of children streamed out. I was listening to Jessica tell me a new joke about a gorilla and a hamster and laughing so hard that at first I didn't recognise the tall figure leaning against the bonnet of the car and talking to Mrs McGaskill.

"What's wrong?"

"It's my Dad," I said. Suddenly I was excited and embarrassed at the same time. Jessica caught sight of her mother standing next to Angus and grabbed my hand, dragged me forward as she called to her mother.

"Hello you two," she said as we ran up, flushed and breathless. "Maudie, I've just been talking to your Daddy."

I felt suddenly shy of them both.

"Hello Maudie," said Angus, holding out his large hand. I took it uncertainly; I wasn't used to him touching me. "And you must be Jessica."

"That's right," said Jessica, bold as you like. "Is it okay if Maudie comes to my house for tea?"

The two adults exchanged amused glances.

"Well now," said Angus. "We thought you might like to come to our house for tea, for a change. How about that?"

I felt an enormous burst of excitement but I said nothing, watching Jessica's face for a clue to her feelings.

She grinned broadly.

"Yes, yes, yes!"

Mrs McGaskill laughed. "Well, that's easily settled. Jessica, I'll drop some clothes off for you later tonight and you can stay the night. How about that?"

We clambered into the back of the Land Rover. I felt a momentary qualm as Jessica perched on the uncovered metal of the wheel arches; it looked so dirty and uncomfortable in the back, the floor smudged with mud and wisps of straw. But Jessica seemed oblivious to it all, almost bouncing with excitement as we pulled away from the school.

The Land Rover crunched over the gravel of the drive as we neared Caernaven. I looked out of the window. It was odd but it was almost as though I was seeing with Jessica's eyes. We rolled to a halt and Jessica fell silent, her almost ceaseless chatter falling away in a sigh. I watched her eyes widen as she looked out of the window.

We walked through into the hallway. Jessica seemed diminished by the house: her usual effervescence gone flat and quiet. I took hold of her hand and pulled her after me, running her through the hallway and the dining room and the other corridor and finally into the kitchen, where Mrs Green was preparing our evening meal.

"Hello Maudie," she said, her hands busy with a vegetable peeler.

I introduced Jessica to Mrs Green and asked whether we could have something to eat.

"You'll have to wait for dinner, love. Why don't you take Jessica out and show her the garden?"

I pulled Jessica, down the kitchen corridor, past the cellar door and onto the side terrace. Heat shimmered up from the flagstones beneath our feet and the air was sweet with the scent of herbs. I picked a leaf from the lemon balm and held it under Jessica's nose.

"Smell."

"Mmmm," said Jessica, sniffing. Then she drew her head back.

"Was that your gran?" she said.

Something in me recoiled. Mrs Green, my grandmother?

"No, silly," I said, trying to laugh. "She's the housekeeper."

"The housekeeper? Are you rich, then?"

"No," I said and then wondered whether that was true.

"Come and see my hiding place," I said, pulling at her arm.

I normally ate my supper at the kitchen table with Mrs Green bringing me my food. On the rare occasions that Angus was home at dinner time, only then would I make my way to the cold and cavernous dining room to sit on his right hand side and eat with him. Very occasionally, if family friends or relatives came to stay, I would also be summoned to the dinner table to sit quietly and listen to the adults talk. As the clock ticked around to six o'clock, Jessica and I scampered across the lawn and the terrace and piled into the kitchen.

Mrs Green was heaving a casserole dish from the oven.

"Not here, children, not here. Come on, out the way."

We jumped back against the table as she whisked the

steaming dish past us.

"Aren't we eating here then?" I asked, confused.

"No, you're dining with your father tonight. Come on, look lively! I bet you haven't even washed your hands."

The dining room table was set with three places. I gestured to Jessica to sit opposite me, on the other side of Angus's chair. He wasn't in the room but somehow, the chair seemed already filled with his presence. We sat down, subdued.

"Are we allowed to talk?" whispered Jessica.

I could hear the faint knock of her sandal against the chair leg. I pushed at my knife and fork, straightening them against the dark, polished wood of the table. Reflected in the surface, faintly grey and ghostlike, was my worried face.

Angus came into the room, rubbing his hands before him.

"Faring well, girls? Hungry, are you?"

I nodded. Jessica said nothing, but simply stared down at her plate.

It was a quiet meal. Angus tried to talk to us, peppering the echoing silence with questions; about school, about Girl Guides, about animals and plants and space travel and families. I was too young to realise he was trying to put our guest at her ease and too young to realise that his efforts were in vain. I just knew that Jessica was quiet, that she muttered her answers and pushed her food about on the plate. After a while, I began to feel my own throat close up in sympathy, and stopped eating too.

After the chocolate pudding and cream (left almost untouched by both of us) we were released. Once we were out of the dining room, Jessica broke into a run. I was so surprised that for a moment I did nothing, just stood and watched her bright blonde hair jump and flip in the wake of her movement. She ran into the garden and out of my sight.

"What's the matter?" I said, when I finally caught up.

She had stopped by the fountain, her hands on the stone wall.

She turned a red and tear-stained face to me.

"Shut up, Maudie," she said fiercely. "I want my Mummy. I want to go home!"

"Why?"

She burst into tears.

"I just do! I want my mummy!"

I can't remember exactly what happened after that. I think Maudie spoke to her mother on the phone and somehow Mrs McGaskill soothed her down. She probably told her daughter she'd be over shortly with Jessica's clothes and she would see her then, and if Jessica still wanted to come home, then of course she could. I'm guessing, obviously, but it's the sort of thing she would have said; practical, sensible, loving. Everything a mother should be. Everything I'd never had.

CHAPTER FOURTEEN

"I can see the sea! Angus - Angus - I can see the sea!"

I bounced in my car seat and pointed at the slice of blue ocean I could just make out in distance. Angus made a 'shushing' gesture with his hand.

I sat back, abashed. We'd been driving for hours and I was cramped and stiff and thirsty but somehow, the first glimpse of the sea had taken all my discomfort away. I craned my neck to see if I could see the other car behind us.

"I can't see Jessica."

"They'll catch us up. Stop worrying about it."

I pressed my nose up against the window. All about the road was glorious, rolling countryside, above us a wide blue cloudless sky. I wondered whether Jessica had seen the sea yet too.

The two stone cottages were nestled into the green curves of a gentle valley, side by side and facing the distant sea. The village itself was tiny, a mere strip of a main street with a pub, a tiny corner-shop and a church. Next to our cottages stood one of the four farms in the area and as we drew up, I could smell the heady reek of cow dung and hay.

"Is this ours?" I asked, wide-eyed.

Angus was busy lifting our bags from the boot of the car. I stood for a moment on the driveway, staring at the flat grey front of the house. Its windows glittered in the sun as if it were winking at me.

I heard the crunching of gravel and turned to see the McGaskills' car draw up behind ours. The wheels had scarcely come to a stop when the back door opened and Jessica tumbled out.

"We're here," she shouted as she picked herself up off the gravel and brushed off her palms.

"So I can see," said Angus.

I pulled at Jessica's arm. I was wild to explore; the house, the garden, the farmyard beyond. I climbed the narrow stairs inside our cottage and into the two bedrooms. The one at the back of the house would be mine, I decided. It had a small wooden bed and a battered old chest of drawers, a small flower-shaped rug on the floor and a brown-shaded bedside light with a pottery base. That was all, except for the yellow curtains at the single window. I struggled with the sash window and managed to shove it upwards, leaning out to look at the cottage that stood beside ours. To my delight, I saw Jessica poke her head out from the nearest window. She was waving and giggling.

"I'm next to you!"

I reached out - we could almost touch our fingers together.

"Can you hear me if I knock on the wall?"

I tried but there was nothing - the stone walls were too thick.

Jessica pouted.

"Shame - we could have had a secret signal."

I was too happy to really mind.

"Meet me downstairs, I want to explore."

We didn't go far that first day. We didn't go to the Men-an-Tol, I'm certain of that. There were too many interesting things closer to home. The cows in the field that came lumbering over to us as we stood by the fence, holding out hopeful handfuls of grass. The ginger farm cat that came twining round our ankles as we stood on the driveway, debating whether to go further. The remains of an old stone shed at the bottom of the garden. By the time we were called in to a late supper, we were drooping, exhausted by the long journey and the excitement of endless discovery.

After supper, the others went next door to their place. I was sent up to bed and submitted without protest, almost too tired to walk up the stairs. As I lay in my new little bed, my last conscious thought was of Jessica, lying near me, just feet away in the soft summer dark.

*

It was Jessica who first found the stones. As usual, she was the one who explored further and faster than anyone else, walking while I lazed about near the cottage. Three days after we arrived, I wandered down to the river one morning after breakfast. I was sitting dangling my fingers in the rippling water when she came panting up, eyes bright and hair flying.

"You'll never guess what I've found," she said, throwing herself down.

"What?"

She flicked water at me, giggling.

"You've got to guess."

"You're a pain," I said, flicking water back at her.

"*You're* a pain. Go on, you've got to guess."

I rolled my eyes.

"Alright. I guess that you've found... a dead badger."

She snorted laughter.

"No. Even better. A magic stone."

I stopped flicking water.

"What?"

Jessica smiled in triumph. "A magic stone. A sort of stone circle, up on the hill. It's probably been there for millions of years."

"Let's go and see it!"

"Wait." Jessica caught my arm as I prepared to gallop away. "We have to tell them we're going. Mummy told me off for going walking on my own yesterday."

It was about a twenty minute walk to the stone, a hard slog up a stony track that became almost vertical on one point. We slithered over loose flints in our summer sandals and rested halfway up, leaning against a rock warm from the sun.

"This had better be worth it," I said, panting.

I'd like to say that the place gave me a cold chill when first I saw it. That I had a premonition, an inkling of what was to come. It didn't. Instead, the emotion I was aware of on my first sight of the Men-an-Tol was delight. We stood looking in silence at the stone. Through the hole, I could see blue sky and, as I watched, a solitary crow flapped its slow dark way across.

"If you walk round here," said Jessica, demonstrating. "This stone lines up with the hole. Go on, do it."

"It does!" I said, amazed.

We stayed there for hours that first day, watching the stone shadows creep across the grass with the movement of the sun. The stone with a hole was furred with mosses and lichen, one side warm beneath our palms, the shadow side damp and cool.

From the start, this holed stone fascinated us. We didn't know its name then – we just called it the magic stone. We were standing before it that afternoon, watching the clouds blow across the space in the middle and I put my hand out to reach through the hole.

"Don't!" Jessica cried.

I nearly shrieked.

"Why? What's wrong?"

"Don't reach through the hole. You don't know what

powers it has. Your hand might disappear.. or when you pull it back, you might just have *bones*."

She had that look I knew well; half mischievous, half earnest. I knew that at least a small part of her actually believed it.

That was when we started to believe the legend. Jessica's words planted a little seed and day by day, our homespun tale began to grow. Soon the stone would become all consuming to us - a grey monolith of myth and legend. We would draw it and photograph it and talk about it endlessly. But that first day, we just wandered about, circling the Men-an-Tol and its companion stone, and watched their shadows move like long black fingers over the whispering grass.

CHAPTER FIFTEEN

Most days, Jessica and I would wander up to the stones. We were fascinated by the ever shifting view through the centre of the Men-an-Tol. We'd stand, one on each side, and look at each other through the hole. As our tales and fantasies grew, there was always the small fear that one day I would look through at Jessica and she wouldn't be there. Some days we walked down to the tiny beach to swim and from the little crescent of pale golden sand, we could stand and look back at the hill and see the faint grey smudges that were the two standing stones.

"I don't want to go home," said Jessica, one day.

I misunderstood.

"We don't have to be home for ages. We can stay out until supper, Angus said so."

"No, stupid. I mean I don't want to go home. Back home. Our real home."

That made me sit up and open my eyes. I was aware of a little finger of cold nudging me.

"What do you mean?" I thought for a moment and then spoke again. "I mean, why don't you want to go home?"

Jessica was silent for a moment. She still had her eyes shut and her blonde hair was splayed out against the grey surface of the rock, drying slowly into stringy little rats' tails.

"I just like it here," she said, eventually. "I like it here with the stones and it always being sunny and never having to go to school. Mummy isn't so cross with Daddy here."

I glanced across at her.

"What do you – "

She didn't let me finish.

"I just wish it could be like this forever," she said.

I hugged my knees and stared out at the shifting blue sea. I was vaguely troubled by her words.

"We have to go back to school," I offered. "It's the law."

Jessica sat up abruptly. "Hey," she said. "I've got it."

"What?"

"It's easy. We have to harness the power of the stones. You know."

"What do you mean?"

"Oh, come on. You know. We do a magic ceremony, just like we've been talking about."

I felt another little cold nudge. She sounded so serious. For a moment, I wavered; I wondered whether I could ask her what she meant. But we'd spent days discussing the magic rituals that the stones had been used for - I knew she wouldn't believe me if I pleaded ignorance.

"Yeah, we could," I said, trying for enthusiasm. I looked back at the stones on the hilltop. My eyes fell on the distant ellipse of the Men-an-Tol and I felt a little shudder pass through me.

Jessica stood up, stretching her arms above her head. She flung her head back and shut her eyes against the sun.

"We'll do it at midnight," she said. "That's the most powerful time of all. We'll sneak out just before midnight and go up there and do our ritual. And you know the Men-an-Tol will be open to the other side, then. Hey Maudie, perhaps we'll even go back in *time*."

I thought of being there at midnight. The enormous black sky stretching overhead. The stones looming up through the darkness, solid, somehow implacable. The cold wind, the blank white light of the moon. I looked down and saw my arms had humped up into gooseflesh, despite the warmth of the sun.

Jessica picked up her towel from the rock and wrapped it around her shoulders.

"I'm going up there," she said. "I want to see what kind of ceremony we can do. I know it won't be the same as it will be at midnight, but I still want to do it. Coming?"

I shook my head.

"I'm going to go home. I'll see you later."

I gathered up my beach bag and towel and began the slow struggle up the hill. The grass was slippery beneath the soles of my sandals and once my foot jagged backwards and I banged my knee on a rock. Eventually I reached level ground and the path that led back to the village. When I looked back, I could see the little moving dot that was Jessica making her way up the circle. She shimmered in my vision.

The stone track gradually led to the rutted, dried mud of the lane which ten yards further grew a skin of tarmac. Despite the heat, I began to run, the soles of my plimsolls slapping against the road. My ponytail bounced and grew looser as I ran faster, past the groups of pink-faced walkers, bent underneath their rucksacks. Soon I was puffing but somehow my legs carried me forward towards home, the home that that been known by that name for two short weeks. I stopped briefly outside the garden gate to tie my shoelace and to get my breath back.

I don't know what made me stop and look up, before putting my hand to the gate. If I hadn't, the gate would have given its long, tortured squeak as I pushed it open and the sound would have alerted them to my presence. But I didn't push it, and so I looked up and saw them, Angus and Mrs McGaskill, framed by the kitchen window and locked in an embrace. They were kissing in the way that people kissed on TV, or in the films that I'd seen; liplocked, pressed up against one another, his hand underneath her jaw.

For a moment, I was dumbstruck, transfixed. My feet felt welded to the hot tarmac beneath them. Then the shockwave hit me and I ducked down behind the hedge out of sight, my face hot and my heart thumping. For a moment, I dithered, wondering whether to walk back through the gate and pretend I'd seen nothing. I knew I couldn't. My knowledge was written in the blood running into my face. Instead I turned and ran back down the lane, back towards the beach. Again, my plimsolls slapped against the dusty surface of the road.

I had some thought of going to find Jessica but instead I found my feet taking me off the track and into one of the nearby fields. I stumbled over the stile that led over the fence and walked along the hedgerow. I felt hot all over, prickly with prurient curiosity and embarrassment. For a while, I stood looking out over the field, hugging my elbows and seeing the kiss again and again. I tried to construct an innocent scenario. Perhaps I'd imagined it? No - I couldn't have, I was seeing it now, unfolding in front of my eyes. Perhaps Jessica's mum had had a fit and needed the kiss of life... even at ten, I could see that that was ludicrous. Did Jessica know? I wondered suddenly. Did *Mr McGaskill* know? I found I had my fingers in my mouth, nibbling at the nails. I could taste gritty sand in my mouth.

There was a pile of wood heaped at the edge of the field, bleaching under the hot sun. I sat down on a log, rubbing my dirty knees. Beyond the hedge, in the next field, I could see a tractor trundling slowly round and round.

For the very first time in my life, I realised that things would change. I realised that we would all get older. One day, Angus wouldn't be here anymore. One day, *I* wouldn't be here any more. A kind of panic took hold of me and I leapt up and began to run. Only, this time, I couldn't run home. I stopped at the edge of the field, at the gate, holding onto its rough wooden spars with both hands, gasping for breath and shaking the gate until its hinges rattled, shaking it with the tears running down my face, and my teeth clenched in sudden fury.

.

CHAPTER SIXTEEN

I stayed in the field until it got dark, roaming the sun-baked edges of the crop, sitting myself down and jumping up again. As the sun sank slowly beyond the darkening horizon, I trailed back home down the lane. Again, I paused outside the gate to our cottage and looked up at the lighted kitchen window.

I could hear cooking sounds coming from the kitchen; the splash of water and the crash of a saucepan onto the stove. There was the pop and glug of a wine bottle being opened. I rubbed my face; it felt tight and hot after being in the open air and sunshine all day and my eyes felt gritty from the tears that had dried along the lids. I could hear Mrs McGaskill calling from the kitchen and froze. A second later, she came out into the corridor.

"Oh, Maudie," she said. "I'd wondered where you girls had got to. Can you go and root out Jessica for me, please? We'll be eating soon."

I didn't answer her straight away. I couldn't take my eyes off her.

"Maudie?"

"S-sorry," I said, stuttering. "I don't know where she is either."

"Well, go and find her for me then, there's a love." She turned back into the kitchen. "Dinner in five minutes."

I dithered for a moment and then walked up to my room. Why should I do anything for her? She wasn't my mother. I'd seen her kissing my father and that was *wrong*. I stomped about my room for a bit and then heard Jessica's voice outside my window. When I looked out she was leaning out from her window.

"There you are," she said. "Where've you been all day? I've been at the stones for hours."

I shook my head. I felt sulky with the whole world, even with my best friend.

"Mum says it's dinner now, anyway. Come on. I'll tell you all the plans afterwards. Come on!"

She whisked back into her room, her blonde hair fluttering behind her like a golden flag. It was full twilight now and the midges were beginning to bite. I made my way slowly down the stairs, not wanting to see anyone but unable to pluck up the courage to stay in my room.

Everyone sat outside, as was usual for our supper time. The citronella candles were lit and a breeze ruffled the paper napkins.

That was the last evening we were to dine in the garden. My eyes kept returning to Angus and Mrs McGaskill, trying to spot a significant glance between them, a softer look, or even a touch out of sight of any eyes but mine. I looked across at Jessica's dad, calmly forking potato salad into his mouth. He caught my eye and smiled at me and I dropped my gaze, feeling hot in the face. All around me, everyone was behaving as they always did; Angus and Mrs McGaskill talking, although not exclusively to each other, Mr McGaskill eating and helping me and Jessica to seconds. I felt as if I were sitting alone, behind a plate of glass; able to observe but totally removed from their world.

After dinner, Jessica and I carried the plates into the kitchen and washed up, as we were expected to do. The kitchen window was wide open and a cloud of moths and insects flew loopily around the unshaded kitchen lightbulb. I went to the kitchen sink and jammed the plug into the plughole. Jessica crashed the plates down beside me and leaned forward, her blonde hair swinging towards me.

"Tonight," she whispered.

I could see the lightbulb reflected in both of her eyes and for a strange moment, it seemed as if the light itself was shining out of her pupils.

"What?"

"It's tonight," she said. "We'll do it tonight. The ritual. It's perfect - it's a full moon. It's the most powerful time. We've got to do it tonight or it won't work."

I struggled to show - what? Enthusiasm? Agreement? In truth, the shock of seeing Angus and Mrs McGaskill had driven any concerns about Jessica's plans out of my head. At last I managed to paste a smile on my face.

"Yeah, okay. What shall we do?"

She looked annoyed.

"Maudie, I've been telling you for the past week. Why don't you listen to me?"

"Sorry," I muttered. I reached for the plates and began to wash them, as much to have something to do with my hands as because I wanted to help.

"What's the matter with you, anyway? I saw you at dinner, sitting all quiet. What's up with you?"

I opened my mouth to tell her. Then I closed it again.

"Nothing."

She lost interest. The stones were all to her; I could tell. She was there already, in her head, under the white moonlight, chanting to the night air.

"We'll sneak out at half eleven," she said, leaning close to me again. She was almost whispering. "Can you get a torch? Oh never mind, don't worry, I know where one is. Meet me out the front of the house... No, that's too close, they might see us. Meet me at the start of the track and we'll go up together."

I nodded, helpless in the face of her obsession. I rinsed the last plate under the tap and watched the glob of dirty foam slide back into the washing up bowl.

"Maudie." It wasn't a question.

"What?"

"You're not going to let me down, are you?"

"No," I said.

"*Are* you?"

For a moment she sounded like her mother and that made me even angrier.

"No."

I slammed the plate down on the draining rack and it broke, clean across. The two pieces fell to the floor, and smashed into smaller pieces. Jessica and I looked at each other in shock and then we both burst out laughing. We were still laughing when the adults came into the kitchen with questions and exclamations and for those few minutes, it was okay.

Most nights after dinner, we all congregated in one of the living rooms, normally the McGaskill's cottage, as they had a small black and white television. Sometimes Jessica and I played cards or occasionally Scrabble, or we read, or talked or squabbled quietly in the corner. Tonight though, Jessica announced that she was going to bed early and so was I.

"Are you sickening for something?" said her mother, laughing and going to feel her forehead. Jessica jerked away.

"No, I'm just tired."

"You're never tired. What are you planning?"

I felt first a thump of panic and then, almost immediately, a surge of relief. Tell your mother, Jessica, and then she won't let us go - and I won't have to walk up to the hill in the dark, small and scared.

"I'm not planning anything," said Jessica in a scolding sort of voice. She managed not to look at me while she spoke. "I want to read my new book."

"Okay, then. Don't stay up too late. I'll be up at nine thirty and I want that light to be out, understood?"

Jessica nodded, her mouth solemn. I felt a giggle build up in me, despite myself.

"What about you, Maudie?" said Angus. I noticed that his sunburnt nose was peeling. "Are you tired enough for an early night too?"

I shook my head. Jessica glared at me from behind her mother's shoulder. I tried to make a 'calm down' face without the adults noticing.

"I'm a bit tired," I said carefully. "But I want to watch TV for a bit."

Jessica grabbed me out in the corridor when I went to get myself a biscuit.

"What did you say that for?" she hissed. "We both have to go to bed early so we can both sneak out."

"I know," I said, shaking off her hand. "But if we'd both gone at the same time they would have known something was up. Come on, Jess, we never want to go to bed normally, do we?"

She looked at me and smiled suddenly.

"Alright, you're right. Smarty-pants! But don't really fall asleep, will you? Remember we're meeting at the start of the track at half past eleven."

Again, I felt a little thrill of fear. I didn't want to do this. I was too scared. I watched Jessica's hand slide around the newel post as she turned the corner. That was the last time I ever saw her.

Jessica needn't have worried that I would fall asleep. I lay in my narrow bed, watching the tree branches outside my window throw their shadows across my bedroom ceiling. My mind would not stop; it threw up a cavalcade of images from the day. My father kissing Mrs McGaskill. Jessica's shining eyes. The endless field of corn where I'd crouched and wandered for hours. I lay on one side, then another, flipping my pillow in a vain attempt to find a cool patch of cotton. I kept squinting at my watch. I heard Angus come up the stairs at about half past ten and the creak of floorboards as he made his way to the bathroom, and then back down the stairs afterwards. Only an hour to go. My stomach was clenched and my hands were rigid fists beneath the covers.

At eleven fifteen, I got out of bed and began to get dressed. The darkness pressed itself around me but I didn't dare turn on a light. I tried to lace up my plimsolls with shaking fingers and couldn't form the knots - in the end I just shoved the ends of the laces inside the shoe. I fumbled for the torch and made my way over to the door.

The house seemed bigger in the dark. The hallway was endless; it stretched off into near eternity. I inched my way along the floorboards, my heartbeat loud in my ears. I was breathing shallowly but despite this, my intake of breath seemed to boom around the house, filling the silent rooms with a rush of noise.

The beam of the torch strobed over the front door, illuminating my shaking fingers as I reached for the handle.

I got one foot outside, onto the cold stone of the doorstep. The night sky was huge and black and shining coldly with stars. I stood for one frozen moment with one leg in and one leg outside. Then I retreated inwards, crying quietly. It was just too dark, too quiet, too scary. I pushed the door so that it almost shut and stood with my head against it, my tears dripping on the floor.

It is here that my memory fades out. The picture in my head of the hallway, the open door, the cold night beyond, bleaches out like an over-exposed photograph and there is nothing beyond. Did Angus find me, crying in the hallway? Did I manage to step outside, out into the moonlight? Did I see Jessica, walking up the hill to the stones?

There is nothing left of the memory, not even the faintest, tattered scrap.

CHAPTER SEVENTEEN

I became aware of an insistent voice and eventually a hand shaking me awake.

"Maudie - Maudie - "

The shaking got more insistent.

Angus was bending over my bed, frowning. When I saw his face, I woke up properly. His skin looked grey and his face was tight, as if his features had been pulled together by an invisible hand.

"What's the matter?"

I struggled to sit up but the bedclothes weighed heavily on me. For once, the sun wasn't shining and, outside, I could hear the faint but insistent patter of raindrops. My bedroom looked grey.

"Maudie, Jessica's missing. She's not in her bed, and we can't find anywhere in the house or the garden. Do you have any idea where she might be?"

"No," I said automatically, not even remembering my panic of the night before. I was still clogged with sleep.

"Are you sure?"

A faint, creeping unease began to seep through me. I remembered what we'd planned and how I'd chickened out. I remembered the hallway, the open door, the blackness beyond. I opened my mouth to confess... and then shut it again.

Angus gave a quick, hard nod.

"Alright, Maudie. Can you please get up and dressed as quickly as possible and come downstairs?"

I was already scrambling out of bed and reaching for my dressing gown. Angus paused in the doorway to my room.

"Try not to worry," he said, and managed a smile. I felt the first sharp pang of guilt. "I'm sure she hasn't gone far."

He left the room, leaving the door ajar. I pulled on my dressing gown. I looked at the door and was suddenly swamped by nausea. My stomach clenched and I ran for the bathroom, kicking the half open door wide open.

I vomited for some minutes. When I stood up, my legs felt wobbly. I washed my face, looking at my red eyes in the mirror. Then I went downstairs.

The kitchen seemed full of people when I came downstairs. In fact, there were five: Angus, Mr and Mrs McGaskill, the farmer from next door and a policeman. I stood in the doorway, hanging onto the frame, eyeing his dark blue uniform.

Angus walked quickly to stand beside me and put a hand on my shoulder. From the safety of his side, I looked at Jessica's mother and flinched. She was pale, her skin almost greyish, rigid with the effort of keeping control. She had her hands clasped in front of her, so tightly her knuckles shone through, chips of bone under translucent skin. Mr McGaskill looked more desiccated than normal.

"Now, don't worry Maudie," said Angus. "This policeman just needs to ask you a few questions about Jessica. You don't have to worry; I'll be with you all the time. Just answer his questions as best you can."

The policeman seemed old to me, although he was probably only about thirty-five. He had a receding hairline and the sun had pinked the exposed skin of his forehead.

"Hello, Maudie," he said. "Now, you look like a clever girl, so you can probably tell we're all a bit worried about Jessica. It's not like her to run off, is it? Do you have any idea where she might be?"

My mouth was dry. I felt as if I'd been eating lumps of dry bread, a whole loaf of bread, with no butter or jam or anything.

"I don't know," I said. My voice sounded like a mouse's voice - thin and wispy and edging on a squeak.

"You're not in trouble, Maudie. It's just that, well, we're trying to find Jessica. You can see her mum and dad are terribly worried. You want to try and find your friend, don't you?"

"Yes," I said. My hands were shaking and I clutched hold of my dressing gown belt.

"So can you tell us where you think she might be? Was she upset about anything?"

I shook my head and then, because some other response seemed called for, said 'I don't know."

"You've no idea? You girls didn't have some secret hiding place she might have gone to? No little hidey-hole?"

I shook my head again. I didn't want to; I knew I should have been telling them the truth, about the stones and our plans to go there last night, but something was making me say and do all the wrong things.

"Well," said the policeman, disappointed. My stomach rumbled, loud enough for us all to hear and I blushed.

Mrs McGaskill got up from the table and walked over to me. She stalked across the room, her body held upright and rigid. I shrank back against the wall but she took no notice. She crouched down and held me by the shoulders, almost shaking me. I could feel her fingers digging into me and the tension that made the bones of her hands judder against me.

"Jane - " said Angus.

She took no notice. Her burning eyes were fixed upon my face. I was afraid.

"Maudie - "

Her voice clogged and she cleared her throat and started again.

"Maudie - if you know where she is, you must tell us. You know that, don't you? You must tell us."

Her nails were digging into my skin. I tried to say something, tried to speak. There was a lump in my throat too big to force words around. Instead I burst into tears.

"I don't know, I don't know," was all that I could say. "I don't know where she is."

I must have convinced them. It was, I suppose, literally the truth - I *didn't* know where she was. Mrs McGaskill released me and stepped back, clenching her fists. Angus patted me as I sobbed into my hands. His palm kept connecting with my shoulder over and over again, as if he were doing it without thinking, without meaning to give comfort, more as if he'd forgotten what he was doing. It began to feel so strange that I managed to stop crying and moved away from him, my sobs tapering off into hiccups.

All of the sudden, the house seemed full of people in blue uniforms. I was sent up to my room and sat on the windowsill, biting my nails and watching people mill about in the front garden. I tried not to look at the window of Jessica's room, right next to mine but it loomed there in my peripheral vision, black and empty.

There was a concerted movement in the small crowd below in the garden and they all began to walk out into the lane, spreading out until they were walking abreast of one another, in a straggling line. I saw Mrs MacGaskill, her face rigid, walking slowly, her husband five steps behind her. I couldn't see Angus.

The door creaked and made me jump. I swung round but there was no one in the open doorway. I was suddenly scared of being left on my own in the house. I looked fearfully again at the door to my bedroom. It didn't have a lock. Supposing - supposing someone had stolen Jessica from her room and now... now they were coming for me? Suddenly, my whole body felt cold. I looked for Angus in the disappearing search party and couldn't see him.

I'd never been frightened of being on my own before now. I'd spent hours and hours roaming the Lakeland countryside on my own. Now quite suddenly, I was terrified.

It was then I heard the creak of a floorboard on the stairs. I froze. I tried to tell myself it was nothing, that I was imagining things. The creak came again - there were footsteps coming up the stairs. A dark figure loomed in the open doorway and I began to scream.

Angus rushed in.

"Maudie, what's the matter?"

I managed to stop screaming by bringing my hands up to my mouth, pressing inwards so hard I could feel the sharp edges of my teeth against my palms.

"Maudie, what's wrong?"

I felt tears rushing up towards my eyes. A sob came out of me and I put my face in my hands, not wanting to see my father's tight face, still grey with shock from all that had happened over the past twenty four hours.

"Maudie - "

He sat beside me, hesitated, and pulled me close. For a second, the fear rose to a peak that was almost unbearable; I thought I was going to choke. I put my face against the wall, the plaster cool against my cheek. I must have made a noise or flinched or something, because I felt Angus move back from me and the fear receded a little.

"Angus -"

My voice came slowly and thickened so I couldn't say more for a moment. I tried again.

"Dad - "

He didn't say anything. He sat unmoving and silent. I told him everything.

CHAPTER EIGHTEEN

That was the first night I had the dream. In the nightmare, I saw the stones and the black figure and Jessica disappearing into darkness. I lay there in the dark with the blankets tangled about my legs and stared upwards. The nights here were so dark, lit only by the moon and the stars. When Jessica had been next door, I hadn't been able to hear her breathing or moving around - the walls were too thick, the distance between our rooms too great. But the silence in my room now seemed somehow deeper and more awful.

Today had been the worst day of my life. I thought that quite dispassionately, staring into darkness. I thought back, unwillingly, to the scene in the kitchen; to Mrs McGaskill's furious anger.

Her face was a dull red, her eyes glittered and her teeth were bared. For one terrifying second, I had thought she was going to bite me.

"You wicked, wicked girl! You little cow! How dare you tell us you didn't know where she was!"

Flecks of saliva from her mouth landed on my face. I was too frozen with horror to move. I saw her raise a hand to slap me and flinched.

Angus was there immediately, pulling her back. She

whipped round and her outstretched hand caught him on the cheek. I heard him give an 'oof' of protest and watched his eyes squeeze shut as her rigid fingers slapped against his face. For a moment, the whole room seemed to rock. Mrs McGaskill and Angus were frozen in a tableau of upraised arms and flying hair. My vision shimmered.

After a moment of stillness, sound and movement came rushing back. She was shrieking, Angus was shouting, Mr McGaskill was hurrying forward, his face creased. I put my hands up to cover my ears but I couldn't stop my mouth from opening and the screams emerging. I shut my eyes to block out the chaos going on before me and screamed and screamed.

It worked, for a moment. I couldn't hear the shouts of the adults, or see them and their twisted up faces. For a moment, all I could hear was myself screaming, wordlessly at first and then repeating 'stop it, stop it, stop it!' over and over again. Eventually I ran out of breath and opened my eyes, gasping.

Angus had moved to put his hand on my shoulder - I hadn't even noticed. I was barely aware of Mr McGaskill. It was Jessica's mother who drew my eye. She was standing rigid, in the middle of the kitchen floor, her arms held stiffly by her side. On her face was an expression of such loathing, I flinched at the sight of it.

"That's right, cry," she said, her voice vibrating. "You go ahead and cry. If we've lost her, because of what you've done, if she's gone because of you, I'll - "

She shut her mouth with a snap. Then she wheeled round, stiffly as a soldier on parade and marched from the kitchen.

"Come on, Maudie," Angus said. "Let's leave her for now."

I think that was when we started losing hope. Before there had been shock and confusion, and, on her parents side, a roiling, bubbling anger. But the thought of Jessica gone forever had been too big to grasp.

The search parties went out again, as soon as the sun came up. Again, I sat in my window seat, watching the blue uniforms of the police, and the holiday clothes of the tourists and the sunlight reflecting off of the cameras of the journalists that had gathered to report on the search. Sometimes they rang the doorbell of the cottage and I cringed back against the curtains, hoping they wouldn't spot my anxious face peering from my bedroom window. I stayed there for most of the day, biting my nails, watching and waiting. I kept imagining Jessica coming up the lane, a miracle, her blonde hair tossed about by the sea breeze, smiling and shouting up to me *bet you can't guess where I've been, Maudie....*

After that dreadful scene in the kitchen, Mrs McGaskill never spoke to me again. If I came into the room, she would walk out of it, keeping her face turned away, as if I exuded a stench too disgusting for her to bear. Every time, I would feel my stomach drop and twist, as if a heavy weight was falling through me. I stopped crying, though. If I felt tears prick my eyes, I would hear her voice saying *cry, that's right, cry*, and that somehow stopped me. At night, I would pinch myself under the covers, just to have a different focus of pain. Somehow, physical pain was easier to deal with.

After two weeks, the search parties stopped. The tourists drifted away, the journalists dwindled to one or two from the local papers, desperate for news. The national dailies all had other stories to occupy their front pages. The photograph of Jessica that had smiled at us from every front page gradually disappeared. She dissolved away before our eyes.

I watched her parents set out every morning to roam the fields and hills and comb the beaches, endlessly searching, refusing to give up. The original police search had found only one thing; one of Jessica's hair clips, on the path to the Men-an-Tol.

Before Jessica vanished, we'd all lived in one another's cottages, having breakfast in one kitchen one day and in the other the next, sharing the sunshine in the one big garden, running in and out of front doors without stopping to think whether it was one house or the other. Once Jessica was gone, and her mother had turned against me, that all stopped. It was two houses standing separate; two families living apart. One wasn't even a family anymore, they were just two people who happened to be married. The four of us left were now firmly split into two groups. We ate separately. The doors to the cottages remained firmly closed.

After two more weeks, Angus and I returned home.

Mr McGaskill came to the doorway of the cottage to wave us off. Mrs McGaskill didn't. I caught a glimpse of the pale oval of her face at one of the downstairs windows and then she was gone. We drove away, bumping slowly over the pitted surface of the lane, past the stony track that led up to the stones. I stared desperately up at the hillside, looking in vain for Jessica once more. In our fairy stories she would have been there, a little figure on the hillside, suddenly restored to us whole and sound and healthy. But of course, there was nothing there, nothing except the blue arc of sky and the mass of green that made up the hills. We drove on, out of the village, out of the county, out of Cornwall.

CHAPTER NINETEEN

It was in the village shop that I first noticed the glances. Little fluttering sideways glances, from the two girls standing near me with their mothers. Their mothers were looking too, less obviously. I looked back over my shoulder, wondering what was drawing their attention. There was nothing more interesting there than a shelf full of sweets and chocolate bars and newspapers. Then I realised they were looking at me.

I heard the word 'Jessica' and then I knew for certain. The air in the shop seemed to darken and grow thick. I could feel my face burning and this made it worse because I was sure that they would see and think I was ashamed. I forgot why I'd come into the shop, what I'd planned to buy. My only thought was to get out of there. I managed to get my legs to move, to walk me across the endless acres of floor and out the shop door, all of the time feeling their gazes boring into my back, shearing through the flimsy protection of my cotton t-shirt and burning into the vulnerable flesh of my back.

I dried my eyes before I reached home. I didn't want Angus asking me what was the matter. What had happened was my fault, I knew that, but I didn't want him to think that everyone thought it was his fault, too. I walked slowly towards the driveway. I didn't feel safe here anymore; I felt watched. The wind carried an undertone of whispers.

I stopped going into the village after that. I knew that, after the holidays ended, I would still have to go to school, but it would be big school, a senior school. Not junior school, where everyone would whisper about me and stare, and refuse to play with me. In so much as I was capable of looking forward to anything, I was looking forward to senior school - I'd assumed it would be the one in the nearest town. I was wrong. Angus sat me down one day in the study, and asked me whether I'd thought about going to boarding school.

I stared at him. Although it was the end of August, it was a cold, white-skied day; I looked at the empty fireplace and felt the goosebumps rise up on my arms.

"Why?" was the only thing I could think to say.

"Well," he said, "I just thought you might like to consider it. Perhaps you might feel happier amongst some new friends?"

Jessica's name hung in the silence between us. I blinked and looked again at the blackened space of the fireplace.

"I don't mind," I said, in a small voice. In a blinding flash it had occurred to me; my father wanted me to go, because he was ashamed of me. He didn't want to be around me anymore.

"If you don't like it, you can always come home again," said Angus. He smiled one of his rare smiles. "I'm sure you'll have a great time. Better than being here."

I nodded, unable to speak.

After that things moved quickly. Perhaps Angus pulled some strings to get me into the new school in time for the start of term. I drifted through my few remaining days at Caernaven in a daze, staring out of windows at the distant mountains, watching the clouds blow in over the fields, listening to the distant, mournful cries of the sheep. I thought of all the people in the village and at my old school who would be talking about me and about Jessica. Her parents were still in Cornwall, still searching, still hoping. I wondered whether they would ever come back.

The morning of my departure came. I ate breakfast silently, sitting by Angus's side in the dining room. My toast was cold by the time I reached for the last piece; it felt as if I were swallowing cardboard. I said goodbye to Mrs Green and then we walked out to the Land Rover, Angus carrying my suitcases in both hands. Mrs Green had packed away my clothes but she hadn't seen Jessica slipping in beside them, wisp thin, visible only to me. Angus didn't know he carried her in my suitcase that rode in the back, sliding from one side of the car to the other as we drove around corners. Only I knew she was there. I carried her away with me as I stood waving goodbye to my father on the steps on my new school. I carried her up the steps with me to the room that would be my bedroom for the next eight years. Only I saw her accompanying me that night to the dining room, to the study hall, squeezing in beside me as I lay in that strange bed. I carried her with me from then on.

PART THREE

CHAPTER TWENTY

The music thudded about us. I stood for a minute, frozen, looking at Jessica's eyes, this woman's eyes, this woman who called herself Jessica, searching her face for confirmation. I stared so hard it felt as if my eyes would fall out of my face. She had Jessica's blue eyes, cobalt blue, edged with a fan of brown lashes.

The music was a wall of sound, a thick pulsating force in itself. I could feel it in every part of my body; a tiny beat pulsing through every cell.

"What are you saying?" I said. I think I shrieked it. Dimly, I was aware of people around me looking at me oddly.

Jessica - if it was Jessica - put her hand on my arm. I flinched. I don't know why but I was expecting her to feel cold. Because I'd been thinking of her as dead for so long, I couldn't grasp the fact that she was standing her before me. Real. Alive. Her hand was warm. How could it be her? I put my hands up to my head again and closed my eyes. To anyone watching I must have looked crazed but I was far, far beyond caring about that by now.

"Maudie - "

Still with my eyes closed, I shook my head. I think a small part of me was thinking, hoping, that when I opened my eyes again, she'd be gone. I opened them and she was still standing in front of me. I felt the world begin to recede slowly, my vision narrowing down until there was just the woman who called herself Jessica standing in front of me. There was a rushing noise in my ears, even over the thud of the music from the dance floor.

"Maudie - "

She was pulling me. Supporting me. I felt my legs bow beneath me and the floor suddenly got much closer. For one horrible second, I believed again that she was dead; dead and intent on dragging me to wherever the dead go. The rushing noise got louder and for a long, confused moment, I wasn't able to see or think anything.

Then the air got clearer and the noise lessened. I blinked, aware of the cold. We'd come outside to the back alley Becca and I had visited earlier. I wondered briefly where Becca was and whether she was looking for me.

Jessica let go of my arm and stepped back. She was smiling in a strained sort of way.

"Are you alright?" said Jessica. I realised I was calling her that now, without the caveat I'd used before. Somewhere inside me, it was starting to sink in.

"I'm alright," I said. I wasn't; it was meaningless gabble, just a way of filling up the silence between us.

There was a flurry of movement and noise as a group of smokers came out into the street. I saw Jessica look over at them and shrink, moving back against the wall. Then she saw me looking and her frown became a smile, of sorts.

"Well - " she said.

Her blonde hair glimmered in the light from the open doorway. She was as tall as I was, almost as thin. I dredged up my memories of the ten year old Jessica's face and tried to compare them with the face before me now. It struck me that she looked exhausted. There were plum coloured rings beneath her eyes and the flesh fell away beneath her cheekbones. She looked older than her thirty-three years.

The group of smokers finished their cigarettes and

stampeded back indoors. For the first time, we had the area to ourselves.

I took a deep breath.

"Is it really you?" I said.

She smiled again.

"It's really me."

"I can't believe it."

My voice slipped and I looked away, blinking. There weren't enough words in my vocabulary to start asking her all the questions I wanted to. I put a hand out to her and then drew it back. That odd, light-headed feeling threatened to swamp me again; I wanted to touch her, to see if she was real. Would she feel warm or cold? Was she really there?

She took my hand and I flinched. She kept hold of my fingers, looking at me steadily. Her hand was cold but it felt solid, the flesh of her fingers like something unnatural, plastic or rubber, against mine.

"Maudie - "

"Where do we start?" I said. My voice was ragged. "What can you possibly say? What can I say?"

"You don't have to think about it now," she said, gently. "We don't have to say anything."

The tears were threatening in earnest now. I felt one escape and make its slow way down my cheek.

"Oh Maudie - "

I held up a hand again. I couldn't have any sympathy, any softness; I wouldn't be able to stand it, I would dissolve. I think she realised this. She stepped back against the wall again, hugging her elbows.

I took a deep breath and then another. I felt removed from myself; as if most of me was off somewhere nearby, watching what was happening from afar.

"Don't worry," she said. "It was stupid of me to - to contact you here. I might have known it would be too much."

I felt cold again. This sounded like a dismissal.

"What do you mean?"

"Maudie, it was too much of a shock for you, I know that. I should have realised. I just thought - I knew you'd seen me and when you followed me the other night, I panicked. And then I thought how upset you must have been and so I knew I had to do something. So, when I saw you here, I just - I just - well, you know - "

I stared at her. I was only taking in about one word in four, but something struck a chord with me.

"How did you know I was going to be here?"

She laughed, a little harsh, gasping laugh. "I didn't. It was pure coincidence, believe it or not. I admit that I've been, well, following you around a bit lately but I was here myself, anyway. I just about dropped when I saw you on the dance floor."

I felt the first beginnings of a smile struggle onto my face.

"You weren't the only one."

"No, well - "she sighed. "I've been so stupid. This hasn't gone exactly as I planned it."

There was a short silence between us.

She sighed again.

"I'm going to go now. I think you need some time to let this sink in."

"Go?"

"Yes, go. I'll let you - calm down a bit."

I felt a jab of panic hit me in the stomach. As much of a shock as it had been, I didn't want to lose her. What if I never saw her again?

"You will come back again?" My voice squeaked higher. "You won't go away again?"

She looked me right in the eyes.

"I promise, Maudie. I won't leave you again. I'm not going anywhere."

I was clutching my arms to my body. I was beginning to get very cold; my teeth were almost chattering.

"Do you promise?" I said, feebly.

"I do. I do promise. But - " she hesitated for a moment."I want you to promise me something too."

"What?"

She moved her head a little and her eyes caught the light from the doorway. Her pupils were huge.

"Don't - tell anyone about me. Don't mention me to anyone. Not yet. I don't - it's just that I have to be sure - I mean - look, Maudie, just don't tell anyone about me, okay? Not Angus. And for God's sake, don't tell my parents."

I felt a brief spasm of pain. Now was obviously not the time to tell her that her parents were dead. And Angus, too. She's got no one to come back to, I thought. Except me. I thought of everything we had to catch up on, two and half decades of life lived, of happenings and incident and memories. I felt suddenly very tired.

"I promise," I said. What else could I say?

She touched my hand for a brief moment.

"I'm going now," she said. "Stay here. Shut your eyes for a moment."

I did as I was told, standing there in the night air. I felt a brief movement of air beside me, stirring my hair, and when I opened my eyes, she was gone.

CHAPTER TWENTY ONE

"Where the hell did you *go?*"

I'd had Becca bleating in my ear for five minutes now. I was on the arm of the living room sofa, staring out of the window at the grey day beyond. I took the phone away from my ear for a moment. I could still hear Becca.

"I came back from the bar and you'd just *gone* - "

"Alright," I snapped. "I said I'm sorry."

"I was worried."

I was silent.

"Oh well," she said, after a moment. "Doesn't really matter. It actually turned out okay, you know. I met a man."

There was an exultant kind of giggle in her voice. At any other time, I would have shrieked enthusiastically and pressed for details. Now, I struggled to sound interested.

"Oh yes?"

"Yes, he's lovely. His name's Martin and he's a whole *seven years* younger than me. A proper toy boy! It's very exciting -"

She went on talking but I'd tuned out. I watched a pigeon flap its slow way across a sky that looked like curdled milk. I was thinking about Jessica.

After she'd left me at the party, I'd left the venue myself

five minutes later. I could barely walk to the taxis massed outside, my legs were shaking so much. I'd let myself into a cold and empty flat - Matt was staying at his cousin's house that night - and lay in bed, hugging my knees to my chest and listening to my teeth chatter.

In the morning it seemed even more unlikely. I kept checking the street outside, nervily, expecting to see her standing there in her black coat. All the time I was showering, forcing down some breakfast, flicking listlessly through television channels, I kept asking myself the same questions. I went back over our conversation, our meeting, until I couldn't remember what had really happened and what I'd imagined happening.

"Are you alright?" Matt said to me over the dinner table.

It was the first time either of us had said a word since we'd sat down. I came to with a start, realising I'd been staring off into space, my fork held aloft.

"Sorry," I said, blushing a little. "I was miles away."

"So I can see." He poured himself another glass of wine and took a long sip. "You were so far away you almost disappeared from view."

I hesitated, wondering whether to tell him. But I couldn't - I'd promised.

Later, I lay beside him in the dark, staring up at the ceiling and listening to his breathing. After a while, I got up and went through to the living room and straight to the window. A plastic bag fluttered along the pavement in the wind like a small, ragged ghost. No Jessica. I walked away from the window, rested my hand on the back of one of the armchairs and walked back. Surely this time - but there was nothing, just the orange tint of the streetlight and the massed ranks of the parked cars jammed against the pavements.

Becca invited us over for dinner the following night. She owned the basement flat in a terraced house in Hackney; being sensible, fiscally prudent and all the other things that

I was not, she'd bought it for tuppenny-happenny or thereabouts back in the early nineties. She'd lived there for so long, the flat seemed to have grown around her - it was now the very essence of Becca; warm, chaotic and loud. The rooms were painted in unexpected colours, her bedroom hung with swaying Chinese lanterns, the walls bedecked with sari silks. Once in a while you came across something truly startling, like the fake skull on the mantlepiece in the sitting room she'd stolen from a client's Halloween party.

As Matt and I arrived, Becca's equally Amazonian sister Lauren and her positively gigantic brother Sam were just leaving. There was a confused scrum in the tiny hallway as we all attempted to greet and say goodbye to everyone else at once.

"Don't worry about this lot," said Becca, as if there were hundreds of relatives cluttering up the place. "They're leaving. They were just dropping off the vino for tonight."

"Haven't seen you two for ages," said Lauren, kissing both Matt and I. "Married life treating you well?"

Matt and I both laughed and I made some sort of noise indicating agreement. Sam patted my shoulder as I squeezed past him.

"Phew," said Becca, waving them off and then ushering us into the kitchen. "Sorry about that. This place isn't really big enough for more than one of my family to visit at any one time but Sam just kind of turned up after the football and stayed on... anyway, vino? Lauren's got us some fantastic champagne. Matt, would you do the honours?"

Matt popped the cork of the bottle she proffered while I sat down at the table. The kitchen was at the front of the house and, from one side of the table, you could see up to the street and watch people's feet walk past the railings, rather like being in the burrow of a voyeuristic mole. I sat down and looked up, clutching my wine glass. I had a feeling that soon a pair of feet would come into view, feet framed by the edge of a long black coat. I was sure she would appear.

Matt raised his glass to Becca.

"To our gracious hostess," he said. "How's things? Who's this new man Maudie was telling me about?"

Becca laughed.

"That would be Martin. Has Maudie told you he's a whole *seven years* younger than I am? How about that?"

"A youngster?" cried Matt in mock anguish. "What for? You don't want one of those, you want a sugar daddy, just like Maudie."

Becca grinned.

"So you say. Perhaps all the good ones are taken. Hey, Maudie?"

"What?" I said, pulling my gaze away from the dark street.

Becca enumerated Martin's good qualities for the next half an hour, clattering about with pots and pans as she talked. She only drew breath to drag on her cigarette, finally grinding it out with a decisive jab before she bought the plates to the table.

"Disgusting habit, smoking while cooking," she said. "Sorry. Anyway, Martin wants to take me to Paris for the weekend. It's so nice to have a bit of romance in a relationship for a change. Don't you think, Maudie?"

"Yes, right," I said. Despite the steaming plate of food in front of me, I suddenly had to get up and walk about, I felt so jittery. I walked over to the window again and looked up. Nothing; just the railings and the trailing fronds of a dusty ivy plant in view. I turned back to find both Matt and Becca watching me with concern.

"Is there a problem, Maudie?" said Becca.

I tried to laugh.

"No. It's just – " I couldn't think of an adequate explanation for my nerves, not one that would suffice. I forced myself to walk back to the table and sit down. I poured myself some more wine, spilling a little over the side of the glass. I could see Matt watching me. He was frowning very slightly and I saw his eyes meet Becca's, just for a moment, a split second of unspoken communication.

"I'm alright," I said, with more emphasis. "I didn't sleep so well last night. I'm just a bit tired. For Christ's sake, everyone stop treating me like I'm a baby."

My voice went up sharply at the end of the sentence. There was a moment of silence.

"Okay," said Becca, rather brightly. "Matt, tell me about you. What's been happening?"

Matt put his knife and fork down.

"Rebecca, sorry, would you excuse me a moment?"

"Sure," she said, eyebrows raised.

He turned to me.

"Maudie, could I have a word? In private?"

I nodded. He led me into the hallway and closed the kitchen door gently. I stared at him, my chin up.

"What the hell is wrong with you?"

"What do you – " I began, hotly.

He took me by the shoulders, not quite shaking me.

"Don't ask me what I bloody mean. What is *wrong* with you? You're jumping at shadows, you keep looking for something or someone. You've got bags the size of suitcases under your eyes."

I took a step back, shaking off his hands.

"I'm fine. I'm sick of people asking me."

"For Christ's sake," he said. He had that look on his face that was worse than anger, that helpless, lost look, the one that turned his face into the face of someone much younger and more vulnerable. It turned something in me, digging deep.

"I feel like I should know what's wrong," he said. "There's nothing you can't tell me, you know that, don't you? How can I help you if you won't tell me?"

I spoke above the blood rushing in my ears.

"There's nothing to tell."

He stepped back, raising his hands in a gesture of defeat.

"Is it – " he said and then stopped.

"What?"

"Are you?" he said, and then stopped again.

I could feel the wine churning in my stomach and swallowed hard.

"Are you having an affair?"

I was so surprised and so relieved at his mistake that a shout of laughter escaped me. He looked bewildered. I kept laughing, I couldn't help it.

"Oh Matt," I said. I went up to him and put my arms round his neck, brushing my face against his bristly cheek. "I'm not having an affair. I promise you."

He stepped back and looked at me.

"Sorry," he said after a moment. "I don't know why I said that."

"No, I'm sorry," I said. Relief was making me feel weak and tired. "I'm sorry I lost my temper. I shouldn't have done. There's nothing wrong with me. I'm just tired and I'm – I'm grieving."

"I know," said Matt. He put a hand up to his face, pushing his fingers underneath his glasses to rub between his eyes. He looked as tired as I felt.

"We'd better get back to Becca," Matt sighed. "Just – look, please don't embarrass me again tonight. Or yourself. Please don't have any more to drink."

I clenched my jaw but I made myself nod. We walked back into the kitchen and I pinned a smile on my face. Rebecca sat with the elaborately casual air of someone pretending they hadn't heard a word of the argument.

I sat down, keeping my back to the window so as not to have to look out. I forced myself to listen to Becca and Matt, smile at appropriate places in their conversation and all the while, run over my strange meeting with my lost best friend, again and again and again.

CHAPTER TWENTY TWO

It was in one of the few moments of the day that I wasn't thinking about Jessica when she reappeared. I'd just left the flat, heading for my gym and a swimming session. I'd been neglecting my exercise routine lately and it was making me feel uncomfortable; not only did I feel fat and unfit, but gentle regular exercise was one of the many ways I kept the demons at bay. Matt and I had spent Christmas very quietly, just the two of us eating a meal at home and watching old films on TV, but I'd over-eaten, drunk far too much, and I was feeling the effects. It was time for me to start being a bit more self-denying. I was looking forward to the warm water, the echoing footsteps of the other swimmers as they walked beside the pool, the wobbling light reflected onto the ceiling. I would swim thirty lengths, shower and treat myself at the gym's café.

So my mind was elsewhere. I was walking away from the building when I heard my name spoken and, simultaneously, a hand on my shoulder. In the two seconds it took me to spin round and recognise her, I felt my heart give a gigantic thud. I breathed in sharply, the reverse of a scream and my hands went up to my face. A man walking towards me must have seen my panic as he hesitated for a second and then obviously thought better of asking me if I was alright. Jessica stood there on the pavement in her long black coat. She put the hand she touched me with back into her pocket.

"Sorry," she said. "Didn't mean to scare you."

I managed a shaky laugh. She put her head on one side. Her blonde hair glowed in the dull light of the winter afternoon. She looked better than before; healthier, somehow.

"Are you going somewhere?"

"I – " I opened my mouth and shut it again. My head buzzed with the backwash of adrenaline. "I was, but it's not important."

There was a short silence.

"Will you come and have a drink with me?"

We went to a pub two streets away; I'd passed it often but not been into it. There were tables outside on the pavement and Jessica gestured to one of them.

"Mind if we sit outside so I can smoke?"

I nodded. I was feeling light-headed again. I pinched a fold of my coat between my fingers; something tangible that I could keep hold of. I kept staring at the table while Jessica went to get our drinks. Perhaps she wouldn't come back again and I'd be sat here alone, as minutes lengthened into hours…

A glass of wine appeared on the table before me, Jessica's hand placing it carefully on the weathered wood. She had long, curved nails, unvarnished, a chunky silver ring on the middle finger of her right hand. I had no recollection of ordering wine but I had no recollection of almost anything of the past ten minutes. My head felt as if it were stuffed with angry wasps. I put both hands up to my temples, pressing inwards, closing my eyes for a brief moment.

The table rocked as Jessica slotted herself into the opposite seat and a splash of wine fell from my glass to land in a bloody little smear on the tabletop.

"Sorry," said Jessica. She had a glass of white wine in front of her, which had also spilt. I watched as a thin, clear trickle flowed towards the little puddle of red.

"So," she finally said, her head on one side again, looking at me and smiling slightly.

I took a shaky sip of my drink, resisting the urge to gulp.

"What do you want?" I blurted out.

Jessica raised her eyebrows.

"That's blunt."

"Sorry. It's just -"

"It's alright, Maudie," she said, speaking rather slowly. She didn't try and touch my hand. I stared up at the white sky, stretching my eyes wide and breathing deeply. Jessica took a sip of her drink, just sitting there opposite me, quietly.

I kept hold of my fold of coat, pleating it and releasing it. The palms of my hands were sweating.

The silence became too much.

"How did you know I was going to come out of the house? Were you waiting?" I said.

She shook her head, breathing out smoke.

"Pot luck," she said. "I'd waited for you a few times before but I never caught you. I'd only been there about five minutes today before you appeared."

"Why didn't you ring the doorbell?"

She gave me a half smile and a one-shoulder shrug.

I nodded, although I didn't really understand.

"Do you live with anyone?" she said.

"Yes, my husband." I took another sip of my drink. "His name's Matt but he's out at the moment."

Her eyebrows went up.

"Your husband? You're married?" She shook her head. "I can't believe you're married. My God – how long for?"

"Almost three years now." I looked down at my bare hands and saw her look too. "I left my ring at home today – I was off to the gym."

She nodded and there was a short silence.

"Are you?" I said.

"Am I what?"

"Married?"

She gave a short bark of a laugh.

"No."

I decided not to ask about children, because I didn't want her to ask me. We both sipped our drinks in silence. Jessica stubbed out her cigarette and almost immediately lit another one.

"Maudie, I'm sorry," she said. "I'm finding this as difficult as you. I just don't know – I don't know where to start. Where do you start, with this situation?"

I shook my head.

"I don't know."

"It's too – " she said, and then stopped abruptly.

"Everyone thought you were dead," I said. The smoke from her cigarette drifted across the table and into my eyes, making me blink.

"I know," she said. "I know they did. They must have done."

"Jessica – " I used her name for the first time. "Jessica. What happened?"

She looked at me for a long moment.

"It's a long, sad story," she said. "How much time have you got?"

I opened my mouth to reply but, before I could, she suddenly sat up and shook her head.

"Not now," she said. "Not today. It's too much. Tell me about you. Tell me all about you."

"Oh – " I looked down at my half empty glass. "Where shall I start?"

Jessica smiled. For the first time since we'd met, I felt a lightening of the spirit, a feeling that perhaps I could cope after all. We were just two women sitting together outside of a pub on a winter's day. It helped me to think that. Don't think about Cornwall, and Mrs McGaskill's hand raised to slap me, and the search parties and the yawning empty window, and the constant, acid guilt. Don't think about the nightmares running on an unending loop in my head, the closed door with the abyss behind it. Don't think about people coming back from the dead. We're just two women, having a drink outside a North London pub.

"Tell me about your wedding," Jessica said.

"My wedding?"

"Yeah, you said you were married. Tell me about your wedding. Was it a big white thing? We always used to talk about having one of those, remember?"

"My wedding..." I looked down at the foamy depths of my cup. "God. It seems like a long time ago now."

"Was it?"

"Not really. Only three years or so. God - time flies."

"So what was it like?"

"It was - amazing. Well, you know, a bit stressful, and all that - " I trailed off. How could I begin to condense all those different emotions down to a couple of coherent sentences? "It was a bit surreal, really. I had a wedding planner for everything - "

Jessica exploded with mirth.

"A wedding planner? Get you!"

I started laughing too. "I know, it's ridiculous, isn't it? Angus really pushed the boat out though, he insisted."

"I suppose, you being the only daughter, and all that – it makes sense," said Jessica, still grinning.

"It was a great day, though," I said. The good memories made my voice soften. "But you know, it was weird too. There were so many – I don't know – so many undercurrents of emotion running under the surface." I stopped, surprised at myself. Where had that come from?

I lifted the glass to my lips to hide the sudden tension in my mouth.

Jessica was watching me keenly.

"What do you mean?"

"Well," I said, and hesitated. Then I plunged in. "I remember during the service looking over and noticing this empty pew at the front. I mean, it was empty, right in the middle of mass of people." I paused, unsure of whether to go on.

"Yes?" said Jessica.

I spoke slowly.

"I had a thought – well, more like a wish, a fantasy – that – that you were there. That that was your pew. That you were sat there, with – with my mother. Except, it was empty because the two of you had just popped outside for a bit of air." I could feel the heat coming up into my face. "It's a bit stupid, I know."

"No," said Jessica, slowly. "It's not stupid. It's nice."

I looked down at my half-full glass, embarrassed.

"Well – "

"I mean it," she said. "Really, Maudie. I think it's lovely."

Her eyes had a suspicious shininess. I quickly looked back down at the table again, not wanting to draw attention to it.

"What's your husband like?" she asked.

"Matt? He's great. He's a bit older than me but I think that works sometimes, you know?"

"You're really in love with him?" she said, leaning forward slightly.

I was embarrassed again. I didn't like quantifying things like that, I told myself, explaining away my discomfiture.

"Well, of course I am. When I married him it felt like the biggest adventure of my life but also – also like coming home. Does that make sense?"

She nodded. There was an odd expression on her face, part wince, part smile. I suddenly felt as though I'd embarrassed her and felt awkward.

"Well, that's good," she said. She dug around in her bag for her cigarettes. "God, I smoke too much."

As she lit a cigarette, I thought of my wedding; my lovely dress; Angus's speech; Becca dropping the bouquet when I threw it to her and rolling her eyes; Aunt Effie's discreet tears, Matt's words to me in our wedding bed; all that crazy stress and anxiety wrapped up in a set of twenty four hours. It was ridiculous, really. One thing I hadn't told Jessica was my overriding impression of the day was that it was happening to someone else. Perhaps that was normal.

"How's your dad?" said Jessica.

I felt it hit me again, right in the pit of the stomach. How long does it have to be since a death, for that to stop?

"Oh – he died," I said.

Jessica's face twitched.

"Oh, Maudie," she said. She sounded close to tears. "Oh, *no*. How – how – I mean, when?"

"Just recently. This autumn, actually."

I surprised myself. I could talk quite matter of factly about it. There was something about her obvious distress that made me want to soften the blow.

Jessica ground her cigarette out.

"That's upset me," she said, almost in a mutter. "That's really upset me. I can't believe it."

I felt a little finger of cold nudge me in the ribs. If she reacted like that to Angus's death, how would she react to the news of her own parents' fate? I held onto my glass, feeling the condensation on the smooth curve of the bowl slip between my fingers.

"Yes," I said, meaninglessly. "It was very quick, though. Quick and painless. I mean, relatively."

Jessica smoked furiously, dragging on her cigarette as if it had personally offended her. I looked at her face, covertly, trying to drink her in, the concrete, flesh reality of her after so long in the ether. Her eyes were still shadowed beneath; marked with a smudge of darkness. With a shock, I realised she was beautiful. I watched her mouth close on the filter of her cigarette, the gasp inwards, the long wavering blue exhalation.

She felt my gaze and looked up, catching my eye.

"Sorry, Maudie," she said. "This is just weird, you know? I mean, I knew it would be weird, but I didn't know how much."

"I know," I said. We looked at each other, properly. In her eyes, I caught the first faint glimmerings of the old Jessica, my ten-year-old companion, the impishness that had once been there.

"Fuck," she said, breathing out smoke.

"Fuck," I said.

There was a moment's silence and then we both began laughing. It was thin, wheezy, gasping laughter, the laughter at something that's not particularly funny. Just an outpouring of emotion with no other exit. I put my hand out over the table and touched hers. She flinched.

"You are real," I said. I could hear myself, my wondering voice. "You *are*. I can't believe it."

"I came back," she said.

"I knew you would."

A car horn blared in the street and we both jerked in shock. She drew her hand away to pick up her glass.

"How many times can I say I can't believe it?" I said.

I sat back on my bench, holding on to the edge of the table. I leaned back, looking up into the sky and breathed out. I felt suddenly filled with hope.

"It's a miracle," I said. "That's what it is. It's the sort of thing the Sunday papers write articles about."

Jessica looked alarmed.

"I hope not."

"Oh, don't worry," I said. "I'm hardly likely to go running to them, am I? Jesus, it's as much as I can do to take it in."

Jessica leaned forward.

"Maudie," she said, very seriously. "I meant what I said the other night. I can't – I mean, I don't want you to tell anyone. Not your husband, or – or anyone. It's too – it's too personal. To us. You understand. I'm not – I'm not ready to have anyone else know, you know? Do you understand?"

I nodded. I was almost laughing, I felt so elated. I would have promised anything.

"I promise," I said. "Don't worry. Jesus, if I tell anyone about this, they'll really think I'm – "

There was a short silence.

"They'll really think what?" said Jessica.

"Nothing," I said, my elation gone. The sun had not been shining but I felt as if it had gone behind the clouds anyway. "Nothing."

I waited for her to push me on what I meant, but she simply sat back and breathed out smoke. She was such a contrast to all the people I knew. It made a strange and refreshing change to be sat opposite someone who *would* just let me be, who would leave it, who wouldn't make a fuss.

"I've never been back, you know," she said, suddenly.

I raised my eyebrows.

"Never been back where?"

"Cornwall."

It gave me a jolt. I'd thought she was going to say Cumbria.

"Nor have I," I said rather slowly, realising it for the first time.

She read my mind.

"I haven't been back – home – either."

"You haven't?" So she still called it home. As did I. When do the houses of your childhood stop being home?

"No," she said, shortly. "I didn't know it was home until recently."

I felt a little chill again, a finger of cold nudging me in the pit of the belly.

"No?" I said, for want of something better.

"No."

She stubbed out her cigarette. The ashtray was piled high with stubs and flaking grey ash.

"Well – " I said, unsure of what I was going to say. The choice was taken from me. I heard a shout from afar and realised, with disbelief, that it was my name being called. I looked down the street to see the distant but recognisable figure of Matt striding towards me.

"It's my husband," I said, panicking. I felt as guilty as if I were sitting there with a lover. "He's coming over here."

The panic in my voice was echoed in Jessica's. She stood up so abruptly, my half full glass fell over, emptying red wine over the surface of the table.

"He can't see me!" she said. She was grabbing up her cigarettes, her bag, her blonde hair falling over her face. "Maudie, I can't meet him, not yet, I can't. I'm sorry – I'm going to have to go – "

She stumbled over the seating bench of the table and almost ran into the pub. I stared after her, open mouthed. Red wine began to drip onto my jeans beneath the table.

"Maudie-"

Matt was almost upon me. I managed to drag my gaze from the door of the pub and brought it to focus on my husband.

"Maudie," said Matt. He was wearing his tweed jacket and the red scarf I'd bought him for Christmas. "Hello, darling. I've been calling you, didn't you hear me? What are you doing here?"

"Oh, nothing much," I said, managing a smile. Belatedly, I realised red wine had soaked into my trousers and cursed, brushing at them ineffectively beneath the table. "Shit. Not much, darling. I just thought – "

"Drinking during the day?" he said, sliding into the place Jessica had so recently and violently vacated. I blinked. He looked so... so real and alive.

I couldn't read his tone; normally, I'd know if he was being serious but my brain felt battered by Jessica's presence.

"Terrible, huh?" I said, smiling. "I've just been to the gym so I was feeling rather virtuous and thought I'd put a stop to that immediately."

"Right," said Matt. He smiled and I relaxed a little. "Who on earth were you talking to, anyway?"

I stopped in the middle of righting my upset glass. I

could feel the blood thumping in my head.

"Oh no-one, really," I said, as casually as I could. "Just someone wanting directions. Some tourist."

"No, I mean *who* were you talking to?" he said, unbuttoning his jacket.

"What do you mean?" I said.

He smiled.

"Well, I couldn't really see clearly but it looked like you were just nattering away to yourself for a while. Talking to yourself. Did you have the phone headset on?"

I felt my heart give a painful jump. My mouth felt suddenly dry.

"That's right," I said slowly, trying to keep my voice under control. I breathed in and out a few times before I went on. "I had to make a few calls. Then someone asked me for directions."

"Right," said Matt, losing interest. He was looking around for a member of the bar staff. I could hear my heartbeat, quite clearly, thundering in my ears as I replayed his casual remark. *It looked like you were just nattering away to yourself.* I would not think about that remark. I would not think, full stop.

"They don't do table service here, do they?" said Matt. He seemed to be talking from a great distance away. I stared at him, at his familiar face, willing my own face not to show my distress. "I'll go in and get us a drink, if you want to stay?"

"That would be lovely," I heard myself say. He stood up and went into the bar.

I sat there on the bench in my wine-stained jeans, trying to think of nothing. I couldn't think of anything other than Jessica at the moment.

"Cheers, sweetheart," Matt said, returning to the table. "Classes finished early today, thank God. It's good to be out and about and not stuck in a bloody lecture hall for once."

"Yes," I said, in my cheerful robot's voice. "Cheers."

Behind his back, the pub door opened and Jessica walked out, her long coat flaring out behind her. My hand twitched and I spilt yet more wine on the already sodden table.

"Whoops," said Matt, mopping away with a tissue.

Behind his back, Jessica looked at me for a long moment. I couldn't decipher her expression; I could barely see. But I saw her nod, a quick, sharp bob of the head, and she began to walk away, down the street, her hands in her pockets, her blonde hair fluttering behind her like a torn golden headscarf. She didn't look back. I watched her until Matt had finished cleaning up the wine, and then I had to look at him. Jessica was gone.

CHAPTER TWENTY THREE

I got through the next couple of days quite successfully by not allowing myself to think. It was a good test of mental stamina. Every time my thoughts went to Jessica, I ruthlessly headed them off. I looped an elasticated hairband about my wrist and snapped it against my skin every time I thought about her, saying to myself 'stop'. Nothing else, just 'stop'. If that didn't work, I sang lyrics to Beatles songs under my breath until I'd tricked my mind into thinking about something else. Sometimes I thought of my brain, my mind, with something approaching hate. My body had never let me down – indeed, in one particular way, although it hadn't seemed so at the time, it had quite spectacularly not let me down - but my mind... It felt like the enemy; as if there were someone else stuck in my head. It gave me a grim pleasure to trick it into doing what I wanted, for a change.

Things between Matt and myself were rather better than they had been. Perhaps it was my own behaviour that had made the change; I was so determined not to give into my darkest thoughts that I was almost relentlessly cheerful, even if I didn't feel it. I was careful about drinking. I still drank, but not so that Matt could see. I went to the gym and swam, I bought new clothes and had my hair done, I bought new books and films and music. I began looking at property websites, working out what was out there, what could be done. I had quite a clear picture in my head of what I wanted. A country house but not a huge, stone pile like Caernaven, with acres of grounds. A manageably sized house, old but not too old, not too remote. Close enough to a big town so that we would still be able to shop and have dinner and see a film when we wanted to, but far enough away from the hustle and bustle for some peace and solitude.

I hadn't decided what to do about Caernaven. I spoke to Matt about it over dinner one night.

"Difficult," said Matt. He laid his knife and fork down precisely in the centre of his plate. "It's your childhood home, Maudie. What do you want to do?"

"I don't know."

"Come on, darling. You must have some preference."

I took a sip of wine and thought. What I wanted to do was for someone else to tell me what to do and then to do it for me but I thought I had probably better not say this.

"Not sure," I said. Matt sighed and I went on quickly. "Maybe – well, rent it out. I mean, once it's sold, it's sold forever."

"If that's what you think is best."

"What about the Board?" he said.

I shrugged.

"I have absolutely no idea."

"Has Mr Fenwick mentioned it again?"

"Not yet. But I've got to give him an answer sometime."

"What do you want to do?"

I put my head into my hands.

"I don't know," I said.

Matt got up to clear our plates. I could almost hear the forbearance sighing out of him as he went past. I would have to do something, anything; his patience was wearing thin.

"There's still a lot of stuff to sort out up there," I said, slowly. "I might need to take another trip up there."

This happened sooner than I thought. The next evening we received a phone call from Aunt Effie's housekeeper, Jane. Aunt Effie had had a fall, broken her collarbone and sprained her ankle, and was in hospital for the next couple of weeks. She was asking for me to come and see her.

"Why?" I asked Jane. "I mean, is there any reason in particular? Apart from, well, just wanting to see me?"

"I don't know, Maudie. She's on quite heavy duty painkillers and she's sometimes a little – well, confused. She just insists she has to see you. Will you come?"

I promised to drive up the next day or two. After I put the phone down, I went into the kitchen, hungry for a glass of wine. Matt had disappeared into the study and I could see a thin blue ribbon of smoke drifting from its wide open doorway. He was smoking a lot more these days and I knew why; he was stressed about work. He was stressed about me.

Our dinner plates were stacked on the kitchen counter. I rinsed them and put them in the dishwasher. It was one of Mrs Dzinkska's days tomorrow but I drew the line at leaving her a pile of encrusted dishes. I shut the door and switched on the machine, drawing a little comfort as always from the reassuring hum as the washing cycle began. I let my gaze drift across the room, coming to rest on the window. Immediately I thought of Jessica.

I reached for my wristband but I'd taken it off when I'd showered earlier. I pinched the skin of my wrist instead. It didn't work. I kept seeing her face as she turned away from me, outside the pub, and her long, flat back disappearing down the road.

Still at the sink, I caught sight of myself in the glass-fronted cupboard above it. At the sight of my rigid face, I suddenly realised how idiotic I was being. How self-pitying. I straightened up properly and took a deep breath.

That night Matt and I made love for the first time in

days. I lay in his arms afterwards, listening to his breathing returning to normal, and thinking, for once, of something different. I wanted to talk to him about what had been happening. No matter what Jessica had asked me, I knew I had to tell him.

"Matt," I said softly. He made a low, inarticulate noise in his throat. Encouraged, I went on.

"I know things have been a bit odd between us, lately," I said, almost whispering. "I know that sometimes - well - I'm a bit odd and I do silly things and I know you find it frustrating."

"You're okay, silly thing," he said in a sleep-slurred kind of voice. I laid my head back against his shoulder, listening to the steady pound of his heartbeat in my ear.

"It's just that, strange things have been happening," I said. I could feel my own heartbeat start to speed up as I thought of what I was about to say. "Very strange. Actually, it's only just really sinking in for me how strange they really are."

My mouth was drying up. I coughed softly to loosen my throat.

"Jessica – "

My voice failed and I coughed again.

"Jessica – she came back."

It sounded so ridiculous. I almost blushed, as if it mattered in the dark. For the first time, I confronted the essential strangeness of it – that Jessica, left for dead, back in the distant past, had been resurrected. Just for me. Not for the first time, I felt a flicker of unease.

"She says she's come back," I said slowly. I could feel the slow rise and fall of Matt's ribcage against my cheek. He hadn't said anything. The darkness sucked at my voice, shredding it down to a whisper. It felt oddly confessional. "But I don't know, Matt. I don't know what to think. When you say to me that I'm talking to thin air – and I close my eyes and when I open them, she's there…" I ran out of breath and took a great rasping gulp of air. I couldn't quite believe I was going to say it.

"Sometimes – sometimes I think I'm just losing my mind."

I couldn't say any more for the moment. I looked down at him, trying to make out his face in the darkness. I could see the black fan of his eyelashes lying against the curve of his cheekbone, etched in shadow.

"Matt?" I said, in a more normal voice. He made no answer and I realised he was asleep.

CHAPTER TWENTY FOUR

Aunt Effie was asleep when I arrived. She lay on the hospital bed, her body almost lost beneath the covers; she barely made a mound under the blankets. Her white hair, usually so carefully set, looked limp and yellowed under the harsh strip lights. Her housekeeper, Jane, was sat by the bed reading *Take a Break* magazine.

"I thought you said she only broke her collar bone?" I said, when Jane and I were in the corridor with the door pulled closed behind us.

Jane shrugged helplessly.

"She's a very old woman, Maudie. She can't bounce back like you or I could. If you ask me - " she lowered her voice and moved a little closer to me. "If you ask me, she won't recover from this. It's too much of a shock to the system."

I was shocked again, by the jolt that this gave me.

"But - " I said, not even sure of what I wanted to say.

Jane patted my arm. Her eyes were limpid with sympathy.

Aunt Effie hadn't moved position on the bed but her eyes were open. I stood for a moment by the side of the bed, hesitating, and then sat down.

"Maudie," she said, her voice a hoarse whisper.

"Do you want some water or something?" I asked. I couldn't get the tone of my voice right - I sounded too lighthearted, falsely jovial.

"Maudie," she said. "I'm sorry."

"Don't worry," I said, thinking she was going to apologise for dragging me up here. I said it automatically, without thought.

"I'm sorry," she said again, in her cracked old voice.

I felt something, a tremor of curiosity. Or was it fear? What was she apologising to me for?

"Sorry for what, Auntie?"

She moved her head from side to side on the pillow.

"We were wrong," she said. "I think now we were wrong. You should have been in a hospital, you should have had treatment much earlier. We didn't realise how bad things were."

I went cold. She'd never spoken about that time, never. It was as if it had been rubbed out of existence. It might not have happened.

I was silent. She cleared her throat.

"If I thought you'd ever do what you did, we wouldn't have hesitated. Maudie, you do understand?" Tears were shining in her eyes, the whites webbed with tiny threads of blood. "You don't know how bad I feel that we didn't see what was happening. I should have known what you were going to do."

"It's okay," I said. I couldn't believe we were actually talking about it, the bad time, openly. I had a vision of myself then as they must have seen me; face down in a pool of vomit on the bathroom floor, and winced, as if something sharp had just pierced me.

"I'm sorry," she said again. Two tears welled up and flowed into the wrinkles by her eyes. "We thought we were doing what was right. Your mother - she - "

"My mother?"

My heart was thumping - I could scarcely hear myself above its beats.

"She - she - that's why we were so afraid. They let her out for the day."

"What are you talking about?"

The tears were clogging Aunt Effie's already hoarse voice; I could hardly understand her.

"She ran away with you," she said. "We didn't know she'd done it. We thought she was safe at the hospital and you were in the garden."

"What?"

I felt like taking that frail little body before me by the shoulders and shaking as hard as I could. The strength of the urge to do this shocked me. I had to clench my fists to stop myself grabbing her, shaking her, forcing her to make sense.

"She took you from the garden," she whispered. "We thought she was safe at the hospital but she wasn't. We could have lost you both that day."

I could barely speak for frustration, my teeth clenched, hissing out my words in a slow whisper.

"What are you talking about?"

She ignored me. I thought suddenly that she wasn't even talking to me, not directly; she was confessing to someone else, something else that only she could see. I stepped back from the bed, clenching and unclenching my hands.

Aunt Effie's eyes closed. I could hear her breath rattling through the phlegm in her throat. She coughed and her eyes flew open and closed again. I held myself rigid for a second, terrified that she'd died, but after a moment, I could make out the barely perceptible rise and fall of the blankets on the bed. I put my hands up to my head, pressing inwards. I could feel each heartbeat pulse in my temples.

The door opened inwards and Jane's head poked around.

"Are you okay?" Jane asked.

I nodded. I couldn't be bothered to say anything else. She gave me a look I couldn't fathom.

"Well, I'll just be outside if you need me," she said.

I waited for a little while. I had each elbow clasped in an opposite hand and I could feel my arms shaking. I tried to take deep breaths while I worked out what to do.

Aunt Effie coughed. I could see her eyes opening again and for a moment, I contemplated running away. I steeled myself, pulled up a chair and sat down again by the side of the bed.

"Auntie," I said, gently. I said her name again, more loudly this time. Her eyelids fluttered open and she looked at me.

"What was I saying?" she said, faintly.

I gritted my teeth.

"You were telling me about my mother. What about her, Auntie? What did she do?"

She cleared her throat again.

"I'm not feeling well."

"You started this," I said. "You have to tell me."

I got her some water and helped her drink it. I had to hold up her head but I didn't do it well; I must have been too rough because she winced and the water ran down the side of her neck. She pawed feebly at her wet nightdress and I wrenched a bunch of tissues from the dispenser on the nightstand and thrust them at her.

"Thank you," she said and something in the way that she said it, in a small, childlike voice, got through my anger. I could feel my eyes filling up with tears and rubbed them away.

Eventually, she dropped the damp wad of tissue on the floor and lay still.

"What happened?" I asked.

My anger had passed as suddenly as it had appeared - I merely felt very tired and my head buzzed. I rubbed at my temples.

"Your mother was a very lovely person," said Aunt Effie, eventually. "But she wasn't very - stable. I think we all knew that, quite early on. Your father knew it."

She stopped speaking. I dropped my hands to my lap.

"And?" I said.

She sighed again. "She was always very lively, very animated. Very vibrant. I suppose that's why we didn't notice she was slipping. She was just slightly more - more excitable than she would have been normally. And then all of a sudden, she wasn't there anymore."

"What do you mean?"

She turned her head towards me.

"Oh, I don't mean literally," she said. "But we lost her. She turned into somebody else, somebody quite different." She fell silent for a moment. "We lost her," she repeated, quietly.

"What was wrong with her?"

"I believe the diagnosis was schizophrenia."

I looked down. The word reverberated in the quiet room.

"What happened?"

Aunt Effie shifted a little under the covers.

"She was having treatment," she said. "In the hospital. It seemed to be working. She was very - very distressed to be parted from you." I could feel my eyes begin to fill again and blinked hastily. Aunt Effie went on. "Your father brought her home for the day so she could spend some time with you. He only left her for a moment. When he came back to the terrace, she'd taken you and the car."

"Taken me?"

Her voice cracked a little.

"You were only a baby. You were in your pram on the terrace, Mrs Green had gone indoors for something. When we checked, you were gone."

I could feel dread creeping upwards through me, like a rising tide of ice water. I tried once to ask the question but my voice failed. I felt faint and the room shimmered. I tried again.

"The car crash - the crash - it wasn't an accident, was it?"

Aunt Effie was silent.

"*Was it?*" I barely recognised my own voice.

"No," she said, eventually.

I heard myself sob. It shocked me.

"She meant to do it?"

Aunt Effie reached out a hand to me but I ignored her.

"Oh, my dear," she said. There were tears in her eyes. "She was ill. She didn't know what she was doing."

I stood up abruptly. I had to get out of this room; it was suffocatingly hot. I had my hand up to my scar.

I heard Aunt Effie say my name but, by that time, I was through the door.

I drove to Caernaven. I didn't allow myself to think on the way. I just stared at the road ahead and looked past the windscreen wipers that moved endlessly back and forth. It was raining steadily and the mountains were shrouded in mist. I parked the car outside the front door, gravel spraying up as I braked a little too hard. Mrs Green opened the door before I could use my key.

"Maudie," she said, sounding surprised. "I wasn't expecting you for a couple of hours."

"Sorry," I said. I felt as though I were speaking through clenched teeth, although of course I wasn't. My voice felt strangled. "I got here quicker than expected. Do you mind if I get myself a drink?"

She looked even more surprised.

"No, of course – I'll just put the kettle on – "

"A proper drink." I was past caring what she thought.

In the kitchen, she poured me a modest glass of wine from a newly opened bottle. I had to restrain myself from grabbing it from her.

"Are you alright?" she asked.

"I'm fine," I said. For a second, I thought of asking her about my mother and then thought better of it. I didn't want to hear anything more about it.

"I'm just going up to my room," I said. I took the bottle with me, not caring what she thought.

Up in my room, I sat against the radiator, shivering. I

drank my wine in gulps, choking over it. My head felt as if it had been recently released from a vice.

So, no accident then. No accident. Was it suicide? Or was she just too mad to remember she was driving? I thought of my own brush with death, face down on a vomit-soaked carpet, and groaned aloud. My own mother had tried to kill me. Why? Because she knew she was going to kill herself and couldn't bear to leave me behind? Had she wanted to prevent me suffering the same affliction in the future, snuffing me out before I had a chance to follow in her footsteps? Well, what a failure she'd made of *that*. In the depths of her mental torment, had she forgotten about me, strapped into the baby seat? Had I screamed as the wall rushed towards us? I thought of what her injuries must have been, and flinched. Had Angus identified her? What must he have thought as he contemplated what was left, the crumpled, ragged, ripped-apart body, the parts of it they'd managed to salvage from the wrecked car?

The pressure in my head screwed itself tighter. I could hear myself sobbing on every outward breath. Angus. All these years he'd lied to me. So many secrets in one family. How many more were there, waiting out there, waiting to spring?

I managed to get to my feet. Oblivion had never seemed so necessary. I ransacked my bathroom, looking for something, anything that would put me out for the night. I found three sleeping tablets, Temazepam, rolling around in one of the drawers. God knows how long they'd been there. As I washed them down with wine, I found myself wondering how dangerous a move this was. Perhaps they would kill me. *Good*, was the only answer my mind came up with, and I lay on the bed and waited for sleep, or some other kind of black curtain, whichever came first.

CHAPTER TWENTY FIVE

"You look like death," were Matt's first words to me as I walked through the door of the flat.

"Thanks a bunch." I handed him one of my bags. "Nice to see you too."

"Sorry." He dropped the bag on the floor, drew me against him and kissed me. "That was a bit rude. You don't look like death, but you look very tired. Better?"

I leant against his broad chest, closing my eyes.

"How was it up there?"

I didn't want to talk about. I wanted to forget what I'd heard, push it back down into the shadows.

"I'll tell you later," I said. "I'm too tired right now."

I flopped onto the sofa, groaning softly. Matt handed me a little pile of envelopes.

"Your post," he said. "Want a drink?"

I nodded. On the top envelope, my name and address were written in a hand I didn't recognise. I tore the envelope open and scanned the single page within.

Matt was clinking about in the drinks cupboard. As I stared at the page, I became aware he'd asked me a question.

"What?"

"I said, vodka tonic do you?"

"Yes, fine." I carefully folded the paper up and put it back in the envelope. "Matt, I have to go out tomorrow. I'll probably be out most of the day."

"Oh darling, you've only just got back. I haven't seen you for days."

"I know, I'm sorry." I couldn't face a row. "It's stuff to do with the estate. I have to deal with it."

Matt handed me my glass.

"If you must, you must. But I'll have forgotten what you look like soon. We must make a bit of time for us, Maudie."

I nodded and sipped my drink, only half listening. All I could think about was the note in my pocket and the meeting with Jessica in the morning that it promised.

I had never been to the London Aquarium before. As I made my way slowly through the dimly lit rooms, bathed in a bluish glow, I thought to myself that I must come here more often. It had a peaceful sense to it, despite the hordes of school children that thronged the corridors and pressed their faces up against the glass. I drifted from one underwater scene to another, moving slowly through the dappled light and feeling calmer than I had in weeks. The three fingers of vodka I'd consumed before I left the house helped too. Drinking in the morning was supposed to be a bad sign but the way I was feeling, it was a lifesaver.

Eventually I came to our meeting place. I found a seat on one of the plastic benches opposite the shark tank and rested there, watching the sharks move in their perpetual circles, spiralling up to the top of the tank, and then moving back down to my eye level. There was something hypnotic in their endless circling.

Jessica's arrival was heralded by a slight breath of the perfume she wore. I kept my eyes on the shark tank but I became aware of her sitting next to me.

"Hi Jessica," I said quietly, not looking at her.
"Hi Maudie."

We were quiet for a little while longer. I could feel the warmth of her arm through my sleeve and felt obscurely comforted.

"Horrible, aren't they?" she said, after a while.

I turned to look at her.

"The sharks?"

"No, the screaming kids. Nightmare."

I laughed. "They are a little noisy, yes."

"At least it means we can talk freely," she said, somewhat mysteriously. She shrugged off her long black coat and folded it over her arm. "Thanks for meeting me. I didn't know whether I should phone – anyway, how have you been?"

"For a moment, I considered telling the truth. That I'd found out my own mother had been as mad as I'd once been and had committed suicide whilst trying to murder me. That my family had connived to keep this a secret. That I'd been drinking more and more heavily, more and more secretly since I'd discovered this. I considered telling her this for a millisecond and of course, rejected the idea.

"Oh I'm fine," I said. "Not bad. How have you been?"

She didn't answer at first. She looked upset. I was about to say something and then she caught my eye. Her face smoothed out and she looked normal again.

"I've been okay," she said. "Things have been a bit - a bit of a struggle. A bit. I've been wondering – wondering what to do. I'm okay now though."

She didn't elaborate and I didn't want to press her. For a moment, I wished passionately that we could jump forward in time, to a friendship renewed three years down the track, where we'd got past the awkwardness and the back stories and were simply able to be ourselves again, as we had once been before.

"Let's wander," I said, wanting to break the silence.

We left the shark tank and walked on. Jessica stopped at

a tank filled with jellyfish, floating like gently undulating, translucent balloons in the water. We were briefly alone, and she moved forward to look more closely. The blue light from the tank fell onto her face and as I watched her, I had a sudden sense of horror; it was visceral, like a whole-body shudder. She looked drowned, her skin bleached out, her eyes unseen in black hollows.

I must have made a sound. She turned towards me and the illusion was gone. I stood there with my hand up to my mouth, swallowing.

"What's up?" she said.

I managed to put my hand down, shrug and smile. I could not shake the image of her drowned face.

Perhaps the Aquarium had been a mistake. I'd managed to forget about Matt's words to me outside the pub. Now all my fears were crowding back, flooding back.

"Sorry," I said to Jessica. "I've just got to nip to the Ladies. Will you wait here for me?"

I prayed she wouldn't need to come with me.

"I'll wait here," she said.

I scurried away. I kept seeing her blue, drowned face in my mind. It had been a momentary illusion, caused by the weird water-light. Hadn't it?

A few moments in a locked cubicle were enough to calm me. I took a few deep breaths. I pushed my way back out through the line of women and young children.

"Come on," I said to Jessica, who was where I'd left her. "Let's get out of here."

We began walking along the South Bank, downriver. The Thames was high, its thick, brown waters roiling and churning in the wake of the many boats that sped or chugged along it. A bitter wind was blowing and we both hunched into our coats. We wandered into the West End. We walked aimlessly for a while and found ourselves drifting into New Bond Street.

"Oh, my favourite boutique's up here," I said. "Do you mind if we have a quick look?"

Jessica shook her head. She was looking at the windows of the shops with an odd look on her face, a look that was blank and hungry at the same time. Daylight was fading now and the lights in the windows looked extra welcoming, a soft cosy glow illuminating the wares within. We reached the door of my favourite shop and I pressed the buzzer.

"It's Maudie Reynolds," I said to the assistant. "I'd like to have a look at your new range, if that's okay?"

Inside, the chilly saleswoman thawed and greeted me by name, something that made Jessica's eyes go wide, to my secret inner amusement. I'd shopped here so often I'd opened my own account.

"It's just so much easier," I explained, wondering if I was trying a little too hard to justify myself.

"What was that, madam?" said the saleswoman.

"Oh, nothing," I said. I waited until she'd moved away and then rolled my eyes at Jessica, to make her giggle.

There were at least three dresses that I immediately wanted. I made a beeline for them and then hesitated. It felt odd, somehow, indelicate, to be spending money on myself in front of my best friend. She was standing by a glass-topped drawer of jewellery, necklaces and bracelets and rings in delicate, filigreed platinum, laid out in tempting rows on white velvet underneath the glass.

"Nice, aren't they?" I said, coming up beside her.

"They're lovely," she said. Then she leaned in and spoke in a murmur. Her voice stirred the hair by my ear. "A lovely price too."

"Oh well," I said, a little uncomfortably. "I suppose so."

"Nice though," said Jessica. She squeezed my arm and then went to move away.

"Do you want one?" I said, blurting out my request. It took me by surprise but the second I'd said it, I could see I'd surprised Jessica more.

"You what?"

I pointed. "Do you want one? One of those?"

She came back to the cabinet and looked down, then looked back at me. I could see both incredulity and suspicion competing for control of her face.

"What do you mean?" she said, frowning.

"I mean, do you want one?"

She looked at the cabinet again.

"Well, of course," she said, "But - "

"Because I'll buy one," I said, my words rushing over one another. "I mean, I'll buy you one. Whichever one you want."

She looked back at me.

"You'd buy me one?" she said, and her tone was wondering. "*You* would?"

"Of course," I said. I could feel the smile stretching my face. It suddenly seemed like such a stupid little thing, a gesture I should have made a lot earlier. "Call it - call it a welcome back present."

She started to laugh then. There was still a wondering note in her voice and her eyes didn't leave my face. She was looking at me like she'd looked so intensely beforehand, when we hadn't spoken, when she'd just been a figure in the street, but the message beaming from her eyes was so different. She looked... happy.

"That's very kind of you, Maudie," she said, quite formally but with a bubble of laughter still trapped in her throat.

"You're welcome," I said, and this time I squeezed her arm.

She drew in her breath when they put my credit card through the till reader and the price came up, but I waved her away. "It's a gift!" I said. "Don't worry about it. God knows I owe you some birthday presents - "

Even outside in the street, her hand kept straying to her pocket, where she'd put the little velvet-covered box. I was touched. I wanted to buy her something else, to see that look of happiness on her face again, but thought I'd better not. Not until next time we met, anyway.

"You're very generous, Maudie," she said.

I shrugged, a little embarrassed as I always was when people mentioned money.

"Well, I suppose it's easy to be generous when you've got money."

"Hah," said Jessica. "You'd think that would be the case, wouldn't you?"

We walked on a little further.

"Isn't that the case?" I said.

"Nope," she said. "People with money who are generous are rare. The tight bastards are more usually found."

"True."

"Except for Angus," she said. "He wasn't tight."

There was a moment's silence.

"No, that he wasn't," I said. I tried to keep the bitterness out of my voice. "That's one thing he wasn't."

A crowd of school children swarmed around us briefly, speaking French. We watched them walk and run down the street.

"He lied to me, Jess," I said.

She glanced warily at me.

"Who did?"

"Angus. And Aunt Effie – remember her? They all lied to me."

"They did?"

"Technically, they didn't," I said. I could hear myself, as if I were listening to someone else speaking flatly. "They withheld information, I think is the term. It comes to the same thing, anyway."

"What do you mean?"

I hesitated for a second. It hurt so much to even think of the words to use. I told her what Aunt Effie had told me. As I finished speaking, I could feel the tears start to come.

Jessica grabbed my arm.

"Don't cry," she said. "You're always crying and what good does it do?" I looked at her, startled out of my misery. "Get *angry*, Maudie. Stop being so passive."

"What?"

"Crying never gets you anywhere. I know that. So people treat you like shit – are you just going to sit there and take it?"

I stared at her, taken aback.

"Are you?"

I felt my shoulders slump.

"Probably. I don't know what else to do."

She remained with her hand on my arm, staring at me. Then she stepped back.

"Sorry."

"No, you're right," I said. "I just – oh, I don't know –"

I had the sense she was struggling not to say more. She opened her mouth and shut it again.

"What is it?" I said.

She held her breath for a second and then let it out in a sigh.

"Nothing," she said. "It's nothing. It's just - " She hesitated again. "It's just - I'm sorry, Maudie."

"Sorry?"

"Yes, I'm sorry," she said. "I'm sorry you're upset."

There was a moment of silence.

Jessica lit a cigarette and, as she spoke, wisps of smoke trickled from her lips. "There's a bar, in Hoxton, on Shade Street. It's off Old Street - it's called the Sticks Bar. Can you be there tomorrow night? Eight o'clock?"

"Of course." I said it too quickly, almost talking over her.

"It's time for my story now." She said it again, almost too quietly for me to hear. "Yes, it's time for my story now."

I felt a leap of something; fear, anticipation.

"I'll be there."

She regarded me for a moment, without speaking. Then with a quick sharp nod, she turned away. I watched her walk away from me down the street, before the crowds swallowed her up.

CHAPTER TWENTY SIX

The Sticks Bar was small and dark. I had found the shabby, anonymous looking street fairly easily but had walked the length of the road twice, up and back, before I found the bar. A discarded newspaper blew against my legs and I had to stop and disentangle myself before walking on. I don't mind waiting in bars by myself but I always have to gather my courage to actually enter them. I suppose it's the fear of not knowing what's behind the door.

The walls were painted dark red, and with the low ceiling and dim lighting, it felt like stepping into a cave. I walked as nonchalantly as I could to the bar and waited to be served, glancing about me as discreetly as possible. I was looking for a flash of blonde hair in the gloom. There were few people there but I still stood for five minutes at the bar, feeling utterly invisible, before the barman deigned to notice me.

With drink in hand, I made my way slowly around the bar, peering through the gloom for a sight of Jessica. I couldn't find her. I made my way to a table for two at the back of the room, sat down and leant my head against the dark red wall. I kept my eyes shut for a minute, trying to breathe deeply and not think of much. Then, a little calmer, I opened them.

Jessica sat opposite me. I suppose I must have been getting used to her sudden appearances and disappearances – I hardly jumped at all. The merest squeak came from my mouth, quickly muffled.

"Hi," I said, voice hardly shaking at all.

"Been waiting long?"

"Not long," I said, rather tightly. "Not long in one way."

"I know exactly how you feel, Maudie, believe me."

She had an odd way about her tonight, a kind of suppressed glee. She kept buttoning herself down; I could see her doing it. I was reminded, unwillingly, of the last night I'd ever seen her, before her reappearance – when she stood in the kitchen of the cottage in Cornwall, her eyes gleaming in the naked light of the kitchen lightbulb. I heard her ten year old voice as clearly as I could hear her now: *Tonight, we'll do it tonight.* The ritual. What in God's name had she conjured up?

Her blonde hair was twisted up tonight, in a messy coil on the back of her head. She wore her long black coat and, underneath, a purple velvet shirt. There was a heavy, silver ring on one of her long fingers and she wore the necklace that I'd bought her. It shimmered against the pale skin of her throat.

Jessica took a big mouthful of her drink – I could see it distending her cheeks.

"Where do you want me to begin?"

"At the beginning, of course."

"But which one?"

"For God's sake," I said. "You tell me."

I didn't sound like myself. I sounded like a stranger, a cold, censorious stranger.

Her manner changed. Before she had been wild, fey, fidgeting about in her seat and turning her glass around and around, inking wet rings of condensation on the table top. Now she sagged. I could see the slowly welling gleam of tears in her eyes.

"Begin after Cornwall," I said, more gently.

She looked down at the table and a tear fell. I was pierced by the memory of sitting opposite Becca and telling her the same story. Now here was the second half, Jessica's second half.

"Cornwall," said Jessica, slowly. I couldn't read her voice – it sounded purposefully flat, as if she was trying not to betray any emotion whatsoever. I knew how she felt.

"Cornwall – " I prompted.

She glanced up at me with a flash of anger.

"Alright," she said. "Give me a chance. I'll tell it in my own time."

"Okay," I said, chastened. We both looked at our drinks. I noticed her nails were bitten, the nail polish on them chipped and flaking.

"Cornwall," she said, once more. Then she took a deep breath, steadying herself for the plunge.

*

"I think I was about fifteen when I first realised something was wrong. *Really* wrong, I mean, not just the wrong kind of thing for a teenage girl. Before that, I'd had problems, you know, but I didn't really connect anything with anything. I just thought my – my situation was a bit fucked up. Which it was of course, Christ, so much more than I could have imagined. But I didn't know. I didn't even know I suspected. I think there was just a sense of – of things being – off kilter. As if you're looking at the world through different coloured glasses to the rest of the people. You know that old chestnut about trying to describe a colour to a blind person? I mean, how do you describe *blue* to a person who's never seen the sky, or the sea, or – or cornflowers, or anything like that? You know what I mean? All I knew was that something was *wrong*, something underneath, but I didn't know if I was *right*. God, it drove me mad. Imagine being fifteen, and stuck in a house with – wait, I'm getting beyond myself.

"I was fifteen, or so I was told. I lived in this very sterile, new-built flat, apartment, with my Aunt. She said she was my Aunt but she looked nothing like me, nothing – she had dark wavy hair that was always a bit greasy and was going grey... she used to get it covered up with dye sometimes but most of the time she didn't bother. And she had olive skin and dark brown eyes. I mean, I know genetics can do funny things but you know, Maudie, what I look like. What we look like. We used to pretend we were sisters, do you remember?

"The flat was like a hotel, one of those totally anonymous chain hotels; all beige carpet and magnolia walls and some god-awful landscape painting on one wall. In a mock-gold frame. I saw a lot of those hotels later on in life... but I'll come to that later. It had four bedrooms so was pretty big, and every so often some other kids stayed over. My Aunt – Tracey, her name was – said she was fostering them, short-term, you know, for the council. They were always girls, normally about twelve, maybe a little bit older. Tracey told me that they'd been through horrible situations and they were emotionally damaged, and because of that, they might tell a lot of lies. So I wasn't to take anything they said to me very seriously. But they never said much – they just stayed in their rooms and watched TV. They never stayed long. I think the most time any of them were there was about a week. They used to creep me out a bit, to be honest, they were so silent. I used to run into them in the kitchen when I was getting something to eat, and they'd just look at me with these big eyes, all in silence.

"It's hard to explain just how weird things were. For a start, I had no memory of anything before my time at the flat. I don't even remember arriving at the flat. Do you see what I mean? Well, put it this way, have you ever had a general anaesthetic? It's not like falling asleep and waking up. There's no sense of time having passed. It's like a slice out of time, you're conscious one minute, the next you're not, then you come back to life and in between is nothing. Nothing at all. That's what my life was like. There was me, in the flat with Tracey, and the weird kids, and before that, nothing. Not a single thing.

"Of course, I knew that wasn't normal. I didn't go to school so I had no – what's the word? – no frame of reference, but I knew that most people didn't just pop into being aged fifteen. So I asked Tracey, and guess what she told me? I'd been in a car accident, a bad one. It had killed my parents. I'd survived, but I'd gone into a coma, a long one, six months or something, and only now was I really recovering.

"When she told me that, I sort of accepted it. I mean, I couldn't remember anything anyway, nothing. And I used to get these really bad headaches, migraines, I suppose, which fitted in with the car crash story, and I had weird digestion, lots of stomach bugs and urine infections, nice stuff like that. But I didn't have any scars on me.

That wasn't the worst part, though. The worst was the men that sometimes came to the flat. It was mostly just this one man – Colin, his name was – and sometimes he brought another guy with him, I was never sure of his name. And – I can't really describe it – I'd look at them, or they'd catch my eye and I would just – break. I would go to pieces inside. I can't really describe it… it's as if the second I saw them, a gigantic rush of – of horror would swamp me. They never said much to me but occasionally, they'd laugh together. At me, I think it was. I can't describe how that made me feel. Just – it was so black, this wave, it was like drowning. I used to get really out of it, you know, with booze, if I knew they were coming round and I couldn't leave the house. God, it was –

"I just sort of carried on. I mean, I couldn't put my finger on why I felt so bad, so I kind of buried it and just went on, day to day. There were little, odd things though, that cropped up. I remember asking Tracey if I could have my birth certificate so I could get a passport – I think I had some sort of idea about going abroad, I wanted to escape for a bit, to run away – and she said she didn't have it. She said she'd lost it.

"Anyway, the day I turned sixteen – or the day Tracey told me I turned sixteen – she threw me out. She said it was time for me to take care of myself now, that she'd kept her end of the bargain and kept me until now but enough was enough and it was time for me to make my own way in the world. You can just see it, can't you? A sixteen year old kid with memory loss, out on the streets of London. Yeah, we were in London, some god-awful bit of South London, by the way. The really shitty part, with the pound shops and the bookies and the off-licence with the sign saying 'we can't sell alcohol before eight o'clock', that's eight o'clock in the *morning*, and the crappy, crappy boutiques with their synthetic, awful, fake-jewel-studded clothes in the smudgy window, and the obese, sweating black girls with their fifty screaming, corn-rowed kids in tow, and the scrawny, skaggy white girls with their horrible greasy hair and their toddlers sucking on a can of Red Bull, and the alcoholics trying to buy Special Brew at nine o'clock in the morning, and the mad people, who'd been thrown out of any kind of care home due to being complete arseholes and a complete lack of anyone, *anyone*, who had any kind of class, or dignity, or worth...

"For the first couple of years, I thought I was going to be okay. I had a little bit of money that Tracey had given me and she'd told me to go to this café up in the East End, where someone would give me a job. So I went there, and they did give me a job, and I was a waitress there for a year or so. I lived in this tiny, shitty little bedsit in Walthamstow, and went to work, and came back and slept and did my usual bury-my-head-in-the-sand type thing, so I wouldn't be able to think about anything. I kept getting the black waves, every so often, mostly after men talked to me in the café. I got through it by drinking a lot and smoking and not thinking about what it might mean.

"After a while, I started going out with this bloke, Michael. He used to come into the café – he was the foreman of a building site nearby – and after a while I moved in with him. It was about the same time I got sacked for being drunk at work. Michael said it didn't matter, he'd look after me, and for a while it was fine, I just sort of stayed at his place and we went out and had fun. He was really into his coke and, after a while, I got into it too; it made me feel even better than the booze. After a while, I wasn't getting the black waves anymore, not as long as I could do the white lines. Then Michael started getting a bit arsey with me, having a go at me for taking all his charlie and never paying my way. I said I didn't know what I could do and he said he could think of one thing I was good at…

"The only surprise was how long it took me to become a hooker. I didn't even mind it so much after a while – I liked the attention. I liked the fact that I was getting paid for doing what other girls were stupid enough to do for free. I couldn't understand why anyone – anyone – would want to fuck for fun. But that's what men wanted and so that's what they got, at the right price, anyway. After a while, I left Michael and set up on my own, in Soho. I shared with this other girl, Susie. She was okay. We used to work, and then we'd go out clubbing and pretend we were normal girls on a night out.

"Ironically enough, it was one of my regulars who saved me. He was an older guy, he must have been in his mid-fifties, and he saw that I was getting more and more strung out. He came round to see me but he didn't want sex with me, not that time. Instead, he just made me sit on the bed and tell him what was wrong. And I just broke down; I was such a snivelling, sobbing mess – you should have seen my face, snot pouring from my nose, no wonder he didn't want to fuck me – and he told me I needed to get off the drugs, that I needed to talk to a therapist and that he would make me an appointment with a drugs counsellor. And he did, and I went along and after that, it was okay. Not good, you understand, but better. And it got better, slowly, day by day. Susie came along with me for a while and things were going really well. But then she had a major relapse. I had to get away from her and so I moved down to Brighton. And I kind of pulled myself together, slowly. That's when things really started coming together.

"My therapist in London had recommended another therapist in Brighton. He specialised in repressed memories, recovering them, that sort of thing. That wasn't why I went to him, though – it was more that I needed a therapist and this was the only one I knew of that was any good. So we start the treatment and he does the repressed memory thing on me.

"All my memories were still there, from my childhood. Right up until the age of ten. Not wholly, not completely, but enough. You were there, although I couldn't remember your name. My parents. Our house in Hellesford. Myself as a young girl, an innocent young girl, before all these terrible things had happened to me.

I remembered what happened that night. The night, the night we were going to go to the stones. I remembered walking up the road by the farm, how big the countryside was all about me. It was so cold... I didn't go to the stones, I don't know why. I think I walked to Penzance. There was still a lot missing - I remember vaguely, very vaguely, waking up in an alleyway somewhere, hidden behind cardboard boxes. I went into a cafe somewhere – I remember the steamed up windows and they had plastic ketchup bottles on the tables that were shaped like tomatoes. A man sat opposite me and started talking to me – or did I go there with him? Then there's nothing, a complete blank, for the next few years.

"Well, you can imagine. It was like an earthquake in the middle of my life. But in spite of it, I was glad. Because I'd always known that there was something more to my story that the bits that I could remember. It was like a piece of a jigsaw puzzle falling into place.

"A journalist on one of the national papers did a article on all the famous kid disappearances. I think Ben Needham's name was mentioned, Madeleine McCann and a few others, and just a little tiny paragraph at the end mentioned me. Jessica McGaskill. I was reading it in a coffee shop, and when I got to that bit I – I fainted. Fell right to the floor, got cappuccino everywhere.

"And after that, I knew. I knew who I was, or who I had been. I did my own research and I compared more memories, and I was certain. I was scanning the papers every day, to see if I could find anything else – I almost wrote to the journalist who had written the first piece but I decided it probably wasn't a good idea – anyway, one morning, there was something in the paper about Angus and the school thing that he owns – sorry, owned – a college, right? And as soon as I read that, I remembered your name. And I knew I had to find you."

She stopped talking. We were the last people in the bar and the barman was stacking chairs around us. I unclenched my fingers from the edge of my chair.

Jessica was looking down at the table. She hadn't looked at me once during her recital.

"It's weird," she said. "Being able to remember something and then you hit a complete wall. Like it's a photograph in your mind and then you come to the blank part and it's like the photo fades out. And there's nothing left. Nothing you can see, anyway. But deep down, you do know what happened. You just can't retrieve the memory."

I stood up abruptly. I still couldn't speak. She opened her mouth to say something but I didn't wait to hear it. I ran for the toilets and crashed open the cubicle door.

I didn't vomit although for a few minutes I was sure I was going to. I hung over the porcelain bowl, gagging and gulping. My whole body ached. Eventually, I stood upright, moving like an old woman. I felt faint.

I heard the door to the bar open and Jessica's voice a moment later.

"Maudie, for God's sake. Speak to me!"

I caught sight of my face in the mirror over her shoulder: I looked deathly white.

"Christ," she said. "I'm sorry. I didn't think it would get to you so badly."

"Don't worry." My mouth felt numb – I couldn't form the words properly.

"You're as white as a ghost," she said. "I think you need another drink."

I managed to get back to the bar, walking by her side with her arm under mine. She ordered the drinks for the both of us; just as well, as the barman would never have served me. Jessica steered me back to the table and we drank our drinks, grimacing, as if they were medicine.

"I'm sorry," I said, managing to speak properly. "I don't know what happened there."

"You scared me."

"I scared myself."

I felt as if I'd just avoided a terminal accident, or I'd stepped away from a crumbling cliff top just in time. I drank the rest of my drink and felt the vodka move through me at quicksilver speed, numbing me, protecting me. That awful feeling of panic subsided and I sighed.

"Jessica – " I began.

"Don't," she said. "Don't say anything now."

"But – "

"That's all there is," she said. She sounded very sad. "That's all that needs to be said."

"But – "

Her chin came up again. Her eyes glittered.

"That's it. That's all there is. The whole truth. So now you know."

CHAPTER TWENTY SEVEN

A shadow bent over me. I made a low noise in my throat, something like 'ugh'. I felt the warm pressure of Matt's hand on my shoulder.

"I'm off, darling. Don't get up."

I managed to raise my head two inches from the pillow. "What?"

The hand squeezed my shoulder.

"I'm off, darling." One final pat. I collapsed back onto the pillows. "Go back to sleep. You look all in."

I didn't hear him leave. The next thing I was aware of was the phone ringing. I buried my head in the pillow, wanting to shut out the real world for just a little bit longer.

My eyes remained stubbornly shut but now my mind was racing. I gave up, sitting up in the tangled bedsheets, and reached for the bedside clock. Ten thirty-two. I collapsed back on the bed with a groan.

The phone by the bed rang again, shatteringly, sending me upright and clutching my chest. I reached out a shaking hand to the receiver, then drew it back. I lay back down and pushed my head under the pillow.

The phone rang again. I kept my head under the pillow, listening to the ringing of the phone, once, twice, three, four, five – the answerphone clicked on and I heard the hesitant sound of a voice.

"Maudie, are you there? Maudie?"

It wasn't her. I sat up, catching the next part of Becca's message.

"Maudie – "

I scrambled for the phone, and reached it just in time.

"I'm here –"

"Maudie?" There was a gasp in her voice, as if she'd been crying. My mental antennae went up, quivering. Becca never cried.

"Yes, it's me. What's wrong?"

There was a silence, and then another faint gasp.

"Can I come round?"

"Now?" I looked down at myself, at my stained nightshirt and unshaven legs.

"Please. I need to talk to you."

"Of course."

I said it automatically. Once I'd put the phone down, I rolled back onto my front, prone, face in the pillow. I lay there for five minutes, cursing under my breath. Then I got up, got in the shower, and attempted to smile.

Becca had been crying – it was obvious. The tip of her nose was red, the edges of her eyelids were inflamed, and her face had that puffy, tear-soaked look. I gave her a hug and let her sit down at the kitchen table.

"Tea? Or something stronger?"

"It had better be tea," she said, miserably.

I busied myself with the kettle and mugs. Cravenly, I wished I'd never picked up the phone. I didn't want any more revelations. I didn't want to hear anything bad, not now.

I plonked a mug down in front of her, and sat myself down with my own drink. Mentally, I braced myself.

Becca looked up at me from her red-rimmed eyes.

"I'm pregnant," she said.

I said nothing for a moment. I said nothing because I

felt precisely as if someone had swung a heavy, booted foot into my lower belly.

"Are you sure?"

"I did three tests. I thought the first must have been a mistake, but three – you wouldn't get a false positive from *three*, surely?" She started to cry again and I could feel myself struggling not to grimace. "I can't believe it, – I don't know what to do, Maudie - "

I held onto my hot coffee cup, drawing meagre comfort from the heat of the porcelain. I thought for one awful second I was going to be sick.

"Is it – " for a moment, the name of her recent boyfriend deserted me. "Is it Martin's?"

She nodded.

"Well, you can't have it," I said. The words came out of my mouth, abruptly, without me even thinking about them.

Becca's eyes widened.

"I haven't decided – " she began.

I talked over her. I could hear my voice getting louder with every word.

"You can't have it. I won't let you do this. You can't do this."

"Maudie – "

I stood up abruptly. My coffee cup fell out of my hands and smashed on the floor. A wave of coffee and porcelain shards splashed up against my legs.

Becca was getting up too, her eyes and mouth wide.

"Maudie, for God's sake – "

"You can't have it!" I bawled. "If you have it, it'll die, don't you know that? If you have a girl, she'll die, they always die, you might kill it, you'll kill it without even meaning to – "

She was coming round the table, her arms stretched wide, her face rigid with alarm.

"Maudie –"

"Leave me alone! Just get out!"

She flinched back but I only kept screaming.

She stepped back, raising her hands.

"Alright, alright, I'm going," she said. "I'm going to call Matt."

"No!"

"Alright, alright. Just – just calm down."

I turned and ran into the bedroom, slamming the door behind me. I was choking with tears; salt water was blinding me. I fell onto the bed and pulled the pillow over my head, screaming and hitting out at the mattress beneath me. I thrashed around until I could barely breathe, until I had to stop and just lie there in the semi-dark, crying bitterly.

I hadn't heard Becca leave but I could tell that she had because the flat had the empty feel to it. After a few minutes, the phone started ringing. I heard Matt's voice, his worried voice, come through on the answerphone, repeating the same question. *Maudie, are you there? Are you there?* But I wasn't there. I didn't know where I was but wherever I was, I intended to stay there for a long time. I kept still on the bed, my face buried in the sheets, not moving, not thinking, until I fell asleep.

CHAPTER TWENTY EIGHT

Jessica hadn't arrived yet. This time I kept my eyes open and I saw her come in through the doorway. I'd already bought her a drink. As she walked towards me, I thought she looked more *there* than she had before, her colours brighter, her outline more defined. I considered this for a moment and then shoved the thought away.

"Hey, Maudie," she said, sitting down. "Thanks for the drink. And for meeting me."

"No problem," I said, as if it hadn't been a matter for agonised decision. I had wondered how she was going to play it, our meeting after her horrible revelations of the last. I'd seen people confess something and then act as if the recipient of their confession had done something wrong. I'd done it myself. I remember the first time I told Margaret about what had happened to Jessica, and my part in it, and how I'd felt afterwards – angry at her, Margaret; ashamed, embarrassed. I wondered how I'd react when I next saw Becca. She'd phoned a couple of times but I couldn't face speaking to her.

Jessica didn't seem to be feeling that. Perhaps she'd told her awful story so many times, it had ceased to hurt so much. Perhaps she didn't feel ashamed – and really, why should she *be* ashamed? She'd come through the other side, she had got through it, she'd reinvented herself as a new person. I remembered that she had been through therapy, was, for all I knew, still in therapy. It made me feel another pull towards her — it was something else that we shared. Suddenly, I wanted to tell her about my own breakdown, to show her that there were bad things in my life too, that she wasn't alone.

"You said you'd been in therapy," I said, rather hesitatingly. Jessica nodded. I took a deep breath. "I have too."

"You have?"

"I'm still going - I mean, I have a therapist — Margaret — she's great. I go at least once or twice a month. It's mostly — no, it's all because of what happened. With you."

She looked sober.

"With me?"

Despite my good intentions, I was struggling. I didn't want to say what I was going to say. It brought back all the bad memories, the same feelings surfacing; guilt, shame, misery, despair.

"I felt so guilty. If I'd only gone with you — or I'd stopped you going — or told Angus what we were going to do — or anything — then it wouldn't have happened."

"You don't know that," said Jessica. "We both could have — "

"Could have what?"

"Well, that's just it," she said. "I don't know. I don't know what happened."

"But it wasn't good."

"No, it wasn't."

We both lapsed into silence. I wondered what she was thinking.

"Anyway," she said, after a moment. "You were telling me about your therapist."

"Margaret," I said. "Yes."

"Is that her name? Is she good?"

"Yes."

"And you go – because of what happened in Cornwall?"

I hesitated for a second.

"It's also because of what happened to me when I was twenty-six." I started with the simplest explanation. "I went through a bad time."

"A bad time?"

I stared down at the table.

"That's putting it mildly. I went - I had - I had an episode." It was still so hard to say the words. I tried again. "I mean, I was ill, became ill. Mentally ill, I mean."

"Oh," said Jessica. "That's not good."

I tried to smile.

"No, it wasn't."

"What happened? Did you - what happened?"

I drained my glass. "I need another one of these."

Jessica went and got us both a drink. While she was at the bar, I thought back to that time; the dark figures, the jumble of images in my head. The mess that was left over; the fragments of myself that had to be stitched back together again.

"I saw things," I said, when she was sat back down again. "I saw figures. They were people at first and then as I got worse they started changing. They were dark figures, like they were wearing black cloaks."

"That sounds awful," said Jessica. "Where did you see them?"

"Everywhere. In the street. In the doorway to my bedroom. I had a - I have a thing about doorways too, I can't bear them to be half open, they have to be open or shut, not halfway...." I trailed off. It sounded so stupid said aloud.

"Did you hear voices too?" she asked.

I grimaced. "Not really. Sort of. It was more sort of thoughts, bad thoughts." I was silent for a moment. "I mean, it's still to do with Cornwall and the stones and everything but – it sort of – coalesced. It all began to – weigh on me. "

"It sounds awful."

"It was. I – I was struggling – I kept seeing these figures and I thought - I had these irrational thoughts, horrible thoughts that everyone, well, hated me. Was after me."

I stopped, unable to continue for a moment. Jessica's eyes were wide.

"Everyone hated you?"

I heaved a sigh.

"Well, no they didn't. I mean, the figures weren't real, they were just things my brain was making up out of - of memories and shadows and things. Obviously. But – oh, it was so silly but so real to me then – I got badly paranoid, I thought people were keeping things from me and then I thought they were out to – to harm me. My mental state was – bad, it was really bad."

"No shit."

"At the worst time, the very worst, I thought – I thought they were going to kill me."

Jessica looked at me in silence. We drank quickly, filling the gaps in conversation with nervous gulps.

"What did your dad do?" said Jessica, eventually.

"Do?"

"Yes," she said. "Did he realise? I mean, were you living at home?"

"I wasn't to start with, when it started happening," I said. "I was working at this really boring office job. I got fired. I mean, I was getting worse by the day. I was – acting irrationally."

"So, what happened?"

"I did go home. After a while. I was getting too scared of London, all I could think about where these figures, these people, following me. I didn't know where to go, I didn't know where was safe."

"God, Maudie," said Jessica. "Even hearing that gives me the shivers. You must have been terrified."

"Angus didn't deal with it too well," I said, after a moment. "At least, I don't think he really realised how ill I was. Or that's what I thought until I found out about my mother."

"Your mother? With the crash?"

"Exactly."

She blew out her cheeks and sat back in her chair.

"Angus - Angus and Aunt Effie - they couldn't deal with it. I know why now, because of my mother and what happened to her. I guess -" I could my voice breaking, "- I guess they thought they were doing the right thing. Or maybe they didn't care, maybe they just couldn't deal with another round of doctors and hospitals and general scandal. I guess they thought everyone would say 'oh look, like mother like daughter, they're all mad in that family, what do you expect?' Angus was always one for appearances." I couldn't stop my face twisting at that. "It was always, like, paper over the cracks, hide what really happened, pretend everything is normal -"

I stopped talking. I could hear my heartbeat in my ears, feel it thudding through my forehead.

"Maudie?" said Jessica, after a moment.

I still couldn't speak. I had that feeling, yet again, of having my foot on the edge of a precipice. One false move and I'd be over and falling.

"Maudie?"

I picked up my nearly empty glass - what wine was left sloshed about in my shaky grasp. I drained it.

"I think they were in denial," I said. "They probably couldn't believe they'd have to go through it all again. They should have had me sectioned, they should have at least taken me to the hospital for assessment..."

I stopped talking, unable to go on. Jessica was turning her glass around and around; the glass chimed dully against the wood of the table. I sighed - it was almost all told. Just one more thing to confess to.

"I took an overdose."

I fought to keep my voice even. I could feel my face trying to smile and fought to keep it level.

"Shit, Maudie."

She sat back in her chair, putting a hand up to her face.

"So what happened? I mean, obviously you didn't – die."

We were both speaking jerkily, the words coming out in blurts.

"Angus found me on the bathroom floor. I guess they decided that was something they couldn't deal with themselves although God knows they probably considered it. I got carted off to A and E."

"Shit."

"I was in hospital, I mean a mental hospital, not the A and E, for ages. Six months maybe. I'm over it now. I'm completely better now." I clenched my teeth. "I'm fine now, but I still go to therapy. It does help. As I'm sure you know."

I sat back in my chair and stretched my shoulders up to my ears, easing the ache in my neck.

There was another silence between us. I had the sudden, horrible thought that perhaps she thought I was competing with her – a competition as to who had the hardest luck story, who deserved more pity. I opened my mouth to say something and shut it again. Instead I said I'd buy us both another drink.

When I came back, she took it from me without a word of thanks. I don't think she meant to be rude. She had the inward look on her face of someone whose mind was far from this room. She seemed to be mentally bracing herself.

"You were going to ask me something, weren't you?"

She hesitated.

"It doesn't matter," she said. "It can wait."

"No, go on. I'm sick of talking about myself, anyway."

She looked me in the eye.

"Alright," she said, eventually. I could see her take a deep breath. "Maudie, how are my parents?"

"You don't know?" I said slowly.

"No," she said. "I just haven't felt up to contacting them. It was just that step too far. I needed to see you first to – to kind of break the ice, if that doesn't sound too stupid."

"It doesn't," I said. My heart was thumping; I felt hot and cold with dread.

"I'm ready now though," she said, and I felt something shrivel up inside me. "I'm ready now."

"Jessica, I'm sorry but I don't know how to tell you this." She was looking at me, her face quite unprepared for what I was about to say. I took a quick, shaky breath, and said it.

"Jessica, I'm really sorry but your parents are dead."

I couldn't take my eyes off her face. She hadn't registered what I said, or so I thought.

She blinked a few time, her eyelids stuttering.

"What?"

I took hold of my legs under the table, to stop my hands from shaking.

"Jessica, I'm really, really sorry but your parents are dead."

Her face began a slow, inner crumpling.

"Dead?" she said, in a whisper. "How?"

"I'm afraid your dad had a heart attack." *Like Angus*, I added mentally. "I'm really sorry. It was very quick –"

"And my mum?" she said, cutting me off.

I closed my eyes briefly and took another deep breath.

"She – she committed suicide."

My voice had trailed away to a whisper. I tried to say something else, but my voice failed completely.

Quaking, I looked at Jessica. She had her eyes shut. She held herself like a cat does, quivering, before it leaps.

Then she moved. Her hand went flying out, into her full wine glass. The glass flew through the air and struck my breastbone, drenching me with wine. I gasped, more in shock than in pain. She rocketed to her feet, leaning over the table towards me.

"You *bitch*," she said, her voice vibrating so much I could barely make out the words. "You knew all this time and you never told me? You never told me my parents were dead?"

I stuttered out something meaningless, something useless. Jessica had both hands on the edge of the table, her hair hanging in a lank swathe on either side of her head, her eyes fixed upon mine.

"You were right, Maudie. You were right."

"What?" I said, gasping.

"You were right. You were right, you were right, you were right – " her voice was going up and up, humming upwards like a warning signal. I was shaking my head without knowing I was doing it. "You were right. You are guilty. You are guilty! It was your fault – "

"But – " I said, uselessly.

She thrust her face forward.

"My fucking parents are dead because of you. Because of you, I've been fucked over my entire life! And you sit there and tell me you have problems. You fucking *bitch*. It's your fault my parents are dead, your fault, your fault, your fault –"

I had a terrifying flashback to her mother in the kitchen of the cottage, eyes squeezed almost shut, flecks of spit landing on my face as she screamed at me. As then, I could only shake my head in terrified denial.

Suddenly she fell silent, silent except for her gasping breaths. Slowly, she backed away from the table, shaking her head.

"You'll pay for this," she said, her chest heaving. "I'll make you pay for this if it's the last thing I do."

She turned and ran from the room and I heard the door of the pub bang open and then closed. I sat there in my chair, clothes soaked with wine. I looked as if someone had shot me in the chest. I could only sit there, hands plastered across my useless, treacherous mouth, shaking.

CHAPTER TWENTY NINE

The telephone rang at nine thirty the next morning, as I was sat picking miserably at my breakfast. Matt got up to answer it and I held my breath.

"Hello?"

I knew it was her. Under the table, I clenched my fists.

"Hello? Who is this?"

Matt banged down the receiver and came back to the table. The phone rang again.

"Oh, leave it," I said, unable to bear it.

"I will," he said, reaching for his coffee. "It's getting rather tiresome. Some idiot obviously thinks it's funny."

The phone stopped ringing and the answerphone clicked on. There was nothing on the line, no speaking, just the click and burr of a broken connection.

"This is starting to become a bit more than annoying," said Matt. "Perhaps you could call the phone company?"

"What?"

"The phone company. Perhaps they can – oh, I don't know – put a block on the line? Trace the calls? I don't know what they do but – could you call them?"

I stared down at my empty coffee cup.

"Okay."

"Thanks, darling. It would help," said Matt. He upended

his coffee cup. "Ugh, lukewarm. Anyway, what are you up to today?"

"I'm seeing Margaret at eleven. Then – I don't know – maybe lunch somewhere. I'm not sure – "

My voice trailed off.

"Well, I've got a meeting with the high-ups at work," he said after a moment. "So we could be celebrating later."

I barely heard him.

"Sorry, what?" I said, looking up.

Frowning, Matt rested his hands on the back of one of the kitchen chairs.

"I said, we could be celebrating later. My promotion, I mean. If you want to. Oh, and if I get it." He laughed. "Mustn't count my chickens."

"That's great," I said, dredging up a smile. "Good luck. I'm sure you won't need it."

I watched him walk out the kitchen and waited until I heard the front door close. Then I slumped forward onto the kitchen table.

I had to brace myself before I left the flat. I pulled gloves on over my shaking hands and thought cravenly about taking a taxi. I took a deep breath and marched outside.

Jessica wasn't there. I let my breath out in a shuddering sigh. The relief almost made me nauseous. I walked quickly to Margaret's house, swinging my arms. I tried not to think of Jessica's last words to me but they kept repeating themselves in my head. I couldn't get that look of hatred – and it had been hatred – out of my mind's eye.

It wasn't a very good session with Margaret. I was nervous and distracted and kept running down into silence. I was worried she would smell the vodka on my breath which made me speak more haltingly than usual. I remembered to ask her for a prescription. As she was a psychiatrist, she was able to write them for me and had always done so, saving me a trip to the doctor's surgery.

"Just sleeping pills?" she said. "Or do you think you might need the anti-depressants again?"

I wavered. I probably did need them but it seemed like such an admission of failure.

"Just the sleeping pills," I said, managing to sound quite firm.

I closed the front door without thinking of anything much. I tucked my scarf more firmly into my coat.

Then I saw her. She was waiting for me on the other side of the street. She wore her black coat, of course; it swirled about her in the wind like an ink cloud. Her eyes were fixed on mine. I froze and shut my eyes.

I stood there, blind. The roar of cars passing echoed the thunder of my heartbeat. I opened my eyelids, quaking. Jessica was gone. Saliva rushed into my mouth and I turned aside for a moment, my hand going to my mouth, almost retching.

The worry of what other people would think still won out. I straightened up, putting my hand back in my pocket, trying to seem as if I didn't care. I put one foot in front of the other, the wavering line of the pavement unrolling before my eyes. I reached the kerb and managed to look one way before stepping out into the road.

A horn blared. My legs went from under me, even as they got me to the opposite pavement. I felt them buckle and then the pavement was rough and cold under my palms. I was knee-down in the street, hair falling forward, the pain in my knees nothing to the public humiliation.

"No, I'm fine, thanks – I'm fine –"

I struggled upwards, the kind hands of some passerby shaken off and left behind. I staggered onwards, my knees smarting.

A taxi light glowed ahead of me. I hailed it, and almost fell in through its doors. I didn't dare look round, for fear of seeing her. I shrank back into the back seat of the taxi, shivering. I held onto my elbows with the opposite hand, feeling the bone juddering underneath my palm.

When I got home I locked the front door, both locked, deadbolts - to keep out the dead.

I gasped all the way to the bedroom, to the vodka bottle in my underwear drawer. There wasn't as much left as I thought; there wasn't enough to work properly. My knees went again as I made my way to the bathroom. Vodka wasn't enough. I didn't really take pills, not when I didn't need to, but this was just intolerable... I crawled the last ten yards on my hands and knees, tear drops marking my way, my knees smudging them into the carpet as I finally got there, scrabbling at the bathroom cabinet, fumbling for the pill bottle that had been hidden away, unneeded for so long. Got it, take it, bitter taste in the throat, scramble for the glass, chiming against the tap, water falling coolly over my unsteady fingers. I got the pill down my throat and sat back against the bath, laughing weakly.

After twenty minutes, when the Valium began to percolate through my system, I breathed in and out, in and out, slowing my heart beat, getting myself back under control. *Come on, Maudie.* I dropped my head back against the side of the bath, closed my eyes, and breathed. I conjured up Margaret in my mind, her colourful jumpers, her comforting grey hair. What would she say to me now, if she were here?

Thinking of Margaret calmed me, somewhat. I knew she'd tell me that I wasn't to be afraid, that there was always a logical explanation. What was the explanation here? I was feeling almost normal again. Even propped up as uncomfortably as I was, I could feel myself falling towards unconsciousness. It was an effort to sit up, to shake off the drowsiness. I got up, carefully, holding on to the side of the bath, wobbled my way down the corridor and fell onto the bed.

I slept for a while, or passed out, or something. The ring of the telephone woke me. I scrabbled my way out of a tangle of bedclothes – the duvet had clamped itself stickily around me – and reached for the phone, on autopilot. I had the receiver to my ear before I remembered why I shouldn't.

There was the same crackle and hiss of static. My head was clearing of the sleep-fog – I'd almost got myself together enough to put the phone down. Then, sighing from the receiver came Jessica's voice, insinuating, mocking; *Maudie, Maudie…*

I gasped and slammed the phone down. I felt as if the trail of her whisper had seeped into the room; I could almost see it, a thin, dark wisp of smoke curling and writhing around the room. The phone rang again, bringing a thin little shriek of fright to my lips. I grabbed up the receiver.

"What do you want?"

Silence again. Then a little, soft laugh.

"What do you think?"

Her voice had changed. It was harder, colder, little chips of ice in my ear. For the first time I could hear South London in her voice, a guttural undercurrent.

I took a deep breath.

"Jessica, I'm so sorry. I never meant to hurt you – "

"You bitch, Maudie," she said, almost conversationally, cutting across me. "Don't give me that. How could you do that to me? Do you know how long I've waited for my parents?"

"I'm sorry," I said again, nearly crying.

"It's too late now for sorry."

"What do you mean?" I asked. I could feel myself shrinking, pulling back within myself.

There was a moment's silence. Then she spoke through what sounded like clenched teeth.

"I want you to *suffer*. I want you to suffer like I've suffered."

"But why?" I was almost incoherent, my voice shaking.

"You know why. You're guilty. It's your fault."

She sounded like a different person. Where was the girl I'd laughed with, hugged, sat and drank cocktails with? She sounded as if she were reciting something, a speech she'd learned not particularly well. Perhaps something she'd been telling herself for years.

"You don't mean that," I said eventually.

"Don't tell me what I mean and don't mean," she said. "You don't know me. You don't have any idea what it feels like."

"I don't, but - "

"You met me, again and again, and you never told me. I bet you were laughing at me all that time!"

"No." For a moment I couldn't say anything else.

Jessica pressed on.

"It's your fault, Maudie. Your fault this happened. You know it is. You know it is."

"Leave me alone." Even to my own ears, I sounded ten years old.

She laughed again, and I felt a clutch inside me, as if a giant, cold hand had grabbed my insides.

"I'll never leave you alone. You think I'm going to leave you, now that I've found you? Now that I've *got* you?"

The phone went down with a sharp crack.

What was wrong with me? Was there something about me – some poisonous, glowing halo – which other people could see, to which I was oblivious? What was it about me that marked me out for things such as this? I put my hands up to my eyes, screwing my face up. I tried to think of Matt, as something to calm me, but somehow that just made things worse. I crawled back to the bedroom and under the bedclothes. Perhaps it would be best if I never got up again. With that dark thought to sustain me, I lay there, hearing Jessica's parting words ricochet around my head, until all about me was a mass of jeering malevolence.

Matt came back later that evening. As I heard the scrape of his key in the lock of the front door, I wondered vaguely where he'd been. I'd managed to get out of bed and was sat on the sofa, wrapped around with the duvet.

The heating was on full blast but I was still cold. I'd drunk two bottles of wine and the empty bottles were still on the coffee table. I didn't care if he saw them. I was beyond caring.

Matt stood in the doorway, looking at me. I tried to smile but my face didn't seem to be working properly. He stood looking, for at least three minutes, until I began to feel like something under a microscope, not a bug, nothing so substantial.

"Are you ill?" he said eventually.

I turned my head to him in enquiry. I winced as I did it - my neck felt stiff.

"Yes," I said. It was easier than telling the truth.

"You must be," he said. "You forgot, didn't you?"

"Forgot what?" I said. My tongue felt too big for my mouth and it was hard to form the words.

He was hanging onto the door frame so hard his knuckles were white.

"Our celebration," he said. "I've been calling you and texting you. Why didn't you pick up? Have you even checked your phone?"

I blinked slowly.

"No," I said.

He breathed in through his nose. Slowly he let go of the doorframe and straightened up.

"It doesn't matter anyway," he said. "I didn't get the job."

"What?" I said. "You've got a job. What job?"

"The promotion, Maudie," he said, in a thin voice. "The permanent role. They didn't offer it to me. Cutbacks, they said. No more money for permanent lecturers. That's what they said."

I processed this.

"Oh dear," Part of me wanted to get up and go and give him a hug but I couldn't seem to make myself move.

"Is that all you've got to say?" said Matt.

Under the duvet, I dug my fingernails into my leg. I

needed the flash of pain to clarify things.

"I'm sorry, Matt," I said. "What a shame. But it's not like you need to work, really, do you? Why not give it up for a while? We don't need the money." I tried to laugh but my throat was too dry and it came out as a croak. "Be a man of leisure for a change."

He said nothing for a moment. Then he wheeled about and moved away from the doorway. A second later, I heard the study door slam.

I turned my face back into the sofa, hiding my face from the light. Behind my eyelids, I could see a half-open door, with darkness behind it.

CHAPTER THIRTY

The calls began again the next day. Luckily Matt was in the shower when the phone rang the first time. I picked up the receiver and dropped it back immediately. Three seconds later, it rang again and I did the same thing. Quickly I bent down and yanked out the plug. There. Silenced. I quickly walked to the bedroom and did the same thing to the phone kept there.

For a moment, I felt safe. The doors were bolted and she couldn't get me through the phone. I sat on the edge of the bed, twisting my hands together. At some point, I'd have to leave the flat. Would she be there? Would she follow me?

Matt came into the room while I was still sat on the bed. He was naked except for a towel around his waist. He plucked a shirt from the wardrobe and threw it on the bed next to me. It was as if I wasn't there. For a moment, I thought of asking him if he was angry with me and then dismissed it almost instantly.

Matt reached for the telephone by the side of the bed. I watched in horror as he brought the receiver to his ear and frowned. He pressed the button on the cradle a few times and tutted.

I had to speak up.

"I pulled out the plug," I said, in a faint voice.

He looked at me as if he'd just remembered I was in the room.

"You pulled out the plug? Why, for God's sake?"

"It was – the calls that kept coming – " I trailed away limply as I saw him shake his head.

"For God's sake, Maudie," he said. "What's wrong with you?"

I said nothing. He pushed the plug back into the wall socket with a jerk of his wrist and looked back over his shoulder.

"I am really, seriously worried about you," he said. "I'm even wondering whether I should call your therapist."

"No!" My voice came out louder than I'd intended. I swallowed. "There's really no need. I feel fine. Just a bit fluey."

"But why did you pull the phones out?" he said. He had that helpless look on his face again, the look of someone swimming in unknown and dangerous waters.

"I just wanted a bit of peace," I said. "I was getting fed up of those calls. That's all."

"You didn't call the phone company?" he said.

I swallowed.

"I did, actually," I said, after a moment. "But they couldn't do anything."

I climbed back under the bed covers. Matt stood above me for a moment, hesitating.

"I have to go to work," he said. "I need to sort out a few things."

"That's fine," I said. "Don't worry about me."

I saw his jaw clench.

"Do you even remember what we talked about last night?" he said.

I rolled over, pulling the duvet up around my ears.

"Yes," I said in a mumble.

I could feel him still hovering above me. I heard him

take a deep breath.

"Alright," he said eventually. "I'm going to leave you alone now. I want you to call me if - if you start to feel worse. In any way."

I had the feeling he wanted to say something else but he didn't. After a moment, he left the room.

As soon as I heard the front door slam, I threw back the covers and scuttled into the hallway. I locked it behind him, bolts and deadlocks shot home. Then I ran to unplug the phones.

I hadn't showered, eaten breakfast, or even cleaned my teeth. In fact, I couldn't quite remember the last time I had eaten something but it didn't seem to matter too much at the moment. I wasn't hungry. I went back to the sofa and lay there.

The beep of a text message arriving at my mobile alerted me. I opened the little envelope icon, wary. But it was just a missed call from Mr Fenwick's office. No doubt he'd been trying to get through on the landline. I took a deep breath and rang the number back.

"Maudie," said Mr Fenwick, when I finally got through to him. "How are you, my dear? I've been trying to get hold of you. I've just called Matthew and he said you were at home, ill. Did you know you had a problem with your telephone line?"

"Oh, I'm fine," I said, lying through my teeth. "There's nothing wrong with me. Thanks for telling me about the phone line, though."

"Now, nothing for you to worry about but I need your signatures on a couple of documents. Nothing too exciting, just a few bits of paperwork for the estate. Is there any chance you could pop along sometime today to sign them? Do you feel up to it?"

I showered and dressed, yanking my clothes on clumsily, my fingers stiff. I was getting angrier and angrier, with which person precisely, I wasn't quite sure. It was fury at a host of people; at Jessica, naturally. It was with Matt, for not understanding, for smothering me with his concern, for making me so ashamed of my drinking that I had to hide it from him. It was with Becca, for being pregnant and making me feel things I didn't want to feel. It was with Angus, for everything.

In the kitchen, I looked at the knife block. My hand went out and selected one, small enough to fit in my coat pocket. Just in case.

I banged the front door behind me and went downstairs in the lift, humming a quiet, bitter tune through clenched teeth. As I reached the outside air, I almost wanted her to be there. I was just about ready for a proper, stand up fight.

She wasn't there. I felt the hot tide that had bourn me out of the door and down the storeys ebb and evaporate. Chastened, I hailed a taxi. I didn't even bother looking about me as we joined the flow of traffic that pushed and jostled its way towards the city.

"Good God, Maudie," said Mr Fenwick as I entered his office. I was startled; he looked genuinely shocked. "Are you sure you're feeling alright?"

"I'm fine," I muttered, taken aback. I caught sight of myself in the mirror hanging on the back wall of his office and nearly jumped myself. I was chalky as a ghost, the rings under my eyes deep and plum coloured. My scar stood out like a brand.

We dealt with the paperwork quickly – there was very little to do. I could hear Mr Fenwick begin to make tentative, preparatory enquiries into my state of health and headed them off by pretending not to hear. As decently as I could, I said goodbye and ran from the office.

She was waiting by the steps of the building, ten feet from where I'd emerged. Our eyes locked. She looked as pale as I had just seen myself to be. For a moment, I stood frozen, unable to move. Then I thought I'm damn – I'm *fucking* well not going to see you. I marched down the steps, not looking at her, not looking away from her. My neck felt stiff from the effort of not turning my head away.

When I drew level with her I thought she was going to reach out and grab me, but she didn't. I turned my back to her and walked away.

I became aware I was holding my breath and let it out in a giant huff of air. I looked around for a taxi but there were no friendly yellow lights in sight on the roofs of approaching cabs. I could hear the ring of her high heels behind me, like steel pins going into the concrete. I turned blindly, down some side street. Almost at once, I realised this was a mistake. It was quieter on this road and I could hear her clearly behind me; her breathing, the flap and swish of her bloody black coat, the *thud-thud-thud* of her boot heels. Tears began to leak from my eyes.

Suddenly, she spoke.

"Where are you running to?"

I didn't answer. I tried to walk faster.

"Always running away, aren't you?" she said. She sounded amused. "Never face up to anything in your life, do you?"

I stopped dead. I swung round. I pulled the knife from my pocket.

She didn't notice it for a moment, not until I lifted it high. Her face went even whiter than it was already. She opened her mouth to say something, closed it, turned away.

"Yes," I said. "Now who's running? Now who's running?"

Her blonde hair bounced as she scurried away. I started laughing; she looked so silly, running away like a scared little rabbit. She was scared of me. I started to run after her, waving the knife like a talisman.

"Not so brave now, are you? Not so brave now! Come back, Jessica! You came back once before.. come back again. Come back! Come back! Come back!"

I stumbled over something as I took another step forward. Suddenly the pavement became six inches lower. I fell forward onto my knees, skinning my hands on the concrete. The knife fell onto the ground in a musical tinkle; it span around in a circle, skidding around, and the noise it made was drowned out in a horrible screech, a crescendo of noise that rose and grew and flowed over me like a wave. It must be Jessica screaming, I thought, before something slammed into me hard enough to knock the breath from my body. As I fell sideways I saw the knife on the dirty concrete road, glinting in the winter sun, a yellow star of light twinkling on the blade. The star grew until it filled my eyes, a sunburst of yellow light that blotted out the rest of the world.

*

When I next opened my eyes, white cotton had replaced the glinting knife. I blinked a couple of times. One minute I had been face down on dirty concrete and the next I was... where? I moved my head and a gigantic bolt of pain shot through it.

I may have slept for a little while. When I opened my eyes again, cautiously, I was conscious of time having passed. I managed to move my head a little. I was lying in bed. A hospital bed. For a moment I wondered whether I was dreaming but I could smell that hospital smell; the usual, nauseating mixture of antiseptic floor wash, canteen food and something underneath it all, something rank. Matt was sitting by the side of the bed, looking at me. His eyes were red.

"Door," I said.

He leant forward. "What's that, darling?"

"I said 'hi'" I said. My voice was croaky. "What happened?"

"You got hit by a car, darling," he said, speaking gently. "They think you have concussion."

I shut my eyes, trying to process this. I could hear a gentle creak but I couldn't work out if it was in my head or in the room. I felt as if the entire surface of my skin was covered in bruises and here and there were sharper areas of pain; on my knees, my right elbow, the palms of my hands. I managed to free my arms from beneath the clamp of the hospital blankets and looked at my hands - they were skinned raw.

"Your poor hands," said Matt. "You must have fallen in front of a car. Don't you remember?"

"Sort of," I said, vaguely. "I think I was - " I stopped, remembering Jessica's white face. "I must have fallen over."

Matt looked doubtful. "You gave the driver a hell of a fright. They thought they'd killed you."

"Killed me," I repeated. "No, they didn't. They didn't kill *me*. I wasn't killed."

He looked at me strangely.

He took my hand, carefully. "You poor thing. Listen, I'm going to leave you to get some more rest now but the doctors say you can probably come home tomorrow. You're very lucky, you know, Maudie. I can't believe you got off as lightly as you did."

He kissed me on the forehead and I tried not to wince.

"Oh, sorry," he said.

"The door's open," I said.

"What?" Matt looked at me sharply. "What was that?"

"I don't know," I said. I was mumbling, falling backwards into sleep. "Doesn't matter."

I closed my eyes again, shutting out the light.

When we got home, Matt wanted to carry me to the bed.

"I can walk," I said.

"Maudie, you're as white as a sheet," he said. "Just shut up and hold on for a moment, there's a good girl."

I put my arms around his neck. I felt dreadful, limp as a wet piece of paper. My head throbbed.

"It's like we've just been married," I said, as he struggled over the threshold.

"Yes," he panted, lowering me to the bed. I couldn't sustain my smile any longer as my head touched the pillow. I felt so weak and awful, I began to cry.

"There, there," he said, pulling the duvet up around me. "Just rest. That's what you need."

"I know," I said, voice thick with tears. "I can't sleep while the door's open."

Matt gave me a strange look but he didn't say anything. He tucked the duvet under my chin and patted my shoulder.

"Just rest," he said. "I've got to pop out now to get some stuff; we've got no food in the house. I'll leave you to sleep. I'll be back later."

I heard the front door shut. Immediately, I pushed back the covers. Despite the pain in my head, I couldn't lie still any longer; I buzzed with adrenaline. I was terribly, horribly afraid.

I made my way to the door, hanging onto pieces of furniture to stop myself from falling. In the hallway, I gave up and went down onto my knees, crawling along the carpet. I reached the living room. I don't know where I was going, what I was trying to do; all I could do was try to get away, to crawl away from the fear. In my head, a door was opening and yellow light began to creep out, at first a narrow ribbon, a chink, widening to a strip that grew and grew and flooded my head with light. I could hear myself crying out. *Stop it, stop it*, crying out to an uncaring world, *stop it, stop it...* but it wouldn't be stopped, it was too late. It was too late now, because the door was open.

It's the door in the cottage in Cornwall. But it's not the front door with the abyss behind it, is it? It never has been. I creep along the hallway, I open that door and look out at the night beyond; the rolling black sky, the rustling, creeping countryside. And I close that door. It's the door to the living room that stands half open, faint yellow light spilling into the hallway through the gap. I see the light as I creep back along the hallway. I hear the voices coming from the room; the voices of Angus and Jessica.

Why don't I open it fully? Am I scared I will get into trouble for being up so late? Is it the tone of Angus's voice that scares me; the unctuous, pleading tone I'd never heard him use before? Is it the way Jessica's voice goes hard and angry, the beginning of a shout, a scream - and then nothing, a choking noise, gasps? I push the door just a little, just enough to see into the room. Enough to see Jessica and Angus. Enough to see his large hand over her face, his large hand on her small neck. Her puff of cornsilk hair shaking back and forth. The monster from the stones is here in this room, all bulging eyes and bared teeth. I watch from the doorway, watch as the black cloud flows over her. Her bare legs buckle. I can see the dirty soles of her feet as Angus lowers her to the floor.

I don't scream. I make no sound. I have to get away before I too am swallowed up, eaten by the monster with a taste for small blond girls. I am aware that my trousers are wet, wet with a warmth that rapidly cools. I am climbing the stairs, not daring to look behind me. I can hear sobs coming from the living room, a terrible, harsh tearing noise that goes on and on. I have never heard my father cry before. I am in my bedroom again, but I am not safe - while that door is open, I will never be safe. I hide my wet trousers and pants in a pile of dirty washing in the corner of my room and put my nightdress back on again. I can hear the monster moving about downstairs now, still sobbing. I pull the covers up over my head. The door is open but I can close it. If I close it, I will be safe. For a moment, it resists but I push it with all my might, inside my head. The strip of yellow light shrinks, narrows. One last effort and the light is gone. The abyss has closed. Blackness surrounds me and I surrender to it gratefully. I am safe now. I sleep.

CHAPTER THIRTY TWO

I sat there on the floor, my legs stretched out in front of me, floppy as a rag doll. The light gradually faded from the sky and the room became darker; the air inside gradually thickening until I couldn't see my hands lying limp in my lap. I wasn't aware of much, really; just the gradual darkening of the room, the draining of the light, the quiet rasp of my breathing.

I became aware of a figure standing in the doorway.

"What's going on?" said Matt.

The sound of his voice roused me. I managed to move my head up, wincing. For a moment, I thought I wouldn't be able to speak, that my voice would have been lost completely.

"Why are you sitting here in the dark?"

I dropped my eyes to the floor again.

"I don't know," I said. I cleared my throat. "I think it's because I've gone mad. Again."

Matt didn't say anything. I listened to the swoop and hiss and thud of my blood, pulsing inside me. My temples felt as if they were shut in a vice that was slowly closing.

"Mad," I said, once more.

I was aware of Matt moving towards me. Dimly, I felt his hands under my armpits, pulling me up gently.

"Up you come, Maudie – "

I was on the sofa. There was a rustling at the side of the room and then a warm bloom of light. I recoiled, blinking. Matt had drawn the curtains more firmly and switched on one of the table lamps. He stood in front of me, looking down on me with a slight frown, looking very tall and dark in his tweed jacket.

"What's going on?" he said.

I managed to look up at him. Strangely, I felt like laughing. There was no Jessica. There never had been. I should have known, I thought, I should have known. All the signs were there.

"I've gone mad," I said, once more.

Matt sat down next to me, quite lightly, as if he were about to spring off the sofa at any moment. *I scare him*, I thought. He put his hands out to my shoulders and then drew them back.

"Maudie, darling," he said. "Tell me what's been going on."

I felt a warm, breaking wave of relief. I was going to tell him, finally, at last – I was going to tell him everything I should have told him from the beginning; Jessica, what had really happened in Cornwall, my hopes and doubts and fears, everything. I'd kept the door shut for so long; I'd kept that memory locked away, my ten-year-old mind trying to protect me from the awful truth. But I'd always known, hadn't I? Because the door was in my head and I carried it around with me. The constant fear I'd felt in the presence of my father, the nervous breakdown, the drinking... all a direct consequence of the door in my mind, and what lay behind it.

Matt was watching my face, very carefully. I raised my eyes to his.

"Angus killed Jessica," I said.

He said nothing. He blinked once, twice.

"What?" he said.

"You heard me," I said. "Angus killed Jessica. My father

killed her. In Cornwall, when we were both ten."

He was silent for a long moment.

"What do you mean?" he said eventually.

"I mean what I just said. Angus killed Jessica."

"But - " he licked his lips and tried again. "What do you mean, he killed her? He really killed her? How do you know?"

"I saw him."

"You saw him?" He put his hands out to my shoulders again and drew them back, again. "How could you have seen him?"

"When I went downstairs to meet Jessica. She was already there in the cottage. I saw him do it but I – I made myself forget it, I repressed it – "

"You forgot it?" He looked sceptical. "How could you just forget something like that?"

"I don't know," I said. "I don't know how I did it, but I did. It was like I had a room in my head and the memory went there, and I shut the door on it."

Matt had been facing me but he slowly turned away. He was staring at the floor but then he looked back sharply.

"Are you sure?" he demanded. "Are you sure you're not just – "

"What?"

"Well-"

"I'm not making it up, if that's what you mean," I said. I didn't speak sharply. I couldn't summon up any kind of emotion.

He looked in my face again and he must have seen something to convince him. His face contracted a little.

"Why?" he said.

I closed my eyes.

"I don't know," I said. "I couldn't hear what they were saying before it – before it happened. Perhaps Jessica was – oh, I don't know – threatening him over his affair with her mother. Oh yes – " as Matt looked up sharply, "- he was having an affair with her mother. Perhaps he just went mad for a moment." I gave a small laugh which was half a sob. "It runs in the family, don't you know? Both sides, it seems."

Matt black eyebrows were drawn together in a frown.

"Or perhaps there was another reason," I said, softly. I said it almost to myself. "Perhaps he was – he – "

I had to stop. Did my fear of the open door go deeper than I remembered? I had a vision of myself as a small child, lying in bed, waiting wide-eyed with fear for the opening of the bedroom door. A vision or a memory? That was something I couldn't face, an abyss too deep to ever climb out of. That was one door I would never open. I swallowed and thrust the thought away.

Matt hadn't noticed my recent silence. He looked as though he was thinking ferociously hard. His gaze hadn't moved from the floor.

"I'll tell you about what's been happening," I said, when I was able to speak again. "I should have told you a lot earlier."

He looked up at that.

"Tell me what, Maudie?" he said.

"I need to tell you about Jessica," I said. "Or someone I thought was Jessica. But it can't be, because I know that Jessica is dead. I thought she came back, you see. Perhaps she did. Perhaps she is real, or as real as a ghost can be."

He was staring at me again.

"Maudie – " he said.

I went on, talking over him.

"But she's not real," I said. "She's a figment of my imagination. I should have guessed it from the first – the black coat she wore, the way she just appeared from nowhere. I'd been through it all before. She isn't Jessica, because Jessica is dead. She's a hallucination. She's a symptom of my mental illness."

It took a long time. I had to keep going back over my story, filling in the little details, wondering what to include.

He didn't say much, just nodded, or asked me to repeat a few things. He didn't touch me; he reached out a couple of times but his hands never quite connected with mine. But he scarcely took his eyes from my face. He had never paid such... such *ferocious* attention to me, not even at the start of our relationship.

Eventually, I stopped speaking. I felt limp, wrung out; leached of colour. I was spent. That summed it up for me; spent. I had nothing left in me.

After I finished speaking, we sat in silence. Matt had turned his face away again and was staring into space. Then he got up. He moved like a man many years older than himself.

"I'm sorry," he said, "And I know this is normally something you'd say - but I need a drink."

I didn't watch him moving about the kitchen. I let my eyes go soft and unfocused, and stared into the middle distance. I listened to my heartbeat and my breathing. I'm still alive, I thought. Despite everything. I'm still here.

He came back and stood looking over me again, a brandy glass in his hand.

"Have you told anyone else about this?" he said.

I shook my head.

"Seriously Maudie – you're really sure? You haven't told Margaret? Or Becca?"

"No."

Matt leant forward and put his free hand under my chin, tipping my face up towards him. His eyes searched my face.

"Are you *certain*?" he said.

I shook my head, dislodging his fingers.

"Yes."

He left me again and walked into the bedroom, shutting the door behind him. I didn't blame him. I was just grateful he was still here. I leaned my aching head against the back of the sofa and closed my eyes.

After a while, I was again aware of Matt's presence. I

opened my eyes to find him holding out a bottle of my pills, and in the other hand, a brimming glass of brandy.

"Here darling," he said, "drink this."

I realised he still had his gloves on from when he'd come in from outside. He must have been shocked to forget to take them off – Matt never did silly things like that. I took both things from him. It was odd, but for the first time in years, I didn't feel like drinking. I felt oddly calm, peaceful even. Whatever had festered inside me for so long had been lanced, the poison drained away. Despite my aching head, and my injuries, I felt cleansed.

"Go on," said Matt, "Drink it up."

I took a sip.

"Ugh," I said, almost gagging. "It tastes foul."

Matt sat down next to me again, rather gingerly.

"Well, it's supposed to. Spirits aren't supposed to taste nice."

I took another sip and grimaced.

"I'll have it later," I said, and put the glass down on the floor.

Matt looked annoyed.

"You've had a shock," he said. "Drink it."

"I don't want it."

"You don't want a drink? *You* don't? That must be a first."

I felt a sob start to come up through my chest.

"I'm sorry, Matt, but I just don't want it."

"Well, at least take your pills then."

I stared down at the little brown bottle in my hands.

"These are sleeping pills."

"I know," said Matt. "I think you need a rest."

I fumbled with the cap of the bottle. My hands felt weak as water. Eventually I managed to open it and took out one of the little white capsules.

"You'll need more than that," said Matt.

I stared at him.

"What do you mean?"

He smiled, a gentle, sorrowing smile. I couldn't see his eyes behind the opaque lenses of his glasses. I thought for a second of reaching out and removing them from his face. My hand reached out to do so, but I stopped it.

"I'm sorry, Matt," I said.

He shook his head, still with the same smile on his face.

"Don't you think this has gone on long enough, Maudie?"

"What do you mean? I'm sorry I didn't tell you before – "

He shook his head. Then he must have read my mind. He reached up and took off his glasses, folding them and putting them down on the side table.

"I can't do this anymore," he said.

"What do you mean?" I whispered. I felt a coldness creeping through me. "What do you mean you can't do this anymore?"

He looked away from me. He had his hands folded on his lap, as if he were in church, his head tilted to one side, as if listening to a far-off sermon.

"It's the end of the road, Maudie," he said. "I've had enough."

"Oh – " I said, but that was all I could say without my voice breaking.

He looked back at me then.

"I can't take it any longer."

Unmasked by glass, his eyes were beautiful. I couldn't look away from them.

"I don't understand," I whispered.

He leant forward and put a gloved finger to my cheek. I felt the cold leather pass over my lips and move up to my hairline, tracing the ridge of my scar.

"Take them all," said Matt, very softly.

I stared at him. I put my hand up to touch my mouth, to touch the place his finger had traced.

"What?"

He smiled at me.

"Take them all, Maudie. Stop fighting it. Can't you see this is a sign?"

I drew back. Again, I had the weird feeling, as if I were dreaming awake. I put a hand out to touch him but he drew back.

"What?" I said, again.

There was a creak of floorboards that made me look over at the door. There was no light in the hallway. From the darkness, into the dim light of the living room, came a tall, thin figure. She coalesced out of the inky air, as if her components parts were drawing themselves together. Her black coat moved around her like mist. I shrank back in my seat with a terrified moan. Not here, not in my house, my one refuge... I could feel myself gasping in air, anything to get my frozen body to start working again.

"No," I said. "You don't exist. You're not really here."

Jessica moved forward slowly, one step into the room, another step. Her face was pale. I could hear my high, terrified breathing. It was the only sound in the room.

"I don't believe in you," I said. "You don't exist."

Matt looked at me. Then he turned his head to look in the direction I was staring.

"What are you doing here?" he said.

There was a moment's silence. I turned my head towards him, creakily, moving like an old woman. I couldn't think of how to answer him.

He said it again.

"What are you doing here? I told you never to come here."

"I – " I said, with no knowledge of what I was going to say. Then I realised he wasn't talking to me.

Jessica moved another step forward. Her face was chalky-pale, her eyes black-shadowed. She wasn't looking at me either. She was looking at Matt.

"I know," she said.

It was like watching a play in a foreign language. Like

listening to music underwater. I could feel myself screwing up my face and shaking my head, as if to clear my ears.

"I told you never to come here," Matt said, again. Jessica stopped moving towards him. She hadn't looked at me once.

I took in a gasp of air.

"What's going on? Matt – Matt – can you see her?"

He ignored me. He wasn't looking at me either. I had a sudden, terrifying thought; Jessica and I had swapped places, perhaps even bodies – she was the one everyone could see and hear and speak to, while I had become the ghost. I grabbed at my own arms, pinching the gooseflesh.

"Matt, Matt, can you see me? Can you hear me? Tell me I'm the one you see, I am, I'm the one you see – don't tell me it's her, tell me you can't see her – "

He got up from the sofa and looked at me. At last he looked at me. Something strange was happening to his face. It was lightening, gradually, undergoing a subtle transformation. He looked like himself, but different, somehow; as if he were gradually shedding a mask, or gaining one, revealing a face that looked almost the same.

"Would you for once just *shut up*?" he said. "Every time I think you can't say something stupider than before, you continue to surprise me."

The shock was beginning to hit me now. I didn't understand, not everything, but my body knew. I could feel prickles of sweat breaking out all over my face, as if I was about to be sick.

Matt turned to face Jessica, the woman who said she was Jessica.

"What the fuck do you think you're doing? I told you never to come here."

"It doesn't matter *now*, does it?" said Jessica. She walked a little further into the room. She pulled off her gloves as she did so. Finally, she swung her gaze towards my face, looking at me with a frown.

"Put those back on for a start," said Matt. "You had no

right to come here. I told you I'd handle it."

Jessica – I had to call her that, what else could I call her? – stood in the middle of the room. She hadn't taken her eyes from my face; she hadn't looked at Matt once since he spoke. She kept frowning.

"I was worried," she said.

"Worried?" said Matt. "I told you I'd contact you afterwards. Get out of here, you'll fuck the whole thing up."

Jessica didn't reply. She brought her arms up across her body as if she were cold. I felt the same. I was shivering so hard my body was making the sofa vibrate.

She looked at me, properly at me. Our eyes met. Her hand went up to her throat and I saw she was wearing the necklace I'd bought her.

I tried to speak but nothing came out. I cleared my throat and started again.

"What thing?" I said in a thin voice.

Matt sighed sharply through his nose, his characteristic expression of annoyance. He was looking at me with such contempt that I flinched every time I met his eyes. The face belonged to a person I didn't recognise at all.

"What – what's going on?"

I could feel my voice wobbling as if someone had me by the shoulders and was shaking hard. Jessica took a step to the side, moving out of Matt's shadow which fell across her like a black cloak. I could see her more clearly now. She was still holding onto the necklace.

"Stop trying to work it out, Maudie," said Matt. Every time he said my name, his face contracted as if he were tasting something bad. "Your mind's so fucked you don't know what's real and what's not, you never have. Stop trying to make sense of it because you're incapable of making sense of anything."

"What?" I said.

"What? What? Is that all you can say?" said Matt. His whole face was twisted. The light was behind him but I could see the hate beaming out of him despite the shadow. Momentarily I was reminded of something; the dark figures that had stalked me through the bad time; that was the last time I'd been the target of such concentrated malice.

"You are so pathetic," he said. "Do you even realise how pathetic you are? You do nothing, you know nothing, you're so vapid I'm surprised you don't disappear altogether. And you know what? I think you know how useless you are. I think you realise what a shallow, self-obsessed, neurotic, whining parasite you actually are. Why else do you drink so much?"

He paused for breath. I heard myself say something in a tiny, child's voice that even I could barely hear.

"You thought I loved you?" he said. He started to laugh and then stopped abruptly. "Of course not, don't be ridiculous. You're not capable of being loved."

I think we'd both forgotten Jessica. She took another step forward, further into the light. She was looking at Matt with an odd expression on her face.

"You know what I think?" he said. "I mean, what I really think – I'm not just saying this to hurt you, although Christ knows you deserve it. I think you killed Jessica. I don't know why and I don't know why you can't remember it but that's what I think. That's what you've not been facing for the rest of your life."

"That's not true!" I said, horrified. "That's a lie."

"Is it?" said Matt, sneering. "Well, you'd know all about that. You're the liar, Maudie. You lie all the time, you lie and lie and lie. Do you even know you're doing it? How can anyone trust anything that comes out of your mouth? You're not even that good at it, did you realise? Do you really think I had no idea about your drinking? You're so thick you judge everyone by your own pathetic standards. It's a fucking *insult*. All this guff you've made up about your father, Christ, a child could see through it. I don't know why you bothered." He laughed at my expression.

"It's been like living with a child, a particularly moronic child. I've earned that fucking money, that's for sure. I've fucking earned it ten times over."

Something was rising up inside me. I gripped my legs, trying to control the shaking of my hands. The second he'd uttered the word 'money' I knew the truth – it was heading up within me, grabbing me in the throat, sending my blood thundering. My skin prickled with the knowledge. I looked at Jessica and said her name. She didn't answer. I said it again.

"Jessica."

Slowly, her eyes went from Matt's face to mine.

"What's your real name?" I said. "Because you're not Jessica, are you?"

Her face twitched.

"I can't tell you that," she said.

"Why not?"

"I just can't."

I hadn't taken my eyes from her face.

"Why did you come here?" I whispered.

She looked at me, her hand still up to her throat. I thought for a second she wasn't going to answer.

"I was worried," she said, again.

"You were worried?" said Matt, and the sound of his voice made us both start. "You? You, with your well-tuned moral sense? What a fine upstanding person you are! You must be really proud of yourself!"

She looked at him. I saw comprehension dawning slowly on her face; she looked dazzled, as if she'd just woken from a not particularly pleasant dream. She looked at him the way I was looking at him; as a person never seen before. She didn't bother to reply.

"Tell me," I said, to her alone.

"Don't tell her," said Matt.

She looked at him with what looked like irritation.

"It hardly matters now," she said. "Does it?"

"Just shut up, would you?" said Matt. He was sweating; I

could see his top lip shining even in the dim light.

I looked back at Jessica.

"What's your real name?" I said. "What are you really called?"

She just shook her head.

"I'm not mad," I said, trying out the sound of the words. Then I said it to Matt. "I'm not mad. You tried to make me think I was."

"No I didn't," said Matt, "You know you are. You're not normal. You just don't want to admit it." He bent down and picked up the brandy glass and held it out to me. "Go on, drink this down. You'll feel much better about things afterward. You know you always do, when you drink."

It would be the easiest thing in the world to capitulate. To give in. To keep the peace. My hand moved forward and then something stopped it; I could feel something snapping shut, like a trap within me.

I looked him in the eye.

"I don't think I will."

My blood was up and humming. I was darting little glances at the open door to the hallway. What was the chance that I'd be able to get past him and out the door? I thought for a moment of shouting for help but it was an old building; the walls were thick, the ceilings high. No one would hear me.

I thought faster than I'd ever had in my life. I was in danger here. I looked at my husband. He looked like Matt, he sounded exactly like Matt but he'd been body snatched. He'd been possessed by someone I didn't know at all.

"Why – " my voice cracked for a second. I tried again. "Why did you do this?"

Matt rolled his eyes.

"Was it just for the money?" I said. I had that horrible, sweaty feeling you get when you're about to vomit. I swallowed hard. "Was that all it was about? How could you – how could you be so cruel?"

He didn't answer.

"You were trying to drive me mad," I said. The full meaning of the words hit me for a second and I almost gagged. "Were you going to have me locked away? Was that the plan? You wanted the money for yourself, all of it? You couldn't bear to share it with me?"

"Oh Maudie," he said. He was trying for a bored, incredulous tone, I could tell, but he couldn't quite pin it down. "What are you saying? You're totally insane."

"But that wasn't it, was it Matt?" I said. I could hardly speak, my mouth was so dry. "That wasn't what you had planned at all, was it?" I thought back to the sleeping pills he'd reminded me to get. I thought of how bitter the brandy he'd brought me had tasted.

"Were you trying to get me sectioned? Or was it more than that, were you trying to make me kill myself? Or were you going to do it for me?"

"Oh God, would you just *listen* to yourself?" said Matt. I could see beads of sweat caught like pearls in his stubble. "You're completely insane, you're mad."

Jessica was looking back and forth, from Matt's face to mine.

"I'm not," I said again. "If I'm mad, who's that?" I gestured at Jessica. "Who's that, then?"

Matt's face flickered.

"Who's who?" he said, quietly. "Maudie, there's no one there."

I blinked. For a moment, I thought I'd misheard him.

"Don't be stupid," I said after a moment. "Don't try that. You know she's there. She's *there*."

He was looking at me quite steadily.

"Who's she?" he said. I could see Jessica's head whipping back and forth as she switched her gaze between our faces. "There's no one there."

"You just talked to her! You just looked at her! You told her not to come here."

"Maudie, for God's sake," he said. He was holding both

hands up as if he were warding something off. "You're frightening me now."

"Stop it," I said, my voice trembling. "I know what you're trying to do."

"Stop what?" he said. His voice had got suddenly gentler. "Maudie, you need help. You're seeing things. There's no one there."

"There is!" I said, in what was not quite a shout. The sound made me start to cry, properly, and I heard myself sob with helpless fury. "She's there, she's right there, you were just talking to her, she's there..."

Matt was shaking his head, quite slowly. The disgust was gone from his face: now he simply looked sad. He held out the brandy glass to me again.

"Drink this," he said. "You need to drink this. Don't struggle any more."

I turned to Jessica.

"I know you're there," I said, my voice vibrating so much I could barely understand myself. "This is just part of his plot, that's all. You know that."

"I'm here," she said. "You're not wrong."

I looked her, full in the face. I had to make her understand.

"So was he paying you?" I said. "Did he promise you a cut of the proceeds? Did he say he'd take care of you?"

Her eyes wavered and fell. I saw her fingers close in on one another.

"He told you that," I said. "I wonder what else he told you about me? Do you think he was going to let you just walk away with your money? When you're the only person who knows what he did?"

She looked up again at that and her eyes met mine, wide and horrified.

"Maudie, stop it," said Matt. "Stop pretending. It's embarrassing."

I ignored him.

"No one knows you exist, Jessica, do they? Who is going

to miss you if you disappear? Don't you think he knew that? He knows you're - you're totally dispensable. How long do you think you'd last, once he got what he wanted?"

I stopped speaking and for a moment the room was silent, save for the sound of our lungs labouring for air. Slowly, Jessica turned to Matt. He wasn't looking at her; he hadn't taken his eyes off me. Then, very slowly, she pivoted. She turned back and I saw her mouth something, I heard her whisper something. I think it was 'go'.

I didn't stop to think. My foot went up and out, connecting with the brandy glass in Matt's hand. It went flying, a golden sheet of liquid spread for a second in the air like a shimmering silk scarf. Then the glass hit the floor and shattered. In the same moment, I propelled myself forward, aiming myself between the two of them. My shoulder hit Matt's arm and flung him backwards. I was at the hallway door. I was running down the corridor to the front door. I was free.

I was at the front door, scrabbling at the lock, when he grabbed me around the neck. I shrieked.

"Shut up," he hissed. "Shut the fuck up, or I'll kill you right now, right here."

His arm was pressing on my windpipe. I clawed at his sleeve, gasping. He began dragging me backwards. I could hear my heels thumping and clacking uselessly on the wooden floor as I was pulled remorselessly back into the living room.

He stopped for a moment, panting. His hold around my neck had loosened and I dragged some air into my burning lungs. I was almost too frightened to think, certainly to speak, until I saw Jessica's face. I couldn't stop thinking of her as Jessica. She was biting her lip, looking at Matt and me. Her hand was at her throat again, holding onto the necklace that I'd bought her.

I managed to get enough air in to speak.

"Jess – you - please help me. Please – "

Matt pulled me away. He started dragging me towards the doors of the roof terrace. I started to struggle even harder. I stopped clawing at his arm that lay like a bar of iron across my neck, the muscles tense as stone, and started flailing at anything I could, grabbing for a grip on something anywhere, on anything.

"Don't fucking *struggle*," said Matt, through gritted teeth. He sounded as if he were crying. "If you do, I'm just going to knock you out. Stop struggling –"

I barely heard him. I had my eyes fixed on her, on the fake Jessica. I tried to pour all my terror, all my despair into my eyes, every single bit of concentrated emotion into my gaze; as she'd once done for me, staring up at me from the street outside.

"Jessica, " I croaked. "Don't let him do this -" She said nothing but her eyes were on mine. I couldn't read her expression. My vision was beginning to fog.

My last sentence was cut off with a gasp as I was pulled through the open doorway to the roof terrace. A gust of cold wind thrust against my cheek.

"Straight over," said Matt in a high, strange voice. He sounded hysterical; he was half-laughing, half-sobbing. "It won't hurt, Maudie. It'll be quick."

The next moment, the rough concrete of the boundary wall was up against my chest and my head was being forced over the top of the wall. I heard the tinkle of glass as my knee hit the mirror that stood against the wall. I could see the street far below. It was going to happen, then. I was going to die.

"I'm sorry," said Matt, crying. "It's for the best. I'm sorry - "

I could feel him dip behind me and grasp me around the waist and I felt myself begin to rise. I couldn't scream. My whole being was concentrated on trying to grip the wall, trying to stay alive for one second longer. The far-off road swung dizzily in my tear-filled vision. *God help me.*

The pressure around my waist suddenly slackened. At

the same time, I heard Matt roar out. I was released; the swinging road vanished as I fell backwards away from the wall. My feet hit the floor and my knees buckled, but, oh God, I hadn't gone over, I hadn't fallen…. I gulped in cold night air. My face was burning where the concrete had scraped it and I'd cut my knee on a shard of mirror glass. I turned round.

Jessica had dug her fingers into Matt's eyes. She had her arms around his neck and was forcing his head back. Her teeth were bared in a desperate grimace; she looked as though she was laughing. As I watched, Matt's fist caught her full in the face and he flailed backwards – I watched her nose spout blood and gasped involuntarily. She loosed her hold and dropped to the floor. Matt turned, snarling, his eyes streaming. I saw his fist come up and back as my own hand closed upon a long shard of glass. As his fist came down towards Jessica's face, I drove the glass into the side of his neck.

Blood flew out in a parabola of red. It spattered across Jessica's face as she lay gasping on the decking. Matt staggered and dropped to his knees. He put a hand up to the shining splinter protruding from his neck. His fingers pulled at it and more blood fell, this time in droplets, thickly over his shoulder and onto the terrace.

I realised I had my hands clamped over my mouth. I could feel my eyes bulging.

Matt groaned. A fine spray of blood feathered through the air. His bleeding hand fell away from the mirror shard buried in his neck. He took one shuffling knee-walk step and fell, his face dropping onto Jessica's leg. She cried out and rolled away and he fell onto the floor, face down. The piece of mirror shattered, half of it falling beneath his body, half of it remaining in his neck. It jerked with each bump of his pulse and, as I watched, the jerks grew fainter and fainter until at last the piece of glass grew still. Behind the blood dappling the surface, I could see the night sky reflected; a little sliver of darkness buried in the pale flesh of my husband's neck.

My eyes met Jessica's. Beyond the awful bubble of silence that surrounded us, I could dimly hear the sounds of the city flowing on without us: car horns, a siren, a shout from the street below.

Jessica pulled herself into a sitting position and hung her head forward. She was breathing heavily, blood dripping from her broken nose. She put a hand up to her mouth.

"Shit," she said thickly and as her hand came away I saw a nugget of enamel in her bloodied palm, half a tooth that Matt's fist had knocked from her jaw. It dropped from her fingers and was swallowed up in the lake of blood that lay by Matt's downturned face.

I managed to take my hands from my face; my whole body felt stiff, as if I'd been welded to the spot and hadn't moved for hours. Slowly, I held out a hand to Jessica and helped her to her feet. We stood swaying, holding one another up.

"Are you alright?" I asked.

"Not really." She looked at me, tears welling up. "Oh shit, Maudie. You killed him."

We both looked down at Matt's body, the blood surrounding him, the mirror shard winking grotesquely from his neck. I dropped Jessica's hand and stepped back.

"Oh my God, you killed him. What are we going to do?"

"Just wait - "

"Maudie, we're fucked. What are we going to do?"

I lifted a clenched fist and rested it against my chest, between my breasts. I could hear the study thump of my heartbeat beneath my breastbone, slowing gradually as my breathing grew deeper. The strangest thing was happening. Inside, I felt a core of something hard, and metallic, something steely, unfolding like a metal flower. Filaments were beginning to spread through me, molten iron sending out a root system of strength that straightened my back and lifted my head. For the first time in my life, I had no one to turn to, no one to take care of things for me. I had no one. And yet, for the first time in my life, I knew it didn't matter. I can do this, I thought, I can cope. *Yes*, said a little voice inside my head, a sane voice, a voice of reason. *You can.*

I looked down at my hands. The terrace wall had broken open the scabs on my palms but there were no cuts from the glass I'd held, none at all.

I took a deep breath. I'd made my decision.

"You should go," I said. "Just go. Get out of here."

She stared.

"But what about you?"

"Don't worry about me," I said. I looked at her, standing square-mouthed and crying like a child, and felt again that odd unfolding of steel within me.

"Just go," I said. "I'll deal with this."

EPILOGUE

"I'll have the smoked salmon and the scrambled eggs, please," I said, handing the little plastic menu back to the guard. I looked across at Becca and raised my eyebrows.

"I'll have the same," she said.

I waited until he'd moved off down the train corridor. The carriage was quiet – this was the mid-week morning train to Cornwall and not many commuters or tourists used it.

Becca shifted uncomfortably.

"Just as well it's first class," she said. "There's no way I'd fit into an economy seat with this belly."

I smiled.

"You do look a bit as though you're about to pop."

"Oh well. Only two months to go." She looked down at herself and sighed. "God, me, a mother. Who'd have thought it?"

"You'll be fine," I said. "You've always looked after me, haven't you? You're a natural."

Another guard was moving down the corridor with coffee jugs in either hand. I smiled at him briefly as he refilled our cups and then walked away, staggering a little as the train rounded a curve.

"I'm sorry I haven't been round much," said Becca. "I'm

just so damn uncomfortable I don't feel like walking any further than the kitchen at the moment. Even then, Martin's doing most of the cooking."

"Becs, it's absolutely fine. I'm fine on my own, really. I'm used to it by now."

Matt's name hung in the air between us. Our eyes met for a second and then I looked away.

The guard came back down the corridor, proffering his coffee jugs again. As he moved past from our table, Becca spoke.

"How are you feeling about this?"

I looked down at the table. I tried to be honest about my feelings now, with people I trusted, but it took me a moment to formulate the answer.

"Upset," I said slowly. "A bit churned up inside. Sad. But – but sort of relieved too. That it's finally at an end."

Becca nodded. Then she said, even more cautiously, "And how do you feel about – about the trial?"

I picked up my coffee cup for the comfort of its warmth against my hand. The trial. Every time I heard that word I could see it in my mind's eye, in thick, black capital letters. THE TRIAL. And there were other images that always accompanied it; wood panelled court rooms, a baying mob of journalists on the steps of the buildings outside, myself with my hands clenched on the side of the dock as the judge passed sentence upon me. There were sounds too; the thwack of the gavel as I was given a life sentence, the wail of sirens, the clang of the prison gate. The jeers and catcalls of the other prisoners. The sound of a key turning as I was locked into a cell.

Perhaps it wouldn't be like that. But perhaps it would.

"I'm trying not to think about it much," I said. "My chances aren't good."

Becca looked uncomfortable.

"Surely your lawyer – " she began.

"He's doing his best," I said. I put the coffee cup down as my hand was starting to tremble. "But it's not looking good."

"Oh Maudie – "

"Please," I said. I couldn't deal with her tears as well as my own. "Let's not talk about it now."

We were silent for a moment as one of the other passengers came down the corridor past us. Then Becca spoke again, quietly.

"Do you think Matt always – always meant to do it?"

I put my coffee cup down.

"What I really think? I just don't know. I don't think he planned it from the moment he met me. He must have thought he'd have a comfortable enough life as my husband; he knew he was marrying into money."

"Well, yes," said Becca.

I stirred my coffee.

"He also knew I was vulnerable and a bit - damaged and when he started getting greedy, he saw how he could use that."

"I don't understand people like that," Becca said. "It's just beyond me. How could he be so cruel?"

I shifted uncomfortably, remembering I'd said exactly that to Matt on the night of his death. I always thought of it in those terms – *the night of his death* – as if his death was nothing to do with me, as if it had happened because of someone else entirely. I had to think like that – it was the only way of staying sane.

"I don't know," I said. I looked down at the flat brown circle of my coffee cup. "It's a mystery. He was obviously able to detach himself from what he was doing. That's what Margaret said. He could compartmentalise it all. Perhaps it started off as a game. You know, what would happen if Maudie died? He must have realised it was a possibility, more of a possibility that it would have been for any – " I hesitated, "- any normal young woman. He knew my history, he knew about my past. He knew about my mother and what happened to her. Perhaps he didn't even have to suggest it to himself, perhaps he honestly thought it would happen. Perhaps –" and I hesitated again "- perhaps it was his way of controlling the situation. You know, pre-empting what he thought was going to happen anyway."

"Oh, come on," said Becca. "Please don't give him that much credit. If he really thought that, why go to all those lengths? Why have an accomplice? He was trying to drive you mad."

I hung my head.

"I know," I muttered. "I know he's a bastard. Was a bastard. But seriously, Becca, I was so awful to live with, at the end. I mean, I was *awful*. It probably made it a lot easier for him."

Our eyes met again. I wondered if she was remembering the scene in my flat, when she'd told me she was pregnant, and I'd overreacted. I was the first to look away.

"Maudie," she said, patiently. "Your so-called husband was trying to convince you you were insane. There's nothing that you could have done, no way you could have behaved, that would excuse that."

"Yes – "

"Yes, really. Stop blaming yourself. Haven't you done enough of that for one lifetime?"

"Yes, I know – "

Becca arched her back, relaxed again and sighed.

"You really had a bad deal with the two men in your life, didn't you?" she said.

I looked out of the window at the countryside speeding past us. I could feel my chest tightening, as it always did when I thought about Angus. I tried to breathe deeply, but unobtrusively, as Margaret had taught me. Thinking of her prompted me to speak.

"Margaret said that could be why I ended up with Matt in the first place. You know, why I felt safe with him." I found myself smiling, rather grimly. "Safe, I know. Stupid, isn't it? But she said you're often attracted to people who act in ways you recognise. Or you recognise patterns in their behaviour, without even realising you're doing it."

"Two sociopaths in the family," said Becca. "How convenient for you."

I rolled my eyes.

"It sounds a bit trite, I know. Matt wasn't a sociopath, anyway. He was just a weak, greedy man who wanted more than he had. And I'm not sure you can call An – my father a sociopath either."

"No?"

"No." I looked out the window again. "I don't know what he was."

"Well, I know what Matt was."

"What?"

"A complete and utter bastard."

I couldn't help but laugh.

"True. He certainly had a massive sense of entitlement."

"And don't even get me started on her."

I pleated a fold of my napkin between my fingers.

"She saved my life," I said.

Becca sniffed.

"Yeah, after trying to drive you crazy."

"She changed her mind, though," I said. "I think she realised she couldn't do it. I think she came to warn me."

Our food arrived at the moment and we both fell silent as the plates were placed into front of us.

"Can I get you ladies a drink?" asked the guard.

I fought the usual internal battle. One day at a time, Margaret had said. Just take it one day at a time. Only she knew how bad my drinking had been. Only she and Becca knew about Angus and what had really happened that night in Cornwall. I hadn't told the police. I couldn't have coped with the resulting investigation and the media attention. And there was Aunt Effie to think of. Or that was what I'd told myself.

"Just water for me, thanks," I said.

"Same here," said Becca.

I pushed at the mass of scrambled eggs on my plate. I

wasn't hungry.

"I wonder if anything she told me was true?" I said.

"I doubt it."

"I don't know. She was so convincing. Surely no one's that good an actress? And it would explain a lot... if she'd had that sort of a life."

Becca rolled her eyes.

"Perhaps that's how Matt met her."

I put my fork down.

"Perhaps."

"Ugh."

"Well, yes. I wonder what he told her, about me."

"God knows," said Becca. "It must have been convincing."

I sighed.

"I was so stupid," I said. "That's what hurts most of all."

"Come on. You weren't to blame. You're supposed to be able to trust your husband. That's supposed to be part of the deal."

"I wanted to believe it," I said. "That was the clincher. I wanted it all to be true."

"Well, of course you did," said Becca. "Of course you did. That's natural."

I fell silent. Becca regarded me with sympathy.

"Maudie, he had us all fooled. But don't worry. It's not like you could have spotted what he was doing, could you? Not really."

I stared down at my half-full plate.

"No."

"Your defence will bring that up, won't they? I mean, that is the defence, isn't it?"

"Yes," I said, slowly. We hadn't yet talked about this and I wasn't sure what to say.

Becca gave me a quick, penetrating glance.

"You don't sound too sure."

"Well," I said. I consciously made myself relax my hands. "The trouble is that the prosecutors – "

There was a moment's silence.

"Yes?" Becca prompted.

I took a deep breath.

"The prosecution's case is that there wasn't anyone else there. It was just me and Matt."

Becca blinked.

"What do you mean?"

I could feel my fingers tightening again and I took hold of my legs under the table.

"There wasn't anyone called Jessica there as well. They're saying she didn't exist. It was just me and Matt. Just a common or garden domestic that went wrong."

Becca was quiet for a moment. Then she laughed a little uncertainly.

"That's crazy," she said. "There's evidence – "

"There isn't – " I said, interrupting her. "Or not much. A blonde girl on the CCTV once or twice."

"Well, that's –"

"They're saying it's me," I said, flatly. "It's me on the CCTV. That's their angle."

Becca chewed her lip for a moment. I could see her flicking through the possibilities in her head, just as I had, and felt a rush of affection for her, even despite my anxiety.

"He knocked out her tooth," she said. "Didn't he?"

I felt the corners of my mouth pull in, in what was almost a smile.

"The police couldn't find it."

Becca was quiet for a moment. Then she sat up a little and smiled.

"Well, I'm sure it'll be fine," she said, trying for briskness. "You and I and your lawyer know the truth, don't we? We know she was there, don't we? She *was* there, wasn't she, Maudie?" When I didn't answer immediately, she asked again. "Wasn't she, Maudie?"

"Of course she was," I said. I cleared my throat and said it in a firmer voice. "Of course she was there."

"Right then," said Becca. I saw her bite her lip again as she looked out of the window. Then she faced me, and smiled again. "I know it's hard, but try not to worry too much. I'm sure it'll all work out fine in the end."

I tried to smile back.

"I know. Thanks Becs."

The train rattled on. Beneath the table, my palms were marked with eight little reddened half smiles.

The sun was shining when the train drew into Penzance although a strong breeze buffeted us as we stepped out onto the concourse. The harbour was a mass of yachts, boats, dinghies and fishing trawlers, all bobbing on an azure sea. I took a deep breath, throwing my head back against the dazzle of the sunlight.

We picked up the keys for our hire car and found it in the car park. I slotted myself behind the steering wheel. I drove carefully, tensely, looking out at the little stone cottages, the holidaymakers eating ice-cream, the far-off white peaks of the waves out in the bay. So familiar, yet so alien. I was glad Becca was there. I looked across at her and smiled when I saw she'd fallen asleep, her head lolling against the tatty fabric of the car seat, her mouth inelegantly agape. I looked back out of the window, and at the distant countryside beyond the houses and roads of the town.

We'd booked into a little guesthouse in the village, two streets over from the cottages Angus had once owned. One of them had become a bed and breakfast place, but staying there would have been too much for me. All the same, I stopped the car on the road outside for a moment. The two houses hadn't changed much. One had grown a small extension and the creaky old wooden gate at the front was gone. The hedges had grown but not as much as I would have thought. Or was it just that I myself was taller? I could see my old bedroom window from where I was parked. I wondered what the reaction would be if I knocked on the door and told the occupants there had been a murder in their front room.

Becca had been sleeping deeply, lulled by the movement of the car. She woke up quite suddenly with a snort.

"Ugh," she said, wiping her hand across her face. "Sorry, I was fast asleep. Where are we?"

I put the car into gear and drove away.

"Nowhere," I said, "It doesn't matter."

The owner of the guesthouse was an elderly, bespectacled lady. I saw her looking at my scar as we signed the guest register.

"It's from a car accident," I said and smiled inwardly when she blushed and muttered something to cover her confusion. It no longer bothered me when people looked. Why would I care what they think?

We ate at the local pub that evening, the only one in the village, still thronged with ruddy-faced walkers sinking pints of stout. Afterwards, we walked slowly back to the guesthouse.

"Are you sure you don't want me to come with you?" said Becca, puffing a little as we climbed the stairs to our rooms.

"Thanks, but no," I said. I smiled at her. "Seriously, thanks Becs. I do appreciate you being here, more than you might think. But I have to do this on my own."

I gave her a quick hug and she hugged me back. I could feel the tight roundness of her belly; the hardness of it was always a small shock.

"Have you thought of a name, yet?"

She put her hands on her bump, moving them in a slow circle.

"Not yet." She looked at me, considering. "Maybe I'll call her Jessica."

When the time was right, I got up off the bed where I'd been lying, and put my shoes on. I pulled on a coat and picked up my torch. I checked my watch again. Then I left the room, quietly, shutting the door behind me.

The night was cool but not cold, the night sky huge, indigo-hued and ragged with rapidly moving clouds. A thin slice of moon shone little light over the dark countryside and I was glad of my torch. I made my way up the track, stones slipping under my feet. Every noise I made sounded loud in the expectant hush of the countryside. As I reached the end of the track, my teeth began to chatter.

The stones looked so small. I walked over to the Men-an-Tol and put my hand on it, feeling the chill of it beneath my palm. Through the hole, I could see a few faint stars twinkling against their black velvet backdrop, before they were blotted out by cloud. I held my breath. If there really had been a ritual to take me back in time, to whisk me back to that night before everything fell apart, would I perform it? Would I have been able to stop what happened, a ten-year-old child? Perhaps somewhere, in another universe, perhaps I had. In this one, all I could do was watch the sky through the hole in the stone and mourn my friend.

"I'm sorry, Jessica," I said. I whispered it to the night and the stones and the sky. "Wherever you are. I'm sorry."

My farewell said, I turned and made my way back to the track. I kept my eyes on the small circle of light cast by the torch. I didn't look behind me.

THE END

ACKNOWLEDGEMENTS

Big, huge, enormous thanks must go to the following fine people:

Clare Conville, for expert advice and editorial support and suggestions; Chris Howard for the brilliant cover designs for print and eBooks; Kathleen and Pat McConnell, Ross McConnell and Anthony Alcock, who are otherwise known as my wonderful family; Naomi White, Lee Benjamin, Bonnie Wede, Sherry and Amali Stoute, Cheryl Lucas, Georgia Lucas-Going, Steven Lucas, Loletha Stoute and Harry Lucas, my equally wonderful extended family; the most highly esteemed members of The Schlock Shack, David Hall, Ben Robinson and Alberto Lopez, Lara Hafez and Reem Shaddad for creative bonding and more bad films ever needed in a lifetime; the two Helens in my life, Ms Parfect and Ms Watson; Emily 'Agnes' Way; Sandy Hall, Kristýna Vosecká; and probably a whole heap of people I've forgotten; and last but definitely not least, my lovely Chris and equally lovely Mabel, Jethro and Isaiah.

WANT MORE CELINA GRACE?

Enjoyed this book? An honest review left on Amazon, Goodreads, Shelfari or LibraryThing is *always* welcome.

You can read more from Celina Grace at her blog on writing and self-publishing http://www.celinagrace.com. Download a free short story, **Salt**, exclusive to subscribers to Celina's newsletter and be the first to be informed of promotions, giveaways, new releases and subscriber-only benefits.

http://www.celinagrace.com
Twitter: @celina__grace
Facebook: http://www.facebook.com/authorcelinagrace

Celina Grace's first novel, **The House on Fever Street**, is also available on Amazon. Shortlisted for the 2006 Crime Writers' Association Debut Dagger Award, **The House on Fever Street** is a chilling study of the violent impulses that lurk beneath the surfaces of everyday life.

Thrown together in the aftermath of the London bombings of 2005, Jake and Bella embark on a passionate and intense romance. Soon Bella is living with Jake in his house on Fever Street, along with his sardonic brother Carl and Carl's girlfriend, the beautiful but chilly Veronica. As Bella tries to come to terms with her traumatic experience, her relationship with Jake also becomes a source of unease. Why do the housemates never go into the garden? Why does Jake have such bad dreams and such explosive outbursts of temper?

Bella is determined to understand the man she loves but as she uncovers long-buried secrets, is she putting herself back into mortal danger?

Read the first two chapters here...

The House on Fever Street

CELINA GRACE

© Celina Grace 2012

PROLOGUE

It began down in the tunnels. He was walking, coughing, half-blind; stumbling through the dark over the sleepers, the air a wall of heat and thick, choking dust. The muscles of his shoulder were aching from the drag of her weight on his arm. Even over the shuffle of their steps and the distant moans and screams of the people who had been in that carriage of the train, he could hear her breath sobbing in and out of her lungs. He coughed again; he couldn't stop coughing, spitting blindly into the darkness. Once he stumbled and fell to his knees, cutting his hand on the protruding edge of a metal bolt. Above the flash of pain in his palm, he heard her panicked gasp as their hands were wrenched apart.

"It's all right," he said. 'I just fell down. It's all right."

"It's not."

He heard the tremor of tears in her voice and groped for her in the darkness. She came to him silently and they held each other for a moment; she thrummed in his arms, her heartbeat a fast gallop beneath the soft swell of her breasts. Then one of the others behind them stumbled against them both and cursed and they let go of each other, reluctantly.

"Don't leave me. Don't let go of me, please."
"I won't."
He tightened his grip on her hand. He was very frightened, trembling on legs that shook with the backwash of adrenaline. He kept walking. He held onto her like a lifeline, their palms slipping against one another's and he thought *this is punishment for what I've done. This is the start of it.*

They came out into daylight and watery sunlight, walking into a frenzy of noise and confusion. Sirens chopping at the air, camera crews and police tape, someone shouting, a staring crowd rigid with tension. He turned to her and looked her in the face, for the first time. Her blue eyes were bloodshot. He cupped her dirty jaw with his dirty hands, his fingers smoked black with soot, but he didn't kiss her, not then. For the first time since the explosion, he thought of the others. Were they trudging through purgatorial tunnels, far beneath the city? Or were they dead? He tightened his fingers against her face and looked again, into her eyes. *Save me*, he thought, and bent to put his blackened mouth against hers.

PART ONE

Chapter One

Bella lay awake. She put a hand up to her face, feeling the thin film of sweat overlaying her skin. Her eyelids fluttered and she dropped back into sleep for a second, just for a moment but then she was back there, in the tunnels, in the dream, in the dark. She heard herself moan a little and pressed her hand more firmly against her forehead, feeling the minute jerks of her fingertips as her hand shook. She concentrated on breathing in and out, staring up at the familiar cracks of her bedroom ceiling, glad of the sunshine coming through the window.

Gradually, her heart rate slowed. She blinked away the tears that had come back again, hot and unwelcome, and tried to breathe normally.

When her legs were steady enough, she got up, wrapped her dressing gown around her shoulders and fumbled her way downstairs. She paused in the kitchen doorway, one hand on the wall, and her mother, busy at the sink, looked up sharply.

"Are you all right?"

"I'm okay. I'll survive."

She could feel her mother's gaze intensify, and she looked away, down at her bare feet. Her toenails still bore the remnants of the pink polish that she'd applied on the very morning of the bombings. She remembered doing it; admiring her summer feet neat in her best high-heeled sandals, ready for her interview.

"Have you been crying?" said Mrs Hardwick.

"I'm okay."

"Bella –"

"I'm *fine*." She took a deep breath, swallowed. "Sorry. It's just - I keep having bad dreams."

She shuffled into the kitchen, belting her dressing gown more tightly about her waist. She'd lost weight; even in the short space of a week, she'd lost weight. Her mother was looking at her again, the same look she'd had ever since they'd left the hospital – anxiety, anguish and glorious relief all vying for precedence on her face.

"Nightmares? Well, that's understandable."

Mrs Hardwick reached for a tea towel and wiped off her hands with brisk efficiency. Something about the movement made Bella feel tired. She stood for a moment in the middle of the kitchen floor, staring dumbly across the room.

They sat down to breakfast in silence. Bella looked at the square slices of toast on her plate, veiled in melting yellow grease.

"Come on, eat something. You've not had a square meal since it happened."

"I'm not very hungry."

"Come on, love," said her mother, in a softened tone. "You have to try and get on with things, you know. It's no use giving in."

Bella took a reluctant bite and jumped as, behind her, the phone rang suddenly. Mrs Hardwick answered it, spoke, frowned, turned to her daughter.

"It's for you."

Bella struggled with her mouthful of toast and managed to

swallow it. She took the receiver from her mother.

"Hello," she said.

"It's Jake."

For a split second, the bright, sun-filled kitchen darkened as, in her head, the explosion thundered once more. She gripped the receiver.

"Jake?"

"It's me. From the – the tunnels."

He'd kissed her in the street, the two of them locked together at the mouth, locked together at the hands. He'd looked like a boy then, a young smooth-faced boy, pale with fright under a black mask of soot. When their lips had parted, she'd begun to say something; she could no longer remember what. The paramedics had descended, rustling with foil blankets. There had been a chorus of soothing, no-nonsense voices. Bella and Jake were separated, gently prised apart by well-meaning hands. She'd felt the loss of his fingers, the sudden departure of his warmth, as if a part of her had been torn away.

And here he was, on the end of a phone line. Bella closed her eyes for a moment, listening to his breathing. He'd been, to this moment, someone almost mythical, a guardian angel who'd appeared in the murk of that tunnel to guide her to safety and light. She'd felt his warmth, felt the touch of his mouth against hers, all so physical and real – and then he was gone, pulled away from her. Leaving her in the tumult of the streets, leaving her to travel alone to the makeshift hospital. She hadn't cried until she'd seen her mother's face, pulled tight with anxiety.

He rescued me, she thought. And then he was gone. And now here he was, on the end of the phone, resurrected.

"How are you doing?"

Bella considered for a moment. How was she doing?

"I'm okay." She felt shy with him, even though he couldn't see her. She had to struggle to keep her voice at a normal conversational level, fought not to let it drop down to a silly little whisper.

"Are you having bad dreams?" said Jake. "I'm having awful dreams. Fucking horrible. My brother says it's just my brain trying to make sense of bad memories. Whatever…. It's awful. Are you sleeping badly?"

He was chatting to her so easily, as if they'd known each other for years. Bella felt herself begin to unbend, opening up under the spell of his easy talk. She was suddenly aware of her mother in the room, listening to every word. She shook her head at Mrs Hardwick's lifted eyebrows. Her mother shrugged and moved away, out of earshot. Bella shifted the handset against her ear and turned away, pressing herself against the kitchen wall.

"Hello?"

"Sorry – I'm still here – it's just – "

"It's okay. It's hard to talk about it. I know."

The two of them were silent for a moment, listening to each other's breathing.

"Are you still there?" said Jake. He suddenly sounded unsure of himself.

"I'm here. I'm sorry. What did you ask me?"

"Um – was it about sleeping?"

"Yeah, that's it. I'm not too bad. I – it's more that I can't sleep. I go to sleep and then I wake up, for no reason, and then I can't get back to sleep. I feel so tired all the time."

"Must be hard for you at work."

"I'm not working." Bella shifted her weight from foot to foot. "I only left university this summer and I haven't really got – I haven't really thought about what I was going to do. That's why I was in London that day, I had a job interview. That's why I was on the train – I stayed at my Dad's place so I could get the tube in the morning – my interview was in the West End and I didn't want to be late, so I ran for that train – the train – and I almost didn't make it, the doors nearly shut on me, but I did get on and I thought wow, just about made that in time, and then we were just going into the tunnel…"

She tripped over herself; the words were coming too fast

for her to speak properly. She'd not talked about that day with anyone, not really, not even her mother. But she could talk to Jake. It was as he was tugging speech out of her, each word emerging like a knotted rope of coloured silk handkerchiefs flourished by a magician. She stopped eventually, more breathless than her speech had warranted.

There was a long moment of silence between them, long enough for Bella's comfort. She was suddenly afraid she'd said too much, and spoken too wildly. The handset slipped a little in her damp palm. Then, after another beat of silence, she heard Jake's intake of breath at the end of the line.

"We should meet," he said.

"Meet?" she said, stupidly.

"Would you like to? I mean – only if you want to." Again, he suddenly sounded unsure of himself and that gave her the courage to answer.

"No! I mean, no, I'd love to. I want – there's – it's hard to say everything that I want to say on the phone."

He chuckled and she smiled at the sound, relieved.

"There's so much I want to say to you. I thought you might think I was a complete nutter ringing you up out of the blue. I bet you don't even remember giving me your home number."

Bella groped through the fog of memories. Had she given him her number? She must have. She took a deep breath. "Where shall I meet you?"

Jake hesitated.

"Could you – could you bear to come to London?" He began to rush his words, much as Bella had done before. "I'll understand – I'll completely understand if you don't. I could understand if you never wanted to set foot in the fucking place ever again. But if you don't mind –"

She did mind. She minded terribly. For a moment, she couldn't answer. Could she bear it, being there again? She was so scared of London, terrified of the capital. She tried to imagine being on a train again, thought about being underground. No, she couldn't go underground. She couldn't go anywhere near a tube tunnel. Her pulse thumped in her ears. She would be so scared… but she longed to meet him again, this rescuer, this stranger, her mysterious tunnel vision…

"I don't mind," she said, surprising herself with the firmness of her voice.

"Oh, that's great. That's fantastic."

She interrupted him. "It's just –"Her voice failed her for a second. "As long – as long as – can we meet somewhere where I don't have to take the tube?"

He actually laughed. "Of course! God – of course. Of course we can, Bella."

There was the usual tangle of suggestions, retractions and final confirmation. A little pub near Waterloo, so she could take the overland train – near enough to walk from the station, said Jake, and quiet enough to talk properly. Bella fumbled for a pen to write down his directions.

"So I'll see you on Saturday, then," said Jake. He began to say something else but stopped himself. Then he said, with an oddly fervent tone, "I'm really looking forward to seeing you again, Bella. See you then. Goodbye."

"Goodbye," said Bella, shakily. Her mouth suddenly felt coated in acrid underground dust. She swallowed and said goodbye again, more firmly.

"See you then, Jake."

She put the phone down and leant against the wall.

For the rest of the week, she thought mainly of two things – the bombing and Jake. Saturday, three o'clock. Saturday, three o'clock. She went through her wardrobe, looking for the right thing to wear, a piece of armour that would take her to London and back unscathed. The idea of getting on a train again, even an overland train, made her hands shake and her breath come short and fast. But yet, she had to. It was either that or spend the rest of her life cooped up here, safe behind the walls of her mother's house.

There were other, smaller anxieties. How would she recognise Jake? Even when they'd emerged into daylight, she'd been half blinded by dust and smoke. His face had been blackened by soot and before that, she'd only glimpsed him as a dark shape in a darker tunnel. She didn't even know his last name. She wondered about looking up newspaper reports of the bombings to see if she could find out, but couldn't bear to read them. What if she couldn't find the pub, or was late and he didn't wait for her? What if he didn't turn up at all?

Then there was the actual meeting. Bella was horribly afraid she would burst into tears on seeing him. Would she scream, faint, wet herself? There were too many what-ifs. The thoughts chased themselves around in her head, stuck in an endless merry-go-round; she shouldn't go – she should go – she shouldn't go – she should. At night, in her dreams, she walked the tunnels of the Underground, wandering lost and scared through an endless black maze, dragging herself back to consciousness in a fever of sweat. She tried to eat the meals her mother placed in front of her, pushing the food around the plate with a fork, chewing and swallowing past the tension in her throat. The days ticked relentlessly away and quite suddenly it was Saturday and she was sat in a near-empty carriage, on a train bound for Waterloo.

Being on a train again wasn't quite as bad as being on the tube would have been, but it was still pretty bad. She sat rigidly by the window, staring out at the fields flashing past, the gradual encroachment of bricks and mortar as the train drew nearer London. I'm being brave, she told herself, trying to find some comfort in the thought. Soon, she could see the giant arch of the London Eye and felt the train begin to slow, shuddering its way into the station. Immediately, the tension inside her screwed a notch tighter. Bella felt sick. She fumbled for her bag with shaking hands and stepped onto the concourse on legs that felt as if they were made of rubber. She walked stiffly through the tumult of the station, flinching at the loudspeaker announcements, hardly breathing.

Walking calmed her somewhat and being out in the open air was better. She stiffened at the sight of the first red bus she saw, remembering the footage of the bombed Number 30, the roof peeled back like the lid of a giant sardine can, seating ripped apart as if by enormous, careless hands. She found the pub, tucked away on a little back street, just as Jake had said. As she approached the entrance, she made herself breathe slowly and deeply. She put her hand to the handle of the saloon door and pushed.

She saw him immediately and recognised him straight away. The sight of him, sat up by the bar opposite the door, caused such a wave of feeling to crash over her that she heard herself give an audible gasp. She staggered forward, crumpling at the waist like someone shot in the stomach.

Jake reached her in half a second. She felt one warm hand under her arm, the comforting muscular bulk of him beside her. She felt herself lifted and propped. She gripped the edge of the bar with one hand, put her head down and breathed deeply.

"Okay?"

He was better looking than she remembered, his eyes darker, his hair longer. Bella looked up at him, trying to control her breathing. His eyes were red-rimmed. *His face is clean though*, she thought confusedly and then she slipped off the stool and they fell into each other's arms, quite naturally. She kept her face against his chest. His arms were tight around her and she felt the tension and sickness she'd carried around with her for the last three weeks fall away.

They held each other for a long moment and then, simultaneously, released their grip. Bella realised she was dangerously near to crying and tried to stretch her eyes wide to stop the drops from falling.

"Are you okay?"

Her 'yes' squeaked out and he reached out and put a steadying hand on her arm.

"You're not okay, you look like you're about to drop. Here – "

Bella was tucked back onto the bar stool; lifted and set down before she realised what was happening. She gripped the cool edge of the bar, steadying herself. She was too churned up to blush properly but she could feel the heat struggling to surface in her face.

"I'm okay." She said it again to convince Jake, and herself. "I'm okay. Really, I am. I just had – had a – "

"A wobbly moment?"

She looked quickly at him to see if he was laughing at her. He had a smile on his face but his eyes were kind.

"Don't worry, Bella."

She liked the way he said her name. Jake, she thought. His name is Jake.

"We're both having wobbly moments lately. Believe me, the whole of London is having a two week long, wobbly moment. It's nothing to be ashamed of."

She smiled weakly, feeling a little better.

"Now, can I get you a drink?"

Bella nodded fervently.

"Gin and tonic, please."

He turned away from her slightly as he gave the order and she studied his profile, covertly. His nose was prominent but matched by a masculine jaw, now faintly smudged with shadow. His hair was thick and fell in a heedless black tangle over his eyes. He was obviously older than her. How much older? The height of him, the breadth of his shoulders, his stubble, the almost invisible creases at the edge of his eyes... Not a smooth-faced boy, after all. She felt breathless again but this time it was nothing to do with fear.

Jake paid for the drinks and folded his battered leather wallet back into his pocket. Bella took the one that he offered her, feeling the cold slippery glass against her fingertips.

"Tell you what, let's move somewhere more comfortable. You look as if you're about to fall off that stool."

Bella laughed but felt embarrassed. She was over the first shaky hurdle but she couldn't relax, not yet. The ice cubes in her drink chinked against each other as she followed Jake through to the back of the pub. There was a tiny, walled garden at the back, and miraculously, an empty table by the far wall. They sat down opposite each other, smiling across the unsteady table.

"Is the sun in your eyes?"

"No – well, a bit, but –"

"Here, let's move round a bit – "

"I've got some shades – "

They talked over one another, realised simultaneously what they were doing and both laughed. Bella felt a little easier now, her legs steadier beneath her. She looked at him, squinting a little in the bright sunlight and realised again how good looking he was. She lifted the glass to her mouth to cover her sudden intake of breath.

When they were finally settled, there was a moment of silence that threatened to become awkward. Bella cast around frantically for something to say. She was just about to come up with something fatuous about the weather when Jake spoke.

"How are you sleeping?"

The question was so unexpected that for a moment she just gaped at him. Then she tried to answer.

"Well, I – not very well – I mean, it's not always easy –"

He interrupted her.

"I can't sleep. I don't think I've been able to sleep properly since it happened."

For a moment, his face darkened. He looked suddenly forbidding, his dark brows lowered, his shadowed jaw suddenly set. Bella swallowed and tried to think of an answer but he went on.

"I have terrible dreams. They're the worst – they're the

worst dreams I think I've ever had. Or if not ever, then certainly since – "

He stopped talking and lifted his glass to his mouth abruptly.

Bella licked her lips to try and get them to part.

"I have bad dreams too. I don't dream about the explosion but I dream about the tunnels. I constantly dream that I'm back in the tunnels, walking through the dark."

He looked at her intently. It was almost as if he was seeing her, really seeing her, for the first time.

"I thought it was just me. Those endless black tunnels, and the dust and the heat and smoke, stumbling over everything, waiting for the next explosion…"

"Yes."

They looked at each sombrely and then Jake smiled.

"I'm glad to see you. I feel better talking to you, I feel better already."

"Me too."

There was another moment of silence but this time, Bella felt no awkwardness. The gin and the sun began to spread a delicious warmth through her body and she relaxed back into the hard slats of the chair. She could hear a pigeon cooing faintly over the noise of the traffic beyond the garden wall.

"Want another drink?"

Jake tipped his glass at her in enquiry. She smiled and reached for her bag.

"Let me get this one."

He nodded, seemingly pleased. Walking away from him and the bright, sunlight garden, back into the dimness of the pub, she was momentarily blinded. Bella slowed her walk, letting her eyes adjust to the darkness. As she stood at the bar, she was very aware of her legs, trembling slightly beneath her. The alcohol and the heat, the fear and the anticipation were making her giddy. She lifted the fresh, cold glasses and made her way back outside, running through the conversation that they'd just had, thinking back on what she'd said.

"So what do you do?"
She snorted at the question, it sounded so grown-up; as if they were at a dinner party. It was about three drinks later, and they'd moved their seats twice, keeping out of the sun. Bella's face felt flushed but whether that was the heat, the gin or Jake's presence across the table she was yet to ascertain.
"What do I do?"
"Yeah." He was grinning. "What do you do?"
Bella giggled. "Well, nothing really, at the moment. I'm a lily of the field. Or is a rose? Anyway, I neither toil nor spin – or whatever it is that lilies do. Or don't do."
"What?"
She paused, momentarily embarrassed.
"I'm looking for work, actually. I just finished uni this summer." She hesitated at the student slang but Jake seemed not to notice. He was looking at her again with focused intensity, black brows drawn down in a frown of concentration. Nervousness made her stutter.
"That's what – I mean, that's why I was in London. On the seventh. I had an interview in the West End, an admin role at a big media company. Oh, I've already told you that. But that's why I was in London, that's why I was on the tube in the first place. I mean, I never should have been there in any case but I'd just got a call from the agency the day before and I thought, great, finally, something I might actually be able to do, you know, with a useless arts degree, and I was so fed up of being back home again, having no freedom after having so much, so I just said yes and the next day I took the train up to London and I got on the tube, I was running late so I ran for it and I didn't think I would make it, but I did…"
She trailed off and reached for her drink. Her hand was shaking a little. Where had that torrent of words come

from? Jake reached forward suddenly and took her hand. The shock of it, his palm against hers, made her flinch.

"It's alright."

"Yes, sorry – "

She fumbled for a tissue in her bag with her free hand. She wondered if he could feel the slight tremor in the fingers he was gripping. His hand was warm, the palm slightly damp. The silver ring he wore on his left index finger pressed hard against the bones of her hand.

Bella took a deep breath.

"Sorry."

"Don't apologise, you idiot."

Bella tried to speak normally.

"What about you?"

"Me?"

"Yes. Why were you there? Why were you on the tube? I suppose you were going to work…"

Jake let go of her hand and it dropped to the table, hitting her empty glass with a dull chime. He didn't seem to notice. That darkened look lowered his brows again.

"I was going to meet my brother," he said slowly. It sounded as though the words were coming to him one by one, each one weighed in a moment of contemplation before being spoken. The words hung in the air between them, oddly like a code. Bella raised her eyebrows enquiringly. There was a moment's silence.

"My brother," Jake repeated. He was looking at the table, his gaze suddenly blank. Bella made what she hoped was an encouraging 'hmm' sound. He stared at nothing for another moment and then raised his eyes to hers, forcing what looked like a rather reluctant smile.

"Yes, my brother," he said for the third time. "He's my older brother – Carl, his name's Carl. We were going to have a coffee and – and talk about a few things. A few house issues."

"House issues?"

Jake sat up slightly straighter. The sun was behind his

shoulder now, making Bella squint a little to make out his expression. "Yes, we live together, didn't I say? We've lived together for a few years now. We've got this big old house in Highgate. Actually, that makes it sound a bit better than it actually is. It's not technically Highgate, it's Archway. It's big though. God, sorry, that sounds really boastful."

Bella shook her head. "Is it just the two of you then?"

His head moved slightly, silhouetted against the glare of the sun.

"No, there's V – she's my brother's girlfriend. Veronica."

He closed his mouth abruptly over the last 'ah' of the word. Bella was left with the impression that he wanted to say more. Why didn't he? She realised she didn't yet know him well enough to ask.

From the easiness of their first hour of conversation, they now seemed in danger of sinking into a quagmire of awkward pauses. Bella was suddenly aware of how busy the garden had become. They'd been so absorbed with each other that each had failed to notice the gradually thickening crowd that was even now encroaching on their tiny table. As if reading her mind, Jake shook himself and looked around at the tumult about them.

"Shit, it's getting busy in here. I didn't notice."

Bella smiled nervously. "Neither did I. I wonder what the time is?"

"I know what time it is."

Jake smiled slowly, his dark eyes on hers. Bella felt a quick pulse of excitement as he held her gaze and felt suddenly very young and very breathless once more.

"I know exactly what time it is," he said. "It's time for another drink."

*

"You should come back to Fever Street," he said.
"Now?"

It was late and they were both drunk. The air was cooling very slowly, the sun having recently set in a blaze of flamingo pink and lurid orange. London hummed around them, dusty and rank and pulsing with noise.

"Yes, now. Come and see my house. I want you to see it."

Bella grinned. She thought fuzzily of train times and getting back to the station. There was a fleeting pang of guilt at the thought of her mother, home alone and waiting for her return. But just as quickly, a recklessness took hold of her. She felt ready for anything. Partly it was the booze but mostly it was Jake, with his sleepy grin and mobile black brows, his smudge of six o'clock shadow and broad shoulders. For the first time, she felt a strong lusty pull towards him, a plucking sensation deep down in the belly, as if gentle fingers were tickling her there.

She rang her mother and told her she'd missed her last train and would stay at her father's house, managing not to wince at the lie. Jake stood a little apart from her as she talked and she appreciated his tact. They headed towards the tube station, jostled by the early evening crowd that thronged the pavement. Jake took hold of her hand. Jolted, she realised why the touch of his fingers felt so familiar. They'd held hands down in the tunnels. In the same moment, it registered with Bella that they were walking towards the underground, they were almost at the gaping mouth of the station entrance and she jerked away, almost unconsciously. Their hands parted and she came to a standstill, beginning to shake.

It was uncanny, how he knew. He realised what she was thinking, he didn't even have to ask. Jake put his hands on her shoulders and she could feel the muscles of her arms shuddering under his palms, she couldn't stop herself.

"We'll get a cab, okay?" he said quietly.

Bella nodded, not trusting herself to speak. It was amazing, the shivering - it was if someone else was controlling her body. Jake waved down a cab, opened the door, handed her inside. She let herself fall back on the seat upholstery, clasping both hands in front of her, trying to stop shaking.

"Are you alright?"

"Yes -"

It was a lie but as soon as she said it she began to feel better. Jake sat beside her, the length of his thigh warm against her own. He took hold of her hand again.

"I'm fine, really -"

Bella breathed deeply. She was fine, she did feel better.

"It was the tube, I can't go on the tube. I know I should, I know I should just bite the bullet and get back on the horse, whatever the phrase is. But I - I can't. Yet. I can't yet. I will one day."

"It's okay, Bella. You don't have to justify anything to me. You don't have to explain anything. If anything, I'm - "

He was looking out of the window as he was saying this and she didn't catch the last part of the sentence. It sounded like *I'm the one who has to justify myself*, but was it? Bella considered asking again for a moment and then pushed the thought away. It didn't matter.

The streets were busy and the taxi moved slowly, jolting occasionally over speed bumps and coming to a juddering halt at road junctions. Once, stationary at a red light, someone slapped the boot whilst passing behind them, shouting with laughter, and Bella flinched. She felt skinned, her nerve endings exposed to the night air. Jake looked at her and she tried hard to smile back reassuringly.

They didn't talk at all during the journey but Bella didn't feel shy or embarrassed. They were deep into North London now, and she felt a momentary qualm. She had no idea where they were or how to get back to Waterloo. Realising this, she surrendered to the feeling, relaxing back into the seat. It was too late to do anything. If Jake was a mass murderer... well, she'd been through enough this year. She could handle it. Bella giggled to herself inwardly, rising into flippancy, buoyed by the alcohol.

The taxi slowed, the indicator ticking steadily as the car

began to turn. She realised that Jake was shifting beside her, stiffening to attention in the time-honoured manner of the taxi passenger nearing their house. She looked out of the window and saw in a fleeting glance the street sign at the end of the road. Fever Street. She felt a sudden jump of –what? Fear? Excitement? Jake let go of her hand and began to fumble in his pocket.

"Are we here?"

"We certainly are."

The taxi pulled in by the pavement. Bella peered over Jake's shoulder but could see nothing but an overgrown hedge, branches thrusting through railings covered in chipped black paint.

"Come on."

His tone had changed. He sounded – could it be? – nervous. Almost irritable. Bella grasped anxiously at her bag. Unfolding herself onto the pavement, she looked up and saw, above the unkempt hedge, a looming, redbrick wall. A huge window hung flat and black against the bricks. There was not a gleam of light from anywhere.

"This is it."

Jake's voice was flat. Bella wondered if she dared reach for his hand. She didn't.

"This is Fever Street?"

"This is Fever Street. Let's – " he stopped for a moment. She had the impression he was mentally bracing himself for what came next. "Let's go inside."

She hadn't dared take his hand but he took hers. He led her through the gap in the shabby railings and the light from the street lamp was swallowed up by the thick hedge as they moved past it into darkness, stepping as cautiously as travellers in a dark and wild wood.

***

Read the rest of **The House on Fever Street** by Celina Grace on Amazon.

CPSIA information can be obtained at www.ICGtesting.com
Printed in the USA
LVOW062007090113

315059LV00001B/21/P

9 781480 033924